I0663847

Forsaken Drifter

Book Three of the Talus 3 Series

Peter Sandor

Forsaken Drifter, 1st Edition.

06-06-25, Rev. 12

ISBN 978-1-7776387-2-6

Copyright 2021 by Peter Sandor

All rights reserved.

Read other books by Peter Sandor

The Wyld Wynd Trilogy

Book 1 – Wyld Wynd The Rising

Book 2 – Wyld Wynd The Unrest

Book 3 – Wyld Wynd Unleashed

The Wall Plug Boys – a hilarious, adult comedy.

The Talus 3 Trilogy

Book 1 – Arctic EMP

Book 2 – Galactic Illusions

Book 4 – Time Undone

Paperbacks, hardcovers and ebooks are available from Amazon.

Contents

Prologue

I was in the middle of a nonsensical dream when my awareness finally overtook my subconscious. My mind came to the realization that the bed I was lying in was rocking. My eyes shot open to see the lacquered wood ceiling of the state room. My hands were stretched out over my head as I lie on my back—a sleeping position my wife often mocked in a loving manner. At least, that's what I preferred to assume.

However, my wife was not beside me. The luxurious cabin reminded me I was aboard an expensive, sleek, 20-metre-long yacht. I had been brought here the prior morning after being abducted. My unnamed kidnapper was apologetic, explaining his reasons for the forceful abduction, and after listening to his reasons, I accepted them.

I slid my hands under my head while looking towards the chair by the doorway. During the night, someone had placed a freshly folded set of clothes on it. I tilted my face towards the clock on the wooden end table and saw I slept later than usual. It was 7:00 a.m.

After a hot shower, I dressed in the clothes set out for me—a black track suit and grey polo shirt. Feeling refreshed, I moved up the narrow stairs to the main deck and into the comfortable living area surrounded by glass deck doors, pulled wide open at the rear of the compartment, and by large windows on the port and starboard sides. The well-appointed compartment was empty, but in the adjoining kitchen area, I saw one of my supposed abductors, a man I learned was Pascoe. He was focused overtop a sizzling pan on the stove.

From behind a full-height pantry cupboard, a second man, with a smile on his face, appeared. He placed one of the two glasses of orange juice he carried down on the central, glass coffee table. He opened his hand towards the comfortable couch. "Please sit, Yevgeni. I hope you slept well."

I lowered onto the couch. He then politely sat down across from me, taking a deep drink of juice from his own glass. The man was quite the conundrum, and that was quite an understatement. The day before, over seven hours, he told me a ridiculous story originating with my grandfather, Luca Ivanov. Now dead for quite a few years, my grandfather had been a Russian secret service agent. Since I was a child, my grandfather and then my father after him, told me of a covert mission he led in Western Canada.

Incredibly, the story included two alien races: one creating a device on Earth to destroy an inhabited asteroid coming close to the Earth's position, and another race who were those inhabitants, trying to stop them.

My grandfather and the Russian secret service, were working with the second group of aliens who called themselves, *Korians*. Just as my grandfather used the false name, Nick Anderson, the Korian operations leader used the pseudonym, Logan Russell. Led by these two men, their combined forces were able to destroy the machine and avert a disaster that would have lost many lives on the asteroid and on Earth.

During the mission, my grandfather and Logan Russell became good friends. Since Logan was returning to his asteroid as it continued through the universe, searching for a habitable planet they could call home, the two men made a vow. When a planet was found, Logan would find a way to send a message back to the man he knew as Nick Anderson. If it didn't come in their lifetimes, then the story and the vow would be passed down through their descendants.

I always thought of the story as nothing more than a tall tale told to children. However, my abduction by a man claiming to be Korian, having returned to tell the story of his people's search for a new planet, raised doubt in my mind. But it was dispelled when he showed me the colour of his blood was blue, a discerning fact of Korian biology my grandfather recounted in his initial story. As much as my mind told me the story was impossible, I could not refute what my eyes saw.

The smell from the kitchen caused my stomach to grumble. My abductor, sitting across from me, let out a chuckle. "I have come to find Pascoe makes excellent omelettes."

"It's making me hungry."

From under his flowing brown hair, accented by wisps of grey, the man took another drink of juice before placing the glass down on the table. I had difficulty still considering him as my abductor. He did retrieve me by force, but since then had been nothing but hospitable with genuine concern for my well being. Still, it was odd he would not tell me his name. He said that, even though the story was only half complete, divulging his identity would just have me laughing in disbelief—at least until the story was told in its entirety.

"It took me a while to get used to eggs."

The man's words brought me back from my deep thoughts. "Eggs? I don't understand."

He smiled coyly under his blue eyes. "The people on our asteroid, Talus, learned about quite a few Earthen customs. Chickens were unknown to us, and when we heard the people of Earth eat the eggs pushed from chicken's asses, well, to some it was comical, to others—gross."

Pascoe brought over three plates. On each was a section of neatly folded omelette and a toasted bagel. My need for further discussion was displaced by my hunger. As I shovelled forkfuls of egg into my mouth, I looked out the open-air doorway at the back of the yacht.

The rain was falling in a light drizzle. It was the kind of rain I had come to know would last all day long. It prattled off the rear deck of the sleek, white yacht, and Lake Zurich beyond it, creating a bubbling sheet of water. Tilting my gaze upwards, I could see the skyline of Zurich in the distance. In earlier days, the historic character of the ancient city was maintained. So, now, when I looked at the city, on the east side was the Old City, easily recognized by smaller buildings, and even from this distance, I could see two historic, stone bridges.

Now, in 2084, with a growing population around the world fueling a need for vertical living space, the city officials had relented. Panning my gaze to the left, I saw a completely contradictory vision. Towering skyscrapers, covered in glass and steel, rose into the low-hanging clouds. This was the New City, an area given over to what was seen as the imminent, modern world, begrudgingly approved by city officials as long as the Old City was respectfully bypassed.

We ate quickly. I noticed my abductor holding his bagel up in front of an inquisitive eye.

"Is there something wrong with it?" I inquired.

He took a bite, and after several chomps and a swallow, replied, "I don't think so. It's just odd."

"Odd how?"

He shrugged. "Why does it have a hole in it?" Shaking his head, he continued, "You would think, with the technology that allows an expansive space station to be built on the moon and exploratory missions to Mars, the scientists on Earth would find a way to make a bagel without a hole."

My own bagel was frozen halfway to my mouth as I stared across the table. "You're kidding, right?"

"Most donuts don't have holes. Why can't this revelation be applied to bagels?"

My bagel with a hole was suddenly less appealing. I laid it back on the plate, offering, "You know what really is odd?"

Having taken a large bite of his bagel, my abductor managed a muffled, "What?"

"Having been abducted, only to have my abductor tell me incredulous stories of space aliens and inhabited asteroids." I held my finger up in the air. "But then, when I think my sense of reality is surely challenged, my alien abductor complains about holes in bagels and the oddity of eating eggs from chicken's butts!"

My abductor's eyes lit up above the smirk forming on his lips. "Then, you are ready for the continuation of the story."

I eyed the hot coffee Pascoe put on the table in front of me. "It seems I am. From where we finished yesterday, I assume Ryder Gunn and I'lish Mann found the habitable planet they searched for"

He nodded. "Yes, and I should describe it to you, since, as I told you yesterday, our historians wrote the history of the Korians, and since the readers would primarily be Korians living on this new planet, they had no need to describe it in detail."

I took a drink of coffee, crossing one leg over the other, waiting for him to continue.

My abductor leaned forward and held his hands out in front of himself. "The vast armada of almost 1,300 Korian and Sholite ships, safely reached the Alpha Centauri system. As a doctor working for your space agency, you would know there are three suns in the system: two are larger and orbit a point between them, while the third sun is a red dwarf and much smaller in size."

I nodded my understanding of the facts he presented.

"Now, the sun that here on Earth you call, Alpha Centauri B, is slightly more massive than your own sun, but it's luminosity as an orange sun is substantially less. All that said, the planet we found was in Alpha Centauri B's habitable zone."

"Based on your comments, I suspect the planet would be colder than this one," I interjected.

He waved his hand in front of himself. "Yes and no. Your familiarity with space should make you familiar with the term, *tidally locked?*"

I answered, "Of course. A planet is tidally locked when it's rotation matches it's orbit around it's partner."

He nodded. "Yes, the result, in this case, is one side of the planet always faces the sun. This side was very hot—too hot for the newly arrived settlers to live on. Obviously, the far side of the planet was too cold to live on. It was discovered to be a mountainous area of solid ice."

I surmised, "There must have been a zone between them that was moderate."

The rain became heavier, pelting off the roof of the cabin and the open rear deck. It distracted my Korian friend for a moment before he turned back to lock his eyes on mine. "There is a 4,000-kilometre-wide, temperate ring, however, most of this zone is mountainous and not considered an optimum location. We did find a 6,000-kilometre-long section within the ring that was relatively flat, containing several oceans, two large continents and many large, lush islands."

As my interest piqued, I leaned forward. "Did the planet support life?"

The Korian picked up his tablet, tilting it up off his thigh. His fingers danced over the screen. Once his eyes lit up from the screen's active reflection, he said, "I will simply say, the answer to your question is, yes. But now that you have a general description of the world, the rest of the story will be told as the Korian historians have written it."

I could not hold back one last question. "What did you name the planet?"

He flicked his finger across the tablet and glanced up for only a second. "The Korians and Sholites agreed to call the planet, *Haven*. Now, sit back, drink your coffee and listen."

Chapter 1: The Protest

10:15 hours, 3rd day of the 6th Korian month, Haven year 0021

Murcia, capital city of New Kor

Jax Zafar was looking out the floor-to-ceiling window from the terminal of the *Rowan Gunn Airfield*. His best friend, Romy Gunn, was on the flight taxiing into the gate just below him. The aircraft was the latest model designed and built by the Tor family. They had dominated manufacturing for many years and, as such, were experts at building sophisticated *spaceships*. But since the fleet's arrival at the planet, Haven, 21 years earlier, there were many stumbles and errors until the same level of proficiency was achieved in their effort to build aircraft to travel the skies within the atmosphere.

The aircraft Jax was watching was 40 metres long with two sets of swept back wings. The forward set were short and narrow. The aft set were slightly wider and reached to the back edge of the plane. There were six engines spread over the four wings, whereby each could be rotated in a synchronous motion to provide rearward thrust, vertical thrust, or thrust at any angle in between. This allowed for a hover mode in addition to short take off and landing capability.

Jax chuckled when his gaze panned to the tail of the light-blue craft where it was adorned with a 12-pointed, white star. Each point represented one of the powerful families of the Council of Twelve governing the Korian lands on Haven. Jax and now, Romy, were in Murcia to protest this same council because of their oppressive, dictatorial nature.

For many thousands of years, the Korian people had been ruled by a Council of Nine, comprised of the nine matriarchs of the nine most powerful Korian families. The people accepted this system during the unusual circumstances, whereby eight million Korians travelled across the universe, searching for a habitable planet to call home. The Korian cities built into the huge space-travelling asteroid required order, and since each of the primary families provided an essential service towards their survival in space, the people accepted this matriarchal, yet far from democratic, system.

However, with the untimely destruction of the asteroid, Talus, leaving just under a million Korian survivors and very few surviving matriarchs, the time was ripe for change. When the surviving fleet arrived at Haven, the priorities for a population on a planet were much different from that of a space civilization. This fuelled the fire for change, yet the long-entrenched, matriarchal system survived; in fact, it flourished as the membership increased from nine to twelve families.

Deep within the population, dissension grew as the hope of a democracy was envisioned. The Council of Twelve was overconfident and underestimated the will of the people, but eventually, they saw the growing threat. At that point, they acted quickly, identifying the members of the growing movement first as dissidents and then—rebels.

Now, 21 years after the fleet's arrival, a large faction of Korians were attending protests in the capital city of Murcia; this being the fourth in the last four Korian months. Today was expected to be nothing more than a continuation of the message sent to the matriarchs with the hope that each protest would hammer the demand for change further into their unacceptable institution.

A grinding noise brought Jax's attention back to the present. As the aircraft's engines were winding down, two covered ramps extended from an arm of the building. Two flashing, blue lights drew Jax's attention, where he saw an automated fuel tanker drive alongside the plane. As soon as the vehicle hit the magnetic marks embedded in the tarmac, an arm extended up to the belly of the craft where a fueling port was open and waiting. Like watching the flames of a fire, Jax was mesmerised by the automation when he heard a familiar voice behind him.

"Jax!"

Jax turned to see Romy waving a hand above his head as he walked towards him. Once Romy was within range, Jax gave his friend a wry smile. He wrapped his arms around Romy, lifting him off his feet. Romy was six-foot-two inches tall with a stout build, but Jax was a mountain of a man, standing a good head taller.

As they separated, Romy slapped the bigger man on the chest. "It's good to see you. Have you been here long?"

Jax playfully slapped Romy's hand away. "The flight from Villaro was a bit shorter than yours from Torrin House, so I've been here about an hour." He grasped Romy's shoulder, turning him before they walked towards the long aisleway that would take them to the ground transportation hub. "How's your mother?" Jax inquired.

Romy was the stepson of I'lish Mann, past president of the Sholite people. Now retired, she lived in Torrin House, the capital city of Shol.

Romy, although born with the blue blood of a Korian, had many reasons to avoid Korian life, preferring the nondescript life with the Sholites. He tilted his face up to Jax, replying, "She's doing well. Although, even though she's retired, she can't seem to keep her fingers out of the family space mining business."

The long aisleway came to an intersection with three other aisles, the widest of which led to the taxis and monorail boarding area. Romy turned his head from side to side. "There's quite a crowd. It's not at all what I expected. I thought this protest would be the same as the last two." They continued until they reached the monorail boarding area. Romy pointed. "Look at the lineups!"

Jax's lips curled down in a frown. "That's many more people than we saw here at any of the previous protests. Something is definitely different."

After 15 minutes, the two men pushed aside their concerns and packed into one of the monorail cars. There was a whining sound before the ten-car-long train shot out of the terminal into what the people of Haven aptly called the *forever twilight*.

Since the planet rotated at the same rate as the planet's orbit around the sun, the habitable zone always faced away at a right angle from the direction of the sun's rays. Consequently, there was no daytime or nighttime; nor were there seasons—only the indirect light provided from the oblique angle of the sun's warming rays.

Of course, this meant, in what the Korians called the west, the sky was brighter and the temperature marginally warmer, compared to the east where less light and colder temperatures were consistent. For the Korians, it wasn't a monumental issue. The climate in the habitable zone was similar to that within the chambers of their previous asteroid home where there had been very little variation in the artificially created environment. The similarity assisted their assimilation to their new lives on the new-found planet.

As the train rode the elevated monorail away from the Rowan Gunn Airfield, in the distance, Romy saw the second half of the facility. The *Kriton Fyr Space Field,* adjacent to the airfield, was operated by the military which, in turn, was controlled by the Fyr family. At the space field, the military coordinated the launch and landing of the many vessels left over from the armada of spaceships. There was still a healthy fleet exploring their new-found solar system while also hunting for asteroids and comets, filled with a vast array of minerals.

The train passed along a corridor cut into the forest, bordering the urban city. There were also foothills, and in these areas, the monorail tract was carved out, resulting in vertical walls of stone highlighted by sparkling mineral deposits.

The ten kilometres to the outskirts of the city were traversed within a few minutes. Now, on both sides, there were colorful houses and low-rise apartments. Romy knew this area as Joyville, a name carried over from a similar suburb in Talus.

Another swath of forest was passed before the train slowed. Angling down, it entered a tunnel before continuing into the station at the border of the city proper.

At the main pedestrian exit from the station, Jax and Romy waited alongside at least 200 other travellers, most apparently on their way to the same protest planned for the city center. They were packed into the large front atrium as they waited for the rain to subside. The rains typically came three times in each 25-hour-period, pushed by the constant westerly winds generated by the temperature differential between the extreme heat in the west and the extreme cold in the east. The patient citizens knew these rains typically lasted no longer than 20 minutes. When the last drops fell, the doors were flung open, and the throng of people spilled out into the square in front of the station.

A rain-soaked man on a makeshift podium, spoke into a microphone. His hands moved aggressively, helping to convey his mood. "Citizens! Today, we travel to the city center and the Council of Twelve chamber! We'll show them the people have had enough of their dictatorship. We have had enough of their policies promoting their families while subjugating the rest of us to second-class citizens!"

He thrust his hand in the air. The growing crowd did the same. The simultaneous motion of 200 raised fists was joined by 200 voices yelling out their approval. The organizer on the platform pointed down the wide boulevard behind him where, six kilometres away, stood the council chambers. "Our future is there! Go, now!" he screamed.

The throng moved as one, shuffling around the podium and onto the expansive boulevard, allowing the next wave of protesters to enter the square from the monorail station. As the people spread out on the boulevard, thankfully, the claustrophobic condition reduced.

Shops and restaurants filled the buildings on both sides of the boulevard; most were three or four stories high, built from stone blocks and liberally trimmed with wood. Since wood hadn't been readily available in Talus, the builders enjoyed many new found uses, carving intricate designs in the softer woods while using the hardwoods for structural components.

Romy and Jax walked along the east side of the boulevard. There were many side streets, and after a kilometer, they saw a group of twenty-five *Mabuza* from the southern islands of the habitable zone.

Surprisingly, when the Korians and Sholites arrived on Haven, they found it inhabited. The Mabuza were a subdued, friendly population of some 200 thousand people. Whereas the Korians and Sholites had pale skin heightened by thousands of years living under the artificial light within Talus, the Mabuza people were quite a contrast. Although some had light brown skin, the vast majority had skin that was as black as the darkness of space.

The Mabuza leaders said they were from a race called the *Bantu*—a race they indicated lived on Haven as well as several other distant planets. Other than that, due to what the Korians considered their quiet nature, further details of their history weren't forthcoming. The Korians and Sholites, with a raw, new planet in front of them, had more pressing concerns than the history of a small race of people. And since the Mabuza people seemed extremely humanitarian in nature, without a concern regarding the new arrivals settling in, the newcomers did just that—they settled in.

Since almost all the Mabuza lived on islands in the far south of the habitable zone, an agreement between the three races was quickly reached. Although all people were able to move freely anywhere within the habitable zone, the Mabuza would govern the settlements in the southern islands. There was a large central continent the Korians and Sholites divided in half. The southern half was named *New Kor.* The northern half was named *Shol,* inclusive of a second, smaller continent further north of the central one. This would have left the Korians with a smaller area to govern. To equalize the imbalance, a group of larger islands in the northeast corner of the habitable zone was claimed by the Korians. They were named the *New Kor Islands.*

Romy saw the simplistic stereotype most often applied to the Mabuza as he gazed past the group into the side street. There was a mix of homes and shops, the colours of which were the warmer tones typically found in nature. The Mabuza onlookers wore clothes with the same mix of hues: brown and green, with brighter colours used only to accent their attire.

Romy recognized the curiosity on the faces of the Mabuza onlookers who dared not step into the mass of protestors. He gave them no more than a glance, with the exception of a smile to the young Mabuza girl holding her mother's hand.

After another kilometer marching down the boulevard, pockets of police officers could be seen along the storefronts. In their standard cohorts of ten, they wore dark-blue uniforms and shiny, silver helmets. Although they were armed with either air pistols or rifles, they presented a casual posture and demeanour while often joking and laughing with the protestors.

The Murcia police force—in fact, all police forces across New Kor—were coordinated and led by the Jez family. Even though there had been many Jez-coordinated, covert efforts to subvert the Fyr family's position on the Council of Twelve, success had never been achieved. The Jez family remained a powerful yet secondary family—a fact that kept a smoldering anger within the Jez family's leadership.

Two more kilometers were traversed when Romy nudged Jax and pointed. "Have you noticed there are protestors massing in each side street we pass?"

Jax grasped Romy's arm and pulled him towards one of these side streets where another organizer was on a podium, stirring up the protestors. There was no microphone—just the man yelling. Romy and Jax couldn't understand the words, and it didn't matter. As long as the yelling man raised his hand after every sentence, the crowd yelled their approval. As the two men moved closer, Romy saw an air pistol in the organizer's belt.

"Do you see that?" Romy whispered. "He has a gun."

Jax's gaze inspected several men at the base of the podium. He saw several more half-hidden pistols. Two of the men wore long coats, and as Jax squinted, he spied menacing, long rifles slung underneath them. "He's not the only one. Let's get out of here."

As if he heard Jax, the organizer pointed back to the main boulevard and yelled, "To the Chamber of Twelve—everyone!"

Now Romy and Jax had no choice. They were pressed along by the mass of people, the group moving as one. They spilled out into the boulevard only to see it was filled with many more boisterous protestors, all shuffling towards the city center like an unstoppable avalanche of rocks.

At the north end of the boulevard was the *Circle*, as it was known. It was a huge park consisting of a series of grass-covered rings, one on top of the other. The lower ring was 200 metres across and elevated one metre above the wide, stone walkway surrounding it. Ten metres in from the edge of the lower ring, behind a one-metre-high block wall, was the edge of the next grass-covered ring. The pattern continued with each grass-covered terrace being one metre higher and 20 metres smaller. At the pinnacle, the top ring was a well-manicured, 100-metre-diameter, grass-covered patch. Pathways crisscrossed the top tier where statues of past Korian heroes were highlighted under the forever twilight.

Beside the northern tip of the Circle was the bay; opposite to it, was the end of the main boulevard, presently spilling out a seemingly endless mass of protesters. Around the Circle were 13 impressive buildings; the largest was the one housing the Korian Council of Twelve chambers where all important matters of state were decided. The other 12 buildings, slightly smaller but no less impressive, were the embassies of the twelve powerful primary families forming the council's matriarchy.

From a third story window of the Fyr Embassy, three well-dressed officials looked out the picture window of a large floor lounge. An attractive woman with short, black hair, dressed in a military uniform, glared at the growing crowd of what she considered rebels. The four silver buttons on her collar indicated General Shelby Fyr, wife of the Fyr family primor, was the top-ranking military official in New Kor. Beside her were two men; Berny Tor and Chester Mal were, respectively, the primors of the influential Tor and Mal families. Since the primors of the families were the ones usually running day to day activities, they were, arguably, the most powerful people in their families.

Shelby Fyr slammed her fist on the glass. "What are those infernal, useless Jez police doing?"

Along each side of the boulevard, for 200 metres, police stood shoulder to shoulder. In front of the Circle, in an arc, two rows of police stood on guard; they numbered an additional two hundred, armed with shields, batons and a holstered weapon of one sort or another.

Chester Mal rocked back and forth, toe to heel, with his hands clasped behind his back. "The police seem to have everything under control."

Shelby let out a guffaw. She was taller than Chester and used the height differential to talk down to him. "I don't tell you how to deliberate your cases, do I? You're just a fucking lawyer who doesn't know anything about evaluating a tactical position."

Chester shrank back. Berny Tor, trying to placate the situation, offered, "My, there are many protestors—with many more coming. What do you suggest?"

Turning back to the window, Shelby formed a sly, twisted grin. She saw the mob had grown to at least five thousand rebels. They were straining the police lines at several points, and without reinforcements, the east side of the wide police line would soon be flanked. However, General Shelby was sure the Jez leadership were calling in those reinforcements. *After all, they weren't idiots.* The police would hold back the crowd and eventually they would disperse—until the next protest. The destructive, insubordinate cycle would be allowed to continue.

As she sarcastically rolled her eyes, Shelby made a decision. *Enough was enough.* Her thought was relative to both the rebels and the ineptitude of the Jez police force. She lifted her wrist interlink to her lips. "Commander Colby Fyr, come in."

The response was immediate. "Yes, General Shelby."

"Proceed with plan, Alpha 22. Send in the first wave," Shelby Fyr ordered.

Romy and Jax were packed in the crowd, ten rows back from the police line guarding the Circle. Romy had a great deal of respect for the police whose line held while they remained calm through the insults and the random bottles thrown in their direction. Two trucks arrived along a side street from the east. Fifty police officers jumped out to shore up the flank that was on the verge of being overrun.

Undeterred, having practiced this before, the people began a coordinated chant. The left side of the crowd yelled, "We want—" while the right side of the mob finished with "—an election!"

With the vast amount of yelling and chanting, no one noticed the low flying aircraft cruising 500 metres above the Circle. But it didn't take long for more and more people to look upwards where they saw black forms dropping from the sky—25 black forms, to be exact. They became larger, and 80 metres from the ground, a plume of gas could be seen from each jet pack. A few moments later, 25 *Talus Dogs* were on the top layer of the circle. The Talus Dogs were the elite shock troops of the Korian military, controlled by the Fyr family.

No sooner had they landed and jettisoned their jet packs, when a second wave of soldiers could be seen following the first. Aircraft after aircraft flew over the Circle, dropping 25 soldiers each time. Romy held his hand over his eyes, seeing five waves of soldiers had successfully landed. He drew in a sharp breath when he saw each Talus Dog wore full body armour and carried an automatic projectile rifle.

The protestors were incensed, and now, truly turned into a mob. Although only a few carried guns, those that did held them over their heads. A few fired shots in the air, infuriated by the taunting action of the military.

Jax coiled a fist into the collar of Romy's jacket. "We need to leave, now! It's out of control!"

Romy didn't need more convincing. He was dedicated to the cause, but he wasn't stupid. Thankfully, Jax was a big man and was able to push his way back through the throng of protestors. More than once, he had to push people to the ground when they wouldn't move. The two men were almost free of the mob when they heard an explosion behind them. They turned to see the last wave of soldiers coming to the ground. Unfortunately, one of them was consumed by a fireball. No one knew if the jet pack malfunctioned, or if a stray bullet hit the fuel pack—it didn't matter.

There were 150 well-armed Talus Dogs on the high ground. The front row moved to a prone position while a second row moved to one knee behind them. Shots were fired towards anyone in the crowd holding a gun. The police, who up to that point were still holding back the crowd, turned. Seeing the Talus Dogs shooting citizens, the police were incensed. The soldiers had never been used in the city for a military action and, most certainly, never against their own people.

Most of the police line turned and took cover behind the one-metre-high ledge of the first ring. Other officers hopped up, ran across the ten metres of grass, and took cover behind the second ring wall. Shots from air rifles and air pistols began to hit into the Talus Dogs. Four soldiers fell before the Talus Dogs took aim at the police lines and returned fire.

It was complete carnage, but the Talus Dogs held the upper hand. They held the high ground, and their projectile weapons were more lethal than the air guns used by the police. Those within the crowd with guns, joined the police line or fired from behind any obstacle they could find.

Romy and Jax had taken cover behind a vendor's wagon in the middle of the boulevard, 80 metres behind the police line. Bullets whizzed by their position as people ran past, fleeing the vicious firefight. A man and woman burst past them, until the man flew forward, landing face down in the street, propelled by the impact of the bullet in his back. The woman stopped, squatting down to check him, only to be hit with another salvo in the side of her head.

A growing stream of terrified people continued running past them. By now, very few protestors were fighting, leaving the police to deal with the superior military forces. Romy looked over the edge of the cart and saw the Talus Dog line had moved down one tier in the Circle. There were many police officers down, dead or wounded. The remaining police were formed in a line, shields up, backing down the boulevard in a retreating action.

Romy yelled to Jax, "We need to move! They'll be on top of us soon!"

Jax nodded his agreement. "Where to?"

Pointing to a side street 40 metres further down the boulevard, Romy replied, "We need to cover the open ground to the side street. Once we're there, we'll be out of the firing line. From there, we'll head east and away from this mess."

Again, Jax grimly nodded. "On your lead."

Romy took one last look over the wagon and saw things weren't going to get any better. He yelled, "Now!"

He and Jax were in a full sprint before the word finished leaving his lips. They skirted obstacles and hurdled any bodies in their path. They were almost at the corner of the side street when Romy heard Jax let out a scream. He turned to see his friend airborne until his bulky form hit the wall on the far side of the side street. Running over, Romy found Jax groggy with a cut on the back of his head where it had hit the stone wall. He inspected Jax from top to bottom, cringing when he saw the gruesome wound in the large man's calf. There was blood flowing from the jagged hole where the bullet passed through. Unfortunately, the visible bone fragment made it obvious it wasn't a clean through-and-through wound.

Romy put his hands under Jax's armpits. He struggled but managed to pull his friend out of the line of fire. Romy removed his coat and tore a wide strip off his shirt. Gingerly, he pushed the bone in as best he could, while the action brought Jax out of his grogginess with a scream.

"Sorry about that," Romy whispered. He then wrapped the cloth around the wounded leg, tied a knot and pulled it tight.

Jax gave out a second yell, but at least now the leg was somewhat stabilised.

Romy turned his attention to the few people running past. He would never be able to carry his friend on his own. A man was racing past, his face full of sweat and his eyes wide with fear. Romy yelled, "Hey, help me!"

Without breaking stride, the man turned his head, yelling back, "Fuck off!"

"Asshole," Romy mumbled. He lifted Jax up to a sitting position as two more men were jogging by. Romy pleaded, "Help me. I can't carry him alone."

The far man didn't even glance over. The second man, slowed, then with a roll of his eyes, stopped. He strode over, then put his hands under one of Jax's arms. His dark eyebrows lowered as he chastised Romy. "Well come on then—are you coming or not?"

They walked a kilometre east on the side street, Romy under one arm and the yet unknown man under the other. Jax stumbled along, dragging his wounded leg. Ahead of them, they saw a group of vehicles, the dark-blue colour identifying them as medical vehicles. The medical attendants quickly evaluated Jax's leg and bustled him into an ambulance. Romy took a minute to face the man who had stopped to help them. He looked 40 years old and had dirty, blonde hair which seemed an odd match for his dark eyebrows.

"What's your name?" Romy asked.

"Barrett—Barrett Fexman," the man replied.

"I have to go with my friend," Romy offered. "Can't thank you enough for your help."

The man gave a smile, albeit a grim one. "No worries. It sounds like the fighting is almost over."

Romy jumped on the back step of the ambulance and held the grab handle. There was an electric whine as the engine's electric motor sprang to life. He considered Barrett's last words and shrugged. He mumbled to himself. "I don't agree, friend. I fear the fight has only just begun."

Chapter 2: The Deliberation

Nineteen years earlier…

13:50 hours, 15th day of the 2nd Korian month, Haven year 0002

Murcia, Capital city of New Kor

It had been 13 months since the fleet's arrival at Alpha Centauri. The time had passed quickly. Ryder Gunn sat on the patio of the *Lost Leaf* restaurant, one leg comfortably across the opposite knee. His fingers slowly turned the glass of iced fruit wine in circle after circle as he waited. His entire morning had been spent in the Council of Twelve chamber, explaining his reasoning for the deception played over the Korian people for the last 16 months.

I'lish Mann, acting president of the Sholite people, sat beside him. She looked the same as she did when the fleet left the wreck of Talus, and even with the stress of the three-month trip to Alpha Centauri, she didn't appear a day older. Her dark hair was tied back in a long ponytail under a wide-brimmed, light-brown hat, matching her loose-fitting pants and jacket over a white blouse.

I'lish took a drink from her glass of ice water, and without shifting her gaze from the construction work at the south end of the street, asked, "How do you think the hearing went?"

A light chuckle escaped Ryder's lips. "I think we both know how it went." He straightened up and leaned closer to I'lish. "You are a good judge of people. You saw the faces of the twelve vidames and their advisors. Their minds were made up before the day began."

She knew he was right, having read the same message on the Korian council member's faces. She could do nothing but smile at her brother, knowing she was an equal partner in the deed that would provide his fate. She thought back, wondering if there could have been another path. Only two other people in their world knew I'lish Mann was secretly the sister of Ryder Gunn, primor of the powerful Gunn family, and the man who took charge of the Korian survivors after the destruction of Talus.

I'lish, was the acting president of the Sholites as well as the matriarch of the Gunn family. Both she and Ryder knew the asteroid's destruction, predictably, led suspicion towards the Sholites, the ages-old enemy of the Korians. Just before Talus exploded, a truce had been reached between the two warring peoples, but both Ryder and his sister knew it was on the verge of breaking. To reinforce the truce, since the people of both nations knew nothing of the bloodlines between the two young leaders, Ryder and his sister decided to marry. When the people saw the leader of the most powerful Korian family and the leader of the Sholites, could set aside the differences that had grown and festered over thousands of years, the people realized they could at least endure a joint mission to Alpha Centauri.

I'lish changed the subject as she pointed up the wide street. "The difference in the appearance of the buildings after they're completed is amazing."

Ryder's eyes followed the direction of her finger. In the distance, the concrete buildings, varying between three and ten stories high, were neatly finished with colourful, decorative blocks and wood trim. The construction crew, one of many throughout the city, were busy refacing the bland, original building fronts. The completed, colourful buildings in the distance were a stark contrast to the one they sat in front of, and those around it. The refacing was a sure indication the Korian people had arrived on Haven—for good.

When the joint Korian-Sholite fleet had arrived at Haven, the citizens aboard the 1,500 spaceships remaining in orbit were anxious—in fact, so anxious they were almost to the point of rebellion with the sight of their new home so close. However, cooler heads prevailed. There were almost one million Korians on those ships as well as just over two million Sholites. It made no sense to drop people into what the advance explorers had found was a wild, heavily-forested world.

Instead, the Tor and Krl families, dominating the manufacturing and construction sectors, worked day and night for three months to prepare colonization areas. First, massive machines were made to prep a thirty-mile-area along the coast of the central continent. Trees were cleared, natural rock walls were pulverized and soil was leveled. Two water treatment plants were built to support the plumbing infrastructure being installed in a grid throughout the site of the future city.

Nearby, the Krl family discovered vast deposits of sand and aggregate. A concrete factory was soon in full operation, primarily making eight foot high, 25-foot-square cubicles. Massive air machines moved these from the factory to the core of the city where, piled one on top of the other, they provided rudimentary living accommodations. The goal was to provide these basic accommodations in volume, and then come back at a later date to make them aesthetically appealing.

This was the process Ryder and I'lish were watching as the construction crew trimmed out the buildings at the end of the street. Ryder took another drink and had just placed the glass back on the table, when his wrist interlink let out a series of *beeps*. Ryder brought the bionic device, integrated into his forearm, closer to his lips. "Yes—are they ready?"

A voice returned from the interlink. "Yes, Mr. Gunn. They'll be bringing the council back into session in 20 minutes."

After placing two tokens on the table, Ryder rose to his feet, followed by I'lish. The newly constructed Council of Twelve building was just completing some final inspections, so for the last year the building, 200 metres south of the restaurant, had sufficed as the temporary home for the matriarchal council. As they walked towards it, following a discrete distance behind them were four Sholite security guards, and across the road, two men dressed in black suits, mirrored their movements. The two men were Linkin Gunn and Byron Gunn, trusted members of the Gunn family security group.

It was an awkward walk, too quiet for I'lish's liking. "Will you be staying here in Murcia, or do you prefer Torrin House?"

Just as the Korians put a massive effort into building Murcia, so too did the Sholites, building the city of Torrin House, 1,000 kilometres to the north. Ryder replied, "I have not quite decided, but Romy does like the Sholite way of life, and of course, enjoys being near his stepmother."

I'lish had become Romy's stepmother, 17 months ago. She thought it was one of the best things she'd ever done. She had come to love the boy deeply, just as if he would have come from her own womb. To many others, it was odd, seeing I'lish as both aunt and stepmother to Romy. But, to her, the only word that mattered was when the young boy, with obvious love in his eyes, called her, "Mom."

"Both you and Romy will always be welcome in Torrin House, and especially my household," I'lish offered. "Since we arrived on this planet, my space mining business has expanded with the increased need for minerals from within this world. You could join me in that endeavour."

Smiling, Ryder put his arm around his sister. He had known her for just over a year, but had come to love her. He didn't want to patronize her. She deserved better than that. "Let me think about your offer. It's interesting."

The remainder of the walk to the council building was in silence. It was obvious, from the job offer and the response, they both knew what the verdict of the council would be—*guilty*.

Ryder saw the temporary council chamber building ahead of him, reminding him of the flawed matriarchal system, one that was more complicated than most political systems. Even though the matriarch was the leader of a family, she was really nothing more than a figurehead. The real power of each family ran through the primor and a few trusted advisors. Typically, the primor was the eldest son of the matriarch. When he came of age, a wife would be selected for him. This selection was done with intense political influence, most often with the goal to improve family alliances. And hopefully, this would result in increased status on the council. Most importantly, the selected wife would be the next family matriarch, cementing such alliances in blood.

A few minutes later, Ryder and I'lish were sitting in front of the boxes typically reserved for the many Korian, secondary families. The remaining boxes, normally filled for council meetings, were empty. Since Ryder and I'lish had confessed their deceit and illegal marriage a month ago, both the Sholite and Korian councils had made every effort to keep the council deliberations as discrete as possible. However, the media did discover the confession and implored the council for comment. The matriarchs were insistent the council, already marred by the actions of Ryder Gunn, would not be completely humiliated. As such, the deliberations were closed to the media.

The room was eerily quiet. An ominous creak echoed around the large room as the moderator entered the chamber. It was a signal for the vidames of the twelve families to follow. Doors opened behind each of the primary family boxes set in a semicircle opposite to the tiers of secondary seats. The vidame of each family was present, and each of them had two or three senior advisors with them. But Ryder noticed only 11 of the primary boxes were filled. The box assigned to the Gunn family was empty. Ryder sighed, thinking, *That's not a good sign—not even an advisor.*

Once everyone was seated, the moderator hit his gavel on the table in front of him, bringing the meeting back to order. He stood and cleared his throat before saying, "Ryder Gunn and I'lish Mann, the council has come to several decisions. Vidame Pym has been selected by the council to read out their judgements. But before that—" The moderator's eyes shifted to I'lish "—President Mann, I understand you have a statement."

To Ryder's surprise, I'lish rose to her feet. Sensing her brother's confusion, she put her hand on his shoulder. "Yes, that is correct."

"The floor is yours," came the moderator's calm reply.

I'lish kept her shoulders high, her chin tilted up. "Council members, the Sholite Council and I have come to an agreement. My understanding is that this council and the Sholite Council have agreed to these terms as part of the general record." She paused for a moment before continuing. "I, I'lish Mann, will abdicate the presidency of the Sholite people when I return to Torrin House this evening. I agree to not hold a Sholite government position after that time, nor will I return to any Korian governed territory in an official capacity representing the Sholite government."

Just as his sister lowered into the chair beside him, so too did Ryder's gaze lower to the polished, stone floor. He was dejected with the thought it had come to this. He felt his sister's breath at his ear. "No worries. Fuck them," she whispered.

He couldn't help but snicker. He raised his face and the council members saw the Gunn look of confidence they'd become accustomed to over the last 16 months.

Hearing I'lish complete her statement, the moderator continued as he turned to the Pym family box, "Vidame, the floor is yours."

Watching the frail, old woman rise to her feet, Ryder wasn't surprised she had been elected to speak. In fact, it was likely she had volunteered. Such was the venom she held for the Gunn family since their arrival on Haven. The woman had disagreed with every decision sourced from the Gunn family and, specifically, from Ryder. To her, unless it was her idea, it was never good enough. The woman was a *super bitch*, Ryder thought.

Vidame Pym gave a polite nod of her chin to the moderator before she turned her dark gaze towards Ryder. Her lips twisted on an angle, adding a sinister smirk to her wrinkled appearance. "Mister Gunn, first there is a pronouncement regarding the Gunn family. Your family officials have already been notified, hence their absence at this time." She was enjoying the moment and paused, letting the euphoria linger. "The Gunn family is removed from the Council of Twelve, and they cannot make a claim to rejoin for ten years. Their place on the council will be filled by the Bli family. The Gunn family, controlling the pharmaceutical business, will remain a powerful part of our community, but only as a secondary family."

The decision wasn't a surprise to either Ryder or I'lish. Ryder remained emotionless, not allowing Vidame Pym the enjoyment of seeing a reaction.

Vidame Pym was careful with her next words. The woman before her was the president of the Sholite people—a people who they had been at peace with since they travelled to Haven. She didn't want to disturb that. The vidame's voice became softer. "Madame President, I'm sure you can understand the awkward situation the council is in. It's impossible for you to remain as the vidame of the Gunn family. In discussions with your family's senior advisors and this council, you have been replaced by Samata Gunn."

Samata Gunn was a cousin of Ryder and I'lish, three times removed. Ryder thought it was actually an excellent choice.

Of course, I'lish expected this judgment. She rose to her feet. "I humbly accept the decision."

Ryder tried his best to contain his grin. He couldn't remember his sister ever being—humble.

Continuing, Vidame Pym said, "Ryder Gunn, there are also some conditions placed on you. You will be stripped of any official title within the Gunn family. You will not be allowed to hold such a title or hold official office within the Gunn family or their pharmaceutical business. This is for your lifetime." She said the last word slowly, enjoying the sound of it from her lips.

Ryder rose to his feet. He had heard enough.

Raising her voice, Vidame Pym implored, "We're not finished Mister Gunn!" As she watched Ryder urge I'lish to her feet and whisper in her ear, the agitated woman blurted, "There are many more details, Mister Gunn. You need to stay and hear the full verdict of this council!"

Ryder glared at the old woman before he and I'lish turned and walked up the aisle towards the back of the large chamber.

"Mister Gunn, this is unacceptable. You will return, right now!" Vidame Pym scolded.

There were a few snickers from the other council boxes. Not all members had a dislike for Ryder Gunn, and many had difficult histories with the overbearing Pym family matriarch.

Vidame Pym was still yelling when the council chamber doors closed behind Ryder and I'lish. I'lish mumbled, "Finally—I couldn't stand another second of her scratchy voice."

They were both laughing when the door behind them opened for a second time, and a young man rushed through into the atrium area. He came to Ryder's side. "I'm sorry, my friend. I tried to remind them of all you did for the people." He rolled his fingers back through his jet-black hair. "I even told them it was likely we wouldn't even be here without the efforts of the two of you."

Langdon Zaf was the husband of the Zaf vidame, and the most influential person within their family. Since the Zaf's controlled power generation, they were a powerful family, but apparently, not powerful enough to sway the group.

Ryder considered Langdon a close friend and liked his spirit. The man was young, a bit hot-headed, but he was definitely a man of action. As he put his hand on the younger man's shoulder, Ryder stated, "It was time for a change. There are other things yet to be done in my life."

Langdon wasn't sure exactly what Ryder meant, but he saw the sparkle in his friend's eyes. There wasn't anything more Langdon could think of saying that would help the situation.

Ryder saw Langdon's awkward hesitation and saved his friend as he held his hand out to him. "Thank you for everything."

There was an odd, determined look in Langdon's eyes as he grasped Ryder's hand. In a matching, steady voice, he said, "Take care of yourself."

I'lish was on her way back to Torrin House. Ryder had sent Byron Gunn with her to supplement her presidential guard. Ryder kept Linkin with him as they returned to the simple home they kept in the eastern sector of Murcia. Linkin thought their day was over and was about to retire to his room when Ryder said, "We need to go back out."

The lines on Linkin's forehead deepened as he replied, "What's going on, Boss?"

Ryder handed Linkin a piece of paper. "When Langdon Zaf shook my hand after I left the council meeting, he handed me a note."

The note was folded in half. Linkin opened it and read it aloud.

> *"I must talk to you tonight. Meet me at the top of the 20th hour at the Green Forest Bar. Take care. You're being followed."*

Linkin lifted his gaze to Ryder with a raised eyebrow. "What's this about?"

Having moved over to the front window, Ryder made a crack in the blinds as he pulled one aside. Linkin saw what he was doing and turned off the lights in the living area before making his own slit in the blinds to peek through. Both men panned their gaze from one side of the street to the other. They had to be careful. Even though they were obscured by blinds within a dark room, the constant twilight outside minimized their covert efforts.

Linkin was trained in espionage activities. He saw them first. "Look to your left, Sir. Past the laneway, there is a fruit market. The man and woman have been loitering there for too long. They act like a couple, but the woman is fixated on her interlink. The man keeps glancing at this building."

Pulling back from the blinds, Ryder nodded. "We are the same size. You can dress in my clothes and lead them away. Once you're gone, I can go to the meeting with Langdon."

Rolling his eyes, Linkin replied, "With all due respect, Sir, I'm the expert in these matters." He pulled Ryder's coat from the hook on the wall and threw it to him. "Just follow my lead, and we'll lose them on the way to the Green Forest Bar."

Linkin donned his own jacket and led Ryder down three flights of stairs to the main level of the apartment building. Along the way, the bodyguard made a fast call from his wrist interlink. Once they were on the sidewalk, there were many taxis moving in both directions. Although some citizens owned private vehicles, taxis were the preferred mode of transportation. Linkin stood with his hands on his hips as taxi's passed, until he saw one with a bright-blue, flashing light on the roof. Waving his hand in the air, the taxi stopped in front of them.

After Linkin opened the door, allowing Ryder to enter, he slipped into the rear seat beside him. "Take us to Malik's Clothing store near the intersection of 34th street and 81st lane."

The driver nodded, and the electrical whine of the engine began just before the three-wheeled vehicle jerked forward. The taxi was comfortable with room for up to four people in the back seat. This specific vehicle was dark-green with a yellow roof, the bright colour being a tactic the drivers used to draw customers to their vehicles.

As they passed the fruit stand, the suspicious couple were at the curb, the woman frantically waving her hand in earnest for their own taxi. As Linkin turned, looking out the rear window, a white taxi with a red roof pulled over for them.

Linkin mumbled, "They'll be right behind us."

"I hope you know what you're doing," Ryder muttered.

Having arrived at the high-end clothing store, the two men exited the taxi after Ryder gave the driver three tokens in payment. This part of the city had the refacing of the building completed. Consequently, the three-story-high building was adorned with large, pink, concrete slabs. At the top of each floor was a row of smaller, white blocks. Above the double, glass doors and the wide picture window on each side of them, was a cantilevered awning highlighted by alternating red and white stripes.

As they entered through the automatic, sliding door, Ryder noticed there were fashionable, men's suits on mannequins filling the space behind the left window. The right window space was similarly styled with women's clothing. In Ryder's opinion there were far too many mannequins packed tightly into the display areas.

Once inside the store, Ryder followed Linkin past the service area where the man behind the counter flipped a key to Linkin. Without breaking stride, Linkin caught the key and said, "I owe you one, Martin. My thanks."

As the two men continued to walk towards a narrow, rear hallway, Martin's words followed them. "It's dark-blue. You're welcome, and yes, you do!"

Linkin and Ryder continued down the hallway and through the rear service door. Across the narrow, service laneway were many vehicles parked neatly in designated spaces. Several were dark-blue. Linkin pointed the key at the vehicles, and the light bar along the trunk latch of one, flashed. After entering the vehicle, a moment later, they were travelling down the short laneway. A quick left, then another, and they were on 34th street with the clothing shop just ahead.

Ryder lowered his head as they passed by, although there was little risk they would be seen. The couple were both peering through the store window as best they could, bobbing their heads back and forth around the mannequins.

Twenty minutes later, Linkin and Romy arrived on 43rd street in a lower-class part of the city. Here, the buildings had not been refinished, so the vision along both sides of the street were two long expanses of grey concrete. In the distance, a large cloud of concrete dust was billowing into the air. Ironically, in the middle of the drab expanse was a dark green sign with white letters. It read,

The Green Forest Bar.

As Linkin brought the electric vehicle to a stop in front of it, Ryder looked at his interlink. The time was 20:05. He was five minutes late. Ryder said, "Park across the road, and keep an eye out from there. I will call you for pickup."

Linkin nodded as Ryder left the vehicle. Ryder peered down both directions along the sidewalk. Quite a few people were out, many for their dinner, some just for a drink and some relaxation. It took a moment for Ryder's eyes to adjust once he entered the long, narrow room of the establishment. A shiny bar top was along one side, with high stools along the front of it. There were booths along both walls rearward of the bar top, but it was hard to tell because of the lack of lighting. There were only a few people within the bar. As Ryder walked past them, they tried not to be obvious, but their eyes let them down. Ryder noticed their shifty eyes following him. As much as he didn't want to be recognized, he realized the dim light within the bar suited the brand of customers frequenting the establishment.

From a booth near the back wall, a hand motioned out from behind it. Ryder walked towards it and found Langdon Zaf, looking ridiculous in all-black clothing, waiting for him. Once Ryder slid in across from him, Langdon raised his hand one more time, this time with two raised fingers. Ryder had a quizzical look on his face, and opened his mouth to speak. Langdon pulled his hand in, bringing a finger to his lips to indicate Ryder should be silent.

The bartender arrived with two short glasses of blue, hard liquor. Once the stocky man left, Langdon relaxed. He took a drink from the glass and swallowed, causing his eyes to squint just as his lips thinned into a wide grimace. "Fuck, it's good, but it burns going down."

Ryder frowned. "What's going on? Why all the secrecy?"

Leaning forward, Langdon, peered around the corner of the booth before locking his eyes on Ryder's. "Your life's in danger."

"You mean those two agents the council had following me?"

Langdon's eyebrows rose. "You did lose them, right?"

There was an edge to Ryder's voice. He took a drink of the harsh liquor, then wiped his lips. "Tell me why they're following me."

"You heard the verdict of the Council of Twelve earlier today," Langdon explained. "The decision wasn't unanimous, but the majority voted accordingly." Raising a finger, he waggled it at Ryder as he continued. "However, a few wanted more severe action. In their view, they thought you would always be an embarrassment to the Korian people. These officials had more radical thoughts. They joked, 'that was as long as Ryder was alive.' They laughed, but I could tell by the look in their eyes, they weren't kidding. Most of the other matriarchs and advisors also laughed, but no one admonished those bringing forth the notion of your death." The finger stopped waggling and pointed at Ryder's nose. "The moderates could be easily swayed."

Ryder leaned back and let out a deep sigh. "What do you think I should do?"

Langdon spit out the response, interrupting the question before it was finished. "You need to leave Murcia. Take Romy and live in Torrin House with your sister and the Sholites. You could be happy there."

Ryder rubbed his chin. "I'm a Korian. As much as I have come to like the Sholites, I'm not one of them."

Seeing the sparkle in Ryder's eyes, Langdon lifted his chin. "You knew something like this would happen, didn't you?" He crossed his arms. "And I assume you already have a plan."

Shrugging, Ryder replied, "I'm going to go far away from the Council of Twelve, hopefully satisfying their need to have me out of their hair."

"You're not going to live with the Mabuza?"

"No—further."

Langdon's eyes lit up with understanding, matching the brightness in Ryder's eyes. "You don't mean…"

Through a wide smile, Ryder said, "I'm going to go back to space and do something I've always wanted." His eyes became even brighter. "I'm joining the Explorer Corp."

Chapter 3: The Patriotic Forces

Three years after the Murcia uprising…

07:00 hours, 21ˢᵗ day of the 3ʳᵈ Korian month, Haven year 0024

PAT Base 4, 400 kilometres east-northeast of Villaro

Romy woke with a start. As his eyes focused, he saw the wide grin dominating Jax's large face as it hovered over him. Immediately, Romy knew the source of the smirk.

After sliding his hand down his face, Romy swivelled, throwing his feet off the side of the cot. "Was I dreaming again?"

Jax had leaned back and lowered onto his cot across the narrow aisle that divided the barracks in two. "Oh, yeah. You were out for a while, your body fidgeting the way it had during your past dreams, and your eyes were vibrating back and forth under your eyelids." Jax pointed at his own eyes with two fingers, moving them back and forth as fast as he could. "It's freaky."

There was a day's worth of stubble on Romy's face. Lifting his chin, he dragged his hand down his neck. "I need a shave."

Jax frowned, narrow lines forming on his brow. "Aren't you going to tell me what the dream was about? Did you see the stars again?"

"Of course. It seems almost every time I dream, first, I always see an expanse of lights in my mind's eye. I would think of them as stars except they are a mix of red, yellow and blue."

Urging him on, Jax leaned closer. "Which world did you go to?"

"I've dreamt about it before. It's a beautiful world, crisscrossed with canals," Romy replied as he pulled on a tee shirt, then a pair of military pants. The tee shirt was olive green with dark-green long sleeves, while the pants carried a grey and green camo pattern.

Jax, dressed in the same military colours, asked, "Were you flying again?"

Romy pushed his feet into a pair of thick, ankle-high boots before pulling the velcro wraps tight. Most people would've thought Romy was crazy, but Jax had been with him long enough to know his dreams were unique and not just a mental delusion. "You know it. In my dream I was flying over a lush landscape. The cities weren't at all modern, and if that in itself wasn't unusual, there were these short creatures covered in blue fur. Yet, they were walking upright and wearing clothes."

Rising to his full height, a head above Romy, Jax shook his head. "Your brain is fucked up. Maybe this civil war is getting to you?"

Romy heard the slight *woosh* from the movement of hydraulic fluid around Jax's ankle. It had been over three years since the Murcia Uprising. That day, Jax made it to the hospital, but the doctors couldn't save his leg. It was amputated below the knee. Fortunately, with the medical advancements from the Bli family, a bionic leg was mounted to the stump a month later. Jax didn't mind, considering he could run faster and jump higher than he could before the accident.

Many others were not as fortunate that day. The Talus Dogs lost 18 soldiers, while the police dead numbered 83. There were also 20 dead protestors. The two hours of fighting brought all Korians to a point where each needed to decide, do they support the matriarchs of the council, or do they support the growing group, now calling themselves patriots.

Over the next two weeks a massive upheaval occurred. Even though the military was dominated by the Fyr family, only about 60 per cent carried the Fyr name or were closely affiliated with the powerful family. These people remained loyal. The remaining 40 per cent, some of which were actually Jez family members, revolted against their Fyr superiors. Entire military barracks were overrun as these soldiers changed sides and joined the patriots.

The same scenario unfolded within the police with most remaining loyal, but again, 30 to 40 per cent bolted to the other side. Most families chose a side. However, some, especially the secondary and lower-level families, were split in their support. Even in space, most of the military fleet remained loyal to the matriarchal council, but 23 ships ranging from frigates to even a battleship, defected. Of course, being severely outnumbered by the matriarchal forces, they couldn't stay in orbit. Rather, they chose what many considered a suicidal trip as they pointed their noses to deep space, never to be seen or heard from again. Such were the events that began the Korian Civil War.

Romy and Jax had joined the Patriotic forces, known simply as the PAT forces, just as the matriarchal enemy became known as the MAT forces. However, some referred to them simply as *loyalists*.

Slapping Jax on the chest, Romy smiled. "I'm hungry. Let's get breakfast." He didn't wait for a response as he walked down the length of the plastic pipe and sheet-covered barracks. In front of the structure, he saw the rest of his squad sitting at a table. The two women and man were already eating the bland looking food off their grey trays.

Without missing a swallow, Marty, one of the women identifiable by her short, blonde hair, pointed at the two covered trays on the table. "We picked up your trays for you."

Romy sat down across from Jax. "Appreciate that, Marty."

Tilting her face, Marty glared at Romy. "I've been with you for over a year, and still, I can't figure you out. You've led our squad to great success. The generals notice and try to promote you. But in no time, you're broken back down to *Senior*, because you've insulted the same generals, or disobeyed their orders."

Jax swallowed a mouthful of food, adding, "But each time he's disobeyed orders, Romy was right, saved our asses and successfully completed the mission. The generals weren't pissed because their orders were disobeyed. They were pissed because they were wrong, and Romy was right."

Marty glared at Jax, then shifted her gaze back to Romy, pointing at him with her knife. "My point is, at least get yourself together enough to get up in time for breakfast. One day, you'll get up, and there'll be nothing here because we'll be sick of babysitting you."

Stone faced, Romy whispered, "Marty."

"What?"

"I love you too." Romy's face was consumed by a huge, condescending smile.

Marty growled, "You ass!" as she flung herself at Romy, her arm wrapping around his neck. They both fell off the bench, wrestling on the ground. Marty was fit and as muscular as any man; she was giving at least as good as she got. Jax, Ren and Callum, the other members of Romy's squad, were cheering and hooting when a voice bellowed in the background.

"Romy Gunn!"

Marty rolled off Romy, allowing him to see the bulky silhouette of a soldier against the forever twilight. When the dust cleared, he saw the soldier was dressed as a soldier should be, in a pressed outfit with crisp pleats. Propping himself up on his elbows, Romy replied, "I'm Romy Gunn." He tilted his head slightly, wondering how the big man could talk with only his lower lip moving, but he did.

"Senior Gunn, General Brett Jezeer requests your presence in his office at 9:00—sharp!"

Nodding his head, Romy replied, "Of course."

The general's messenger made a sharp turn, clicked his heels and strode proudly off towards the officer's compound.

Marty came over to stand beside Romy, hands on her hips. She mumbled, "Well, la-de-da."

Through a grin, Jax added, "I wonder what you've fucked up now."

"I have no idea, but I better get cleaned up before I find out."

After going back into the barracks for a packet of clean clothes and his washing kit, Romy made his way across the huge military compound towards the shower building. A large hover plane cruised over the camp of over 15,000 PAT soldiers. It made a sweeping turn around the base before vectoring towards the runway along the edge of the compound. Beyond the runway, to the south, was a forest of tall, thick-barked trees—like a line of old, grizzly men watching over the base. To the south were tall grasslands where one could hear the high waves crashing against the sheer cliffs along the coast, five kilometres away.

PAT Base 4 was a strategic stronghold, 400 kilometres east-northeast of Villaro. When the civil war began, the patriots fled Murcia for Villaro. Villaro had long been the source of the protests, but after the insurrection, it became the PAT forces home base. PAT Base 4 was a crucial supply base, well behind their front lines, and it was a key point from which their missions initiated.

The hot water spraying over Romy's body felt comforting. As he washed himself, he felt the scars from the many forays he had led: the ragged scar along his forearm, the longer scar down his left side and the ugly round scar from the bullet that travelled through his left thigh. As much as he was a good fighter, and even more so an experienced survivor, he just wanted the war to end. He hadn't been home to Torrin House for three months. He missed his mother and Valre…Valre! *Shit*, he had almost forgot he needed to call her.

He would have a few minutes before his meeting if he hurried, so he did. He was clean, shaved and dressed in no time. He jogged the short distance to the communications building. He made it just in time to initiate the call home from one of many secure, encrypted video terminals. There were several *beeps* before Valre's face appeared on the monitor. When she saw Romy, her face brightened with a wide smile.

Valre was Romy's caretaker—yes, that was the best word for it. Many people on New Kor employed caretakers to look after their households. Typically, these caretakers were a combination of butler, homemaker, accountant, advisor and confidant.

Romy's father, Ryder, had one for most of his life. Fehyr had been loyal to Ryder, even through Ryder's removal from the Gunn family business. However, Fehyr was older and became sick. When he didn't have long left, Valre arrived. Valre was a distant relative of Fehr's within the Edy family. As much as Fehyr worried about Ryder, his larger concern was for a young Romy to have someone to look after his best interests. That was when Romy was 12. Now, as he looked at Valre's face in the computer, Romy was 30, and Valre was 48, but still eye-catchingly attractive.

"Valre, it's great to see you. I received a message to call you this morning. Is everything okay?"

Smiling, her cheeks rose, brightening her face surrounded by shoulder-length, white hair. "Everything is fine here at Torrin House. Your mother is fine as well."

"I miss you both. Hopefully, this war will be over soon, and I can return home."

Valre's face leaned closer to the screen. She peered from side to side as if someone might be listening. "The Sholite officials are hearing there are peace talks secretly scheduled. Although the MAT forces aren't exactly losing, they're taking heavy losses."

"Is that why you wanted me to call?"

"No. It's simpler. I will be visiting my family in Talus. I won't be able to communicate with you for two weeks."

Valre would go on these two-week trips to visit family a few times a year, so, as odd as they were, Romy was accustomed to them. The city, Talus, named after the destroyed asteroid home, was an underground city in the northeast New Kor Islands. Not all Korians, or even Sholites for that matter, adapted well to the openness, natural light and fresh air Haven offered. After thousands of years living in cities carved out of the massive asteroid, they couldn't accept such a monumental change. Consequently, two years after their arrival on Haven, a group of some 25,000 settlers decided to create an underground city in the image of the asteroid cities that had been the Korian's comfort zone for many lifetimes. Valre's relatives were within that group.

"Valre, as always, be careful."

"You too, Romy, and…" She hesitated.

"What?"

She shrugged, "Well, don't piss anybody off."

Romy frowned. "Love you. Talk to you in two weeks." He pressed a key and the call disconnected.

Checking the time on his wrist interlink, he realized he would need to hurry to make it to the general's office on time. At the officer's compound, he passed his interlink over a scanner beside a burly guard. When the light turned green, Romy was allowed to pass.

He saw the same large messenger, from earlier in the morning, outside the large barracks serving as the general's quarters and his office. The large man flicked his head towards the door. "Go on. He's waiting for you."

Romy had only ever seen General Jezeer from a distance, but that was enough to recognize the man sitting behind the desk. Another soldier was sitting in a metal, cloth covered, fold-up chair, opposite from him. As soon as Romy entered, the general lifted a finger in the air, stopping Romy in his tracks.

The general was intently watching a video monitor on his desk, listening to a report. His face turned red, then he slapped the disconnect key. His other hand, in a fist, slammed down on his desk. "I can't believe it!" He was ranting—to no one in particular. "Another cargo shuttle lost over the Eastern Ocean! Another one of these instant storms or cyclones—whatever you want to call it—gobbles up another one of our vessels. You would think, after 24 years, our scientists could figure out what's happening. Overall, things have been easy since we arrived, except for this civil war and these climactic events. Our scientists search and investigate, but they still have no idea what's causing the storms. First, we would inexplicably lose ocean going ships. So, we stopped that. Then, we only used hover ships and even these, such as the one consumed yesterday, are captured by the storms."

General Jezeer pointed to the empty chair beside the man opposite the general. "*Gunney*, take a seat."

The corner of Romy's mouth twitched before he strode to the front of the desk. "It's Gunn, Sir—Romy Gunn."

The general hadn't yet looked at Romy, but now he glanced up at his eyes. He snapped his fingers and pointed to the chair. "Gunn it is then." The general pointed to the man sitting in the other chair. "Gunn, this is Pilot Matt Demoro."

Demoro glanced at the *G33* on the arm of Romy's shirt and said, "Hello, *Grunt*."

The *G*, in fact, indicated Romy was in Ground Forces, squad 33. Similarly, on the arm of the pilot's black shirt was, *A11*. Romy knew the *A* represented – Air Forces, but he couldn't let the pilot's insult lie, despite Valre's recent pleading not to piss anyone off. Romy poked the man at the *A*. "You know what that really stands for?"

Matt Demoro, with a smug look, answered, "Yup. Word amongst the Grunts is it means, *Asshole*, and I'm proud of it."

"Congratulations. You're succeeding."

"Hold up a minute. Stop arguing even before we get started," the general interjected.

Romy sat down and waited for the general to continue. He could tell by the shades of light passing over the general's face, he was scrolling through several files on the monitor.

Romy understood the general's use of the name, "Gunney." After the insurrection, many of the patriots didn't want to be directly associated with their matriarchal families. That's why the general changed his surname from *Jez* to *Jezeer*. In many cases, the prefix or suffix added was tied to a word worthy of the patriotic fight. For Demoro, once of the Oro family, *Dem,* from democratic, was added.

"You're both here for a reason," Jezeer continued. "You don't have to like each other, but you have to get along." The silence that followed told the general the two men understood. The red tinge on his face faded under his short-cropped hair, black at the top, ringed by even shorter, grey hair at the sides and back. His gaze focused on Romy. "I need you to accept a mission."

"With all due respect, Sir, this is the military, and in the military missions are assigned, not accepted or rejected."

The general had a wide face with a protruding jaw, the kind that looked like it could take a punch. He tried to soften the perpetual scowl as he replied," That's true, son, but this is a difficult mission. We think you're the right man for the job, but only if you're confident you can get it done. If you have reservations, then we'll move on with someone else."

"I'm not sure I understand."

"This mission will take you and a few of your squad deep behind enemy lines. We *don't* need a *yes* man. We *do* need someone who can think quick, since this mission will be conducted under radio silence. Your past record shows you think fast on your feet despite the interference of your superiors."

Romy exhaled, wondering what he was getting into. "There are lots of such men in your division."

After a loud guffaw, the general added, "True, but you have something else. You have attitude and a vast amount of pride. That's why you haven't changed your last name even though your father is a black mark on the Korian people. That's why you wear that bracelet on your wrist even though it's against code. It's your own quiet way of saying, *fuck you*, to my leadership."

Romy glanced at the metallic bracelet. It was silver with a metallic insert of black and light blue, held together by a silver chain. He wore it because it held a strong, sentimental value. His gaze returned to match the general's stare. "Not *your* leadership in particular, Sir."

Matt Demoro had been listening, but couldn't hold back his laughter any longer. It spilled out as he slapped his knee. "You're too much, Gunn. I'm really starting to like you!"

Rolling his eyes, the general rose to his feet. "Follow me gentlemen." He led the two men into the next room behind his office. "What you're about to see is strictly confidential."

In the next room, a large map was displayed on a video monitor hanging from the back wall of what was obviously an operations center. The general turned in front of the map and asked Romy, "Have you heard of General Hayden Fyr of the MAT forces?"

"Can't say I have, General."

"That's not a surprise. He's not in the group of higher-ranking generals, but he is the smartest person they have when it comes to tactical strategies. As such, he plans most of their offensive forays," the general explained. "We've been trying to get him for eight months, but his whereabouts are always well guarded. We know he moves from base to base, and that makes targeting him even more difficult." General Jezeer's finger hit hard on the map. "However, we have reliable intelligence that he'll be arriving *here* tomorrow and be staying for two weeks."

Romy squinted and moved closer to the map. The general's finger had pointed to as remote an area as they came, in the middle of the *Northern Wildes*. The *Wildes* was a large, dense jungle area in the middle of the Korian continent, roughly halfway between Murcia and Villaro. It was 800 kilometres wide and 200 kilometres deep. Jezeer's finger had landed on the far side of the Wildes.

Crossing his arms, Romy said, "Getting there will be impossible."

"Impossible?" the general repeated back.

"Let's say—near impossible."

The general grinned. "I like your optimism." He pointed at Demoro. "Matt's here to help you. There's a clearing here, just inside the *Southern Wildes*. He'll drop you there, but from that point you'll be on your own. You'll make your way across the Wildes and assassinate Hayden Fyr." The general plucked a picture of a man off the pin holding it to a board beside the monitor. He handed it to Romy.

Romy's eyebrows rose as he saw the man in the picture. "What happened to his face?"

"Years ago, a house fire. His wife was killed." The general swallowed hard. "He was lucky to make it out alive."

"He will be easy to recognize."

Romy, as a Senior, was the direct leader of his squad, but he was also in command of four additional squads, so 25 soldiers in total. That was too many for this mission. "I'll do it. I'm taking two squads—ten men in total. The job calls for stealth, so we don't need to be clomping through the jungle. When do we go?"

Slapping Romy on the shoulder, the general replied, "Excellent, son! Demoro will take you in his helocraft at 6:00. The rains usually come around 9:00, so you'll be in a holding pattern, then dropped under the cover of the rain."

Romy nodded. "Sir, I have to ask. There are three levels of command between you and I. Why aren't they here?"

"Because this mission is top secret. We don't need leaks. They know you're going on this mission, but they don't—and won't— know any details."

"Got it."

As they moved back into the general's outer office, Jezeer slapped Romy on the back again. "Good luck, son. Remember, tell your squad, but no one else is to know. Once you leave this base, in the morning, there'll be complete radio silence. Your pick up will be exactly nine days after your drop. Make sure you're at the rendezvous on time."

Once Romy left the office, Demoro scratched his head. "Sir, we've known each other for a while. I'm sure Gunn is a good soldier, but I don't see anything spectacular. I'm not sure he's the right guy for the job."

The corners of the general's mouth turned down. "Matt, he's *exactly* the guy we need for the job. Now go relax, and be in the air at 6:00."

After Demoro left, General Jezeer sat down in his chair, crossing one ankle over the other on his desk. From his drawer he picked out a *smack*, a small candy, laced with a tiny amount of a mildly-euphoric drug. He popped it in his mouth as he thought, *yes, Romy Gunn is exactly the person we need. None of the members of his squad are affiliated with important or high-ranking officials on either the MAT or PAT sides. If they don't return, no one will care.* He grinned as the drug began to take effect. *And who would care if Romy Gunn came back? In fact, if something went really bad, who better to blame than the son of the infamous, Ryder Gunn.*

Chapter 4: Villaro Outpost

02:00 hours, 3rd day of the 1st Korian month, Haven year 0006

Space, 3,000 kilometres from Haven.

"*Haven Control 2*, this is the *Factfinder*, requesting permission to approach."

"*Factfinder*, we verify your ping signature. What are your intentions?" came the reply from the controller on board one of four control tower stations orbiting Haven at an altitude of 350 kilometres.

On the command deck of the *Factfinder*, one of 12 Explorer Corp., Wolf-class spaceships the Korians used to explore the distant reaches of space, the communications officer pressed a button on the panel in front of him. "*Haven Control 2*, this is *Factfinder*, requesting permission to dock at Space Station *Odyssey*."

A few seconds later, a reply came from the controller. "*Factfinder*, *Odyssey* station is at position 35, 100, 185. Slow your speed to *4K* and proceed to their outer beacon."

The *Factfinder* navigation officer, sitting beside the communication officer, pressed a sequence of keys at his station. A blue icon with the word, *ENGAGE*, flashed on his monitor. The navigation officer turned and looked at the captain, "Sir, speed and beacon coordinates are programmed. Permission to engage?"

Ryder Gunn sat slouched back in the well-padded, captain's chair. Their ship had been on a mission for the past month. Although, it was vastly productive, with results that would beg future missions, he was grateful to be almost home. "Ensign Edy, permission granted."

Forty-five minutes later, the *Factfinder* had intersected the *Odyssey*'s beacon laser. The Haven controller's voice came over the speaker. "*Factfinder*, you're at the outer beacon. *Odyssey* Control will take you from here. Good luck."

A second later, a fast-paced, female voice was heard on the command deck of the Explorer ship. "*Factfinder*! Welcome home! Follow *Odyssey* beacon, and dock in bay 15."

"Ensign Edy, lock us onto the beacon," Ryder said. "Bring us in slow—by the book. Start the rotation."

Odyssey station was in orbit, 450 kilometres above the surface of Haven. It was a massive, cylindrical, web-like structure, one kilometre across its diameter and one kilometre deep. Half of the depth was occupied by work decks and living quarters. The rear half of the station was an open framework, encompassing docking bays for up to 18 spaceships.

To simulate gravity, at least to some degree, the entire station rotated on its central axis, thus the requirement for *Factfinder* to slowly begin a spin, eventually matching the rotation of the *Odyssey*.

"Rotation matched, Captain," Ensign Mal offered. We're at two kilometres. Permission to dock?"

"Take us in," Ryder said.

It wasn't long before the command deck officers saw *Factfinder* slide alongside what, from a distance, looked like a thin finger but could now be distinguished as a 50-metre-long docking ramp. There was only a slight jostle as the spaceship made contact with the two boarding platforms suspended from the ramp.

"As always, excellent work, Edy and Mal," Ryder offered. He pressed a button on the arm of his chair and pulled a microphone to his mouth. "This is Captain Gunn. We are docked at *Odyssey*." Through the steel walls behind him, he could hear the whoops of the 80 crew members aboard the ship. "Two shuttles are waiting. I have been informed the shuttle at Dock 4 is going to Murcia and the other is at Dock 6, destined for Villaro Outpost." He paused and grinned before continuing. "And for those of you *children* on furlough, be safe. No running in the aisles, please."

The ten members of the command deck crew were anxiously waiting.

Ensign Tor was Ryder's second in command and also the propulsion officer. Ryder turned to him and asked, "Is the shutdown sequence complete?"

"Yes, Sir."

"Is the docking procedure complete, Ensign Edy?" Ryder asked.

"It indeed is, Captain."

Ryder rose to his feet, making a slow circle as he spoke. "Ladies and Gentlemen, it was a pleasure working with you for the last month. Everyone did an exemplary job." He raised a finger in the air. "Remember, the details and findings of our mission are top secret and not to be divulged to anyone—not until I provide the report—and perhaps not even at that point."

There were a few knowing snickers from the deck officers. The Explorer Corp. was officially part of the Fyr military family, but more akin to an unwanted, bastard cousin. Since the Korian fleet had arrived at Haven, the senior military officers thought the Explorer Corp were even less useful than during their time inhabiting the asteroid, Talus. Ryder was fine with that. It meant, depending what their findings were, sometimes he reported them, sometimes he didn't. No one outside the Explorer Corp. really cared.

Ryder continued. "For those of you on furlough, you are dismissed."

All but three of the deck officers hurried to the hallway at the back of the command room. Ryder walked towards Malik Tor who was viewing temperature readings of the electromagnetic drives as they cooled. Ryder said to his second in command, "Take care of my baby while I'm gone. Check on our preparations, and we'll talk every day."

"Yes, Captain. In a month, everything will be ready."

Putting his hand on Malik's shoulder, he gave it a squeeze before he turned towards the exit from the room. As he walked by his chair set in the middle of the command deck, he retrieved the weathered, maroon, captain's jacket from the back of it. As he slipped it on, he turned down a side corridor towards the front docking door. After being in the cramped quarters of the *Factfinder* for the past month, the station's wide spaces seemed overwhelming, causing Ryder's legs to weaken. He grasped the hand rail and waited a few seconds until his brain adjusted to the open space down the 50-metre-length of the tube. After his mind settled, he walked towards the central moving sidewalk. Half its width was filled with a long row of chairs while the other half was left for walking. Ryder needed his legs to wake up. *Walking it was.*

As the capital and most developed area of Haven, most of the crew were going to Murcia. The residents of Villaro numbered only 30,000 and was considered nothing more than an outpost. Since the matriarchs that stripped Ryder of his family position resided in Murcia, he thought it best to steer clear of the Korian capital. He lived in Torrin House with Romy and his sister. The spacefield at Villaro was a better option than Murcia, and that's where a hoverjet was waiting to take him to the Sholite capital.

Not many of the crew members had the same encumbrances Ryder did. As such, there were only six crewmembers on the shuttle with him when the doors closed and the pilot announced their departure to Villaro.

Other than having a rounded nose and a narrower girth towards the rear of the shuttle, it didn't have a typical aerodynamic shape. However, when the shuttle entered the lower atmosphere, wings were pushed out from the fuselage to a swept back position, allowing for a smooth flight for the occupants.

Ryder tilted his head back and looked out one of the small side windows. Their altitude was approximately 3,000 metres. He could see both the airfield and the spacefield just beyond it. The pilot veered the craft to the right, beginning what was a wide circle to come at the spacefield's landing strip from the opposite direction. This allowed them to land into the wind that came constantly from the east.

An hour from the time they left the *Odyssey*, the shuttle's wheels hit the tarmac. Ryder said his goodbyes to his fellow crewmembers, then walked the length of the terminal to the transportation hub. Normally, Linkin would be waiting for him at the taxi stand, so he was surprised to see Brett Dedman wave towards him. Brett was a Sholite and part of I'lish Mann's security group.

"Hello Brett. Where's Linkin?"

"Linkin thought it was a good idea to have a backup trained in your pickup routine, in case something ever happened to him," Brett replied. "This is a test run." He opened the taxi door, indicating Ryder should enter.

Ryder thought it odd Linkin wouldn't have given him some advance notice of the test run, but even though he didn't know Brett Dedman well, he had been in the employ of his sister for several years. There wasn't a reason to distrust him. Ryder entered the taxi, and Brett closed the door after following him in.

They had to make several turns while covering the four kilometres to the airfield and the waiting, Sholite hoverjet. *Something didn't feel right.* Ryder kept thinking about Linkin not meeting him. His tension increased to anxiety when he saw, in the driver's rear-view mirror, a grey vehicle following them. Brett was oddly silent, and when Ryder glanced at the bodyguard, he saw the beads of sweat on the Sholites brow. Ryder had made this trip many times, so when, a half-kilometer from the airfield's terminal, the driver erroneously veered onto a ramp leading towards an underground parking area, the hairs on Ryder's neck were standing on end. *Something was definitely wrong.*

Rolling his body, Ryder brought his left arm around, pummeling his fist into Brett's jaw. A second later, he had unlatched the door and flung himself out of the vehicle. A grunt was expelled from his lungs as he thought, *Tuck and roll—tuck and roll.* After the flip that wasn't as acrobatic as it should have been, Ryder's mind worked through the pain as he struggled to his feet.

As the taxi skidded to a stop, Ryder ran through the tall grass for the forty metres between the taxi and the half-metre high opening, just above ground level at the parking structure. He turned his head only once, seeing Brett hadn't regained consciousness, but another man from the following, grey car was running after him across the terrain.

Ryder was having difficulty. Not having been in a full gravity environment for a month, not only were his muscles fatigued, but he was also gasping to get air into his lungs. He thrust his legs forward and ducked, sliding through the short opening in the concrete, just as a bullet smashed into the wall above him. Twisting, one hand caught the concrete ledge, breaking what would have been a painful fall. Instead, he held on for a moment before releasing, allowing a more controlled fall to the floor of the parking level, three metres below.

Unfortunately, at this late hour, the parking garage was almost empty. There were ten cars parked between his position and the square, elevator structure, 100 metres away. Ignoring his weary legs, Ryder ran as fast as he could towards the elevator block. Behind him, he heard feet hit the concrete floor. By now, he assumed the man chasing him was an assassin. The assumption turned to fact when Ryder was almost at the elevator block, and a second bullet sent a spray of concrete into the air. Another bullet passed close by his head as he dove behind the elevator building.

With his back against the block wall, Ryder pushed himself to his feet. The assassin had no reason to run. It was 5:00, meaning there were few travellers expected at this early hour. He heard the light footsteps of the assassin echoing off the far wall of the parking garage. It was coming from his left, so, with his back still against the wall, he shuffled to his right. Ryder saw the tip of a gun at the edge of the wall, and he hurriedly slid around the far corner.

Behind him, he heard a chuckle echo through the garage level. "There's no where to go, Mister Gunn."

Ryder knew the assassin was right. His heart was pounding so hard, he didn't notice the vibration in the wall he was leaning against. Instinctively, he continued to shuffle to his right. He was halfway down the length of the wall, when the assassin came around the far corner. A satisfied smirk grew on his face as he saw Ryder out of options. The man's dark grin grew wider, and suddenly, his eyes sprang wide open. A trickle of blood dribbled from the corner of his mouth as he stumbled, then fell to the ground.

Turning his face to the right, a great sigh left Ryder's lungs as he saw a second man, gun in hand—a wisp of smoke at the end of the barrel. Ryder exclaimed, "Linkin!"

"My apologies, Sir. They tied me up. I got here as soon as I could."

"And just in time," Ryder admitted as he walked over, then kneeled down by the assassin.

He was still alive, but when Ryder pulled aside the man's jacket and saw the blood-soaked shirt, he knew it wouldn't be for long. This was the fifth assassination attempt Ryder had survived over the last three years. At least a portion of the Council of Twelve were determined to continue this effort until he was dead.

Ryder wanted to find out exactly who was so incensed. He grasped the man's chin, pulling his eyes to his own. "Who sent you to do this—who!"

The man's eyes rolled, and a spurt of blood jumped from his lips when he tried to speak. He tried again and whispered a frothy, "More than a few."

In a deeper voice, as his fingers increased the pressure on the man's chin, Ryder growled, "Who?"

As blood continued to dribble out both sides of the assassin's mouth, Linkin searched him. He checked both pant pockets and found nothing. He pulled aside the right side of the man's jacket and found something in the inside pocket. As Ryder continued to interrogate the dying man, Linkin pulled out the hard square of paper. When he looked at it, his eyes opened wider than the assassins had when he realized he just received a deadly bullet.

Ryder saw Linkin's surprise and glanced at the card. Now, it was Ryder's turn for his eyes to go wide, but his reaction was one of horror. The assassin saw this and smiled. Eyes open, that's how he died.

Ryder was at a loss for words. He just pointed at the card which, in fact, was a picture. On it was the image of his twelve-year-old son, Romy.

Chapter 5: The Mission

05:00 hours, 22ⁿᵈ day of the 3ʳᵈ Korian month, Haven year 0024

PAT Base 4, 400 kilometres east-northeast of Villaro

The morning looked like every other morning on Haven, with a light-grey haze dominating the sky, broken by intermittent fingers of white clouds. In fact, it looked like any other time of every day. Nighttime on Haven only happened in homes and buildings, where the people needed their minds to be fooled into their biological sleep cycle. So, at those times, blinds were pulled closed and lights were turned off, providing a poor solution. But, at least, it resulted in a semblance of calm.

The wind always blew from the east, sucked underneath the torrid air lifted upwards by the perpetual assault of the sun's rays on the western face of the planet. At 3:40, when Romy's eyes cracked open, it was to hear the thin, plastic cover of the barracks, fluttering between the tube-like, plastic supports. Romy dressed quickly and slapped the slumbering form of Marty as he walked by her cot. He did the same for Ren. There was no need to prod Jax whose bunk was empty. His early rise on the day of a mission was a well-known habit.

Once he was outside the barracks, Romy saw the table under the tarp in front of the barracks next to his had five soldiers seated on the benches. Rico was a man with a thick, square face, made even wider by a liberal, unkempt, black beard. His nod towards Romy was enough for Romy to understand Rico's squad was ready. With a squeak from the bench, Romy lowered down beside Jax and across from Callum, the fifth soldier of Romy's squad. Just as the canteen truck stopped in front of the barracks, dropping off trays of hot, breakfast food, Marty and Ren exited the barracks, joining the three men at the table.

As the kitchen attendant passed the trays to the soldiers, he prodded, "So, you're up early. Is it a special mission?" His eyebrows rose inquisitively.

Romy rubbed the sleep that was still in his eyes before inspecting the man. He was more than skinny, and, right there, he understood why the man was assigned to the kitchen. "Just another surveillance mission. No big deal."

The kitchen attendant cracked an angled smile across his hollow face.

Romy could tell the skinny man didn't believe him, and Romy didn't give a shit. He still needed to maintain the secrecy of the mission. Both sides had spies within the military, so even though the man's physique was less than extraordinary, his position within the canteen would be the perfect hub to gather information from.

"Thanks for the early breakfast," Romy added, indicating the conversation was over. He watched the attendant deliver breakfast to Rico's table. Recognizing Rico was the *Junior* in charge of the second squad, the kitchen attendant could be seen prodding him with similar questions. However, Rico wasn't ever one for many words, and when he did have something to say, usually it was direct, albeit in an eerily subdued tone.

Chuckling, Romy saw the skinny man shrink back. He realized Rico must have given the attendant one of his patented requests to, *fuck off*. Romy had been shoveling mouthfuls of meat and a version of spicy potatoes into his mouth, when he glanced towards Marty and saw she hadn't eaten a bite.

Romy nudged her. "Eat your food. It might be a while before we get another hot meal."

"You know I can't eat before a mission," Marty chirped.

Romy knew better than to make a big deal of it, so he continued to eat while keeping his eyes forward. "I'm sorry, Marty, but you seem to be confused, thinking that was a request. If you need help clearing that thought, just glance at my shoulder and the buttons indicating my rank."

Marty didn't need another reminder. Outwardly, Romy gave the appearance of a casual person, but underneath that layer, his squad knew he was intense and a great leader. She knew better than to make him ask a second time. Instead, she gave a slight growl, letting him know she wasn't thrilled, then started lifting forkfuls of food into her mouth.

An hour later, they were inside one of the large, aircraft hangers beside the runway. The two squads of soldiers under Romy were within a large, locker room. They changed out of their camp garb into the high-tech gear provided for stealth missions behind enemy lines. The trousers and thin jackets were made of a grey and green, camouflage-patterned material. The material was developed from a recent technology where the fibres had a triangular cross section. As such, the colour shades changed depending on the angle of the light reflecting off it, making it very difficult to be pinpointed, and it made it just as difficult for a sniper to lock on the suited soldier through the scope of a rifle.

The helmet and knee-high boots were coated with the same material, completing the combat uniform. At their waist was a wide belt. Attached to it, above one hip, was a small pouch containing an electrical device. When activated, it provided a reflective layer around the soldier that would negate the ability for enemy surveillance to sense their heat signatures. It was a necessity on this type of mission behind enemy lines.

Once the six men and four women were dressed, they went to the armoury where they were each given the latest dual mode rifles. Ammunition magazines for the advanced weapons that could fire either bullets or compressed air charges, were clipped to their belts. The exception was Marty who chose a heavier weapon that shot the conventional compressed air charges as well as mini grenades from the wider, second barrel. Consequently, her belt was different, fitting around her waist and also crisscrossing across her chest, allowing for thirty charges to be carried.

As soon as they left the locker room, Romy heard a shrill whistle. His eyes moved to the source of the sound to see General Jezeer waving his hand over his head. Romy turned his head and said to the troop, "Wait for us outside. Rico, you're with me."

When Romy came within range, the general began to walk towards the hanger opening with a hand on Romy's shoulder. Rico walked a few paces behind them.

Retrieving a smack from his pocket, the general popped it into his mouth. "You know we have a major offensive in eastern New Kor, coordinated out of PAT Base 2?"

"Yes, Sir. I hear we have 20,000 men engaged."

The general's lower jaw slid from side to side as the smack rolled around his mouth. "Every day we flood the area with barrage jamming signals just before we strafe their front line with our fighters. Then the infantry advances." The general pivoted and faced Romy. "We've been making excellent headway—four kilometres a day. It's slow, but in a war like this has been, I would say that type of progress tells me we have them on the run."

"Yes, Sir."

A chuckle escaped the general's lips. "I don't say this to make you worry about the eastern front. I'm telling you this so you understand we're going to use the radar jamming event to hide your drop into the Southern Wildes. The loyalists are so used to looking at what we're doing in the east, we can sneak you in under their noses."

Romy's gaze stayed fixated on a spot in the middle of the general's forehead. "Sounds like a plan, Sir."

The general's hand slapped Romy on the shoulder. "It's up to you, son. It's radio silence from here, so good luck."

Any further discussion would have been useless as the engines of the helocraft were started by Pilot Demoro. The high-pitched whine assaulting Romy's ears was soon replaced by the steady, fast-paced *thump, thump, thump* of the four sets of long turboprop blades, one set attached to each corner of the craft.

Romy gave the general a nod of his chin before he and Rico jogged towards the open side door, then jumped in beside their squad members. Immediately, the vertically facing rotors, powered by two electromagnetic turbines, lifted the craft into the air.

It was 6:00. Looking to the east, Romy saw the line of expected rain clouds still two hours away. He knew the plan. They would fly along the tree tops to a holding position until the rains came. Under the darkness it provided, they would swoop in and be dropped into a small clearing—the clearing in the *no-man's-land* of the Wildes. It was as close as they dared go while still avoiding detection.

The soldiers, seated on a short metal bench, all reached for the handholds suspended from the roof when the aircraft made its first sharp turn. For the first 30 minutes, the forest wasn't as dense, so Demoro could weave a path through the trees. The two gunners, one on each side of the helocraft, each held the end of a powerful laser cannon. Under the rim of their black helmets, they wore modified goggles, electrically charged so that their vision was greatly enhanced. Romy was amazed that, as the craft moved almost on its side while it snaked through the trees, even though the gunners were joined to the craft by a safety strap, they barely shifted. One of them even yawned.

The craft, that had been angled forward, tipped back to a horizontal position and lowered to the carpet of long grass in a clearing just before the edge of the thicker jungle ahead. Demoro brought the engines back to an idling speed, with the rotors feathered and disconnected, before turning over the controls to his co-pilot. He walked back to the main cabin and said to the soldiers, "The rain is still at least an hour away." He turned his gaze to Romy. "You have time to get some fresh air."

Romy nodded, then let the two squads out of the helocraft. He pointed to four of the soldiers, assigning one to each corner of the perimeter. "Keep your eyes peeled."

It would be easy to be lulled into a sense of lethargy. The ground was covered in ankle-high, green grass, broken by twist trees, so called because they spiraled upwards as they grew. At the base of their trunks, blue and red wildflowers grew—the type requiring shade provided by the wide, star shaped leaves.

"A tiny bit of calm before the storm?"

Romy recognized Jax's voice behind him. The branches above the two men rattled as the wind picked up, pushed by the oncoming rainclouds. Turning to face his friend, Romy had the same thought he had at the beginning of every mission. Jax was the only person who he considered a close friend.

It was a relationship that began when Romy was in middle school. It wasn't easy being the son of the infamous Ryder Gunn. His father sent him to a private school in the hope the stricter environment would result in less chiding from the other boys at the school. It probably was, but still, Romy received his fair share of taunts and insults.

In one way, Romy thought it wasn't all that bad as he grew a thick skin and learned some creative ways to avoid some vulnerable situations. Nevertheless, some couldn't be avoided. One day, he was late for a class, so he took a shortcut between two buildings. Three boys came out of the shadows when he was halfway down the narrow laneway. He had a choice. He could run the other way in which case the bullying would just get worse. Instead, he put down his school bag and rolled up his sleeves.

The three boys smirked confidently as they approached Romy, but Romy lunged forward, smacking the confident look off the closest one with a roundhouse right. The boy stumbled before spitting out a mouthful of bloody saliva. A moment later, the three boys attacked simultaneously, and Romy fought back, fists flailing into one, then the next. Yet, there were three of them, so it didn't take long for Romy to be on his back with the three boys kicking into him.

Romy was about to roll into a ball when he heard a grunt from one of the boys. When he opened his eyes, there were only two boys over him. A large hand grabbed the collar of one of them, flinging him backwards off his feet. No sooner had that boy landed in a heap when the same large hand curled into a fist, pummeling into the side of the remaining attacker's face.

As the three bloodied culprits scrambled to their feet and fled, Romy's blurred vision saw the large hand reach down to him. He took it and was helped to his feet. The boy, a good half head taller than Romy, smiled. "Hi, I'm Jax."

"Hi. I'm thankful."

"Huh?"

"I was kidding. I'm Romy." The response came with a wide, ear to ear smile.

From that point, Romy and Jax were inseparable during their remaining year of middle school and then through four years of higher education.

This was the history Romy thought of as he slid down with his back against the tree, his friend right beside him. It was nice to have time to talk as they waited, discussing nothing of real value, just the bullshit banter friends tended to talk about.

Ninety minutes later, they were interrupted by the first drops of rain. The soldiers moved back into the helocraft. Demoro was there waiting for them. "We'll be in the air momentarily. The jet packs are in the back of the helocraft."

The words were muffled as the co-pilot pressed the engine switches causing the rotors to whine. Romy was close enough to understand the direction and led the soldiers to a chest where they found the jet packs. Each of them strapped one around their shoulders before closing the clasp at their chest.

When they returned to their seats, they could hear the drops of rain against the metal shell of the craft were heavier. Demoro, with one hand on an overhead steel member, said, "Okay, we'll be in the air in a minute. The path ahead is dense jungle, so I won't be able to navigate through the trees as well." He pointed to a light positioned over the open side on each side of the helocraft. "When the light turns blue, it means 30 seconds to the target, so get to the opening. When it changes to yellow, it means you'll be jumping in five seconds." His blank, emotionless eyes moved from one soldier to the next. "When the light is green, jump. Don't fucking think about it—just jump. If you hesitate, you'll wind up dead in the trees." Demoro resembled a psychopath as he spoke the words of doom and gloom, while the deluge of rain was rattling on the outer skin of the craft. Demoro turned and mumbled, "Here we go."

The helocraft's engines gave out a deep groan as Demoro pushed the thrust levers forward. The aircraft angled sharply forward and popped out of the trees, then sped forward across the tips of the jungle canopy. If the occupants thought the first leg of their flight was stomach-churning, it didn't take long for their misconception to be verified. The treetops, thick with leaves, looked like a sea of green clouds, with creases between the billowing sections. Demoro found the creases and sped along them, half hidden in the treetops. As such, the helocraft still veered back and forth, but at double the speed of the first leg.

Romy and his two squads didn't say a word. Although the conditions were severe, it was something they had practiced many times over. Thankfully, when the door lights turned blue, Demoro righted the helocraft and reduced their velocity. Rising to their feet, Romy's crew each held the bar across the top of the left door opening. Rico's crew were the mirror image on the right. When the lights turned yellow, each soldier pulled down their goggles and took a bent-kneed stance.

Romy yelled, "green!" and Marty was instantly doing a barrel roll out the door. Each soldier's front foot was out the door as the previous soldiers back foot left the craft. As planned, they jumped at an altitude only 150 metres from the ground. Separation was created between them as they fired their jetpacks. Ten seconds later, they landed safely in a small field of rainbow grass, then they ran for the cover of the trees, 50 metres away.

These clearings were rare within the Wildes. They existed because there were isolated bedrock formations close to the surface, covered by a layer of soil up to half a metre thick. Because of the bedrock, tree roots couldn't take hold. The rainbow grass, thus named because it could exist in colours ranging from yellow to deep-red, depending on the acidity of the soil, thrived in the shallow soil and full sunlight.

Once the two squads were in the cover of the trees, they pulled off their expired jet packs and buried them under a blanket of dry, brown leaves. Romy huddled them together and looked at the map on his wrist interlink. It showed their position and the target camp, 70 kilometres away—70 kilometres of dense jungle and the *Swamp*, as it was simply known.

The Swamp was a half-kilometre expanse of hook trees, rooted in a three-metre-depth of semi-fluid mud. More than a few early explorers of the Wildes had lost their lives to it as the mud sucked in anyone foolish enough to fall in. Legend had it, that if someone did succumb to the mud and water, they would disappear in seconds, after which, almost immediately, the thin layer of muddy water would, once again, be peaceful and calm.

The rain stopped. In any case, thanks to the thick cover, the ground below the jungle canopy was relatively dry. Romy addressed his soldiers. "We have what I estimate is a 35-hour hike through this shit." His eyes turned to Ren. "You've got point, so put on the electroband." His eyes shifted to Rico. "Bring up the rear. I'll go second and keep us in the right direction. Everyone keep a spacing of ten metres." Rising from his squat, he rose and pointed north. "Let's go."

Ren moved beside Callum and retrieved a wristband from Callum's backpack. She locked it on her right wrist before taking her position ten metres ahead of Romy. She flicked a small switch on the band, and a blue-green, one-metre-long discharge of electricity sprung from it. With a circumspect gaze, she found the thinnest portion of the jungle before them and swung the sword-like electrical beam at the overgrowth, making short work of it.

Even with the advantage of the electroband, it was tough going. They stopped every two hours, and after eight hours, they were exhausted and hungry. Romy wanted to continue, but even he was feeling the fatigue affect his focus. Consequently, he gave the order to stop and make camp. Since they hadn't come across another clearing, Ren made one via the electroband.

The others, having been through this many times, also knew their tasks. Beck, one of Rico's squad, started up one of the trees, a wire trailing behind him. He scurried up the trunk, and at the top he locked the small solar panel onto a sturdy branch. He retraced his path to the ground, connecting the end of the wire to a power bar. Ren, having removed the wristband, plugged it in to recharge.

Callum, placed spikes from his backpack into the ground around the small clearing. Additional spikes were hammered into several trees ringing their campsite. Once wires connected all the spikes, Callum yelled, "All clear!" With no objections evident, he plugged the final wire into the power bar. There was a sizzle as the invisible fence was activated. Anything curious enough to touch it would learn a painful lesson.

The jungle floor was relatively dark since the majority of the sunlight was diffused by the wide-leafed canopy. Nevertheless, just as during their six-hour hike, they decided not to use lights. The jungle was filled with life, from insects to snakes and monkeys—lots of monkeys, both small and large. As is the case in most environments, there were predators and prey, so they needed to be both discrete and vigilant.

Romy was searching for a gathering of softer leaves when he heard the scream. He instinctively dropped to one knee with his pistol pointed at the source of the sound. He saw Callum, and even in the dim light, Romy could see his frame shaking as he pointed to the ground in front of him. Rico, who also had his rifle at the ready, sidestepped to Callum, his intense gaze following the direction of Callum's finger.

Rico rolled his eyes as he swung the rifle to his back. Leaning forward, he picked up the lizard.

Callum jumped back and yelled for a second time. "I hate fucking lizards!"

With a flick of his wrist, the lizard was slung towards the invisible fence. There was a blue flash as the eight-legged creature shook before bouncing off a tree on the other side. Rico kept his attention on Callum, berating him. "Some fucking soldier. C'mon—a lizard?"

Marty was lying on the ground, eating a meal from a heat pack. "Check— I think he shit his pants."

"Don't even go there," Callum replied as he cracked open his own meal pack, the heat instantly coming to life.

They all laughed after that—even Callum. Romy thought they needed that. It had been a tough day, and tomorrow would be even worse. He hadn't told them yet, but tomorrow, he wanted to keep pressing forward until they were ready to drop.

After they ate, Rico gave direction as to camp watches, whereby he would take the first two-hour stint. Eight hours later, they were as refreshed as they could be considering the conditions. They packed their gear and were once again continuing on a northerly track, but this time Romy took the lead with the electroband. It wasn't long before they noticed the change in vegetation. The trees were taller with narrow, orange leaves, and increased light cracked through the carpet of foliage. They came across a waist-high stream, easily fording it. They took the opportunity to fill their canteens, and in each they added a purification pill, an innovative chemical created by the Gunn family pharmaceutical company.

After four hours of difficult passage, they got a break. The group came across a well-trodden path, and it was going in their general direction. Romy had a decision to make. Considering the width of the path, it was made by a large creature as evidenced by the deep hoof prints in the dirt. They could risk running into it, or they could bypass the path altogether.

They were behind schedule. That was the deciding factor for Romy. He told the crew they would use the path, but they needed to be vigilant. It seemed it was the correct choice. For the next four hours they made triple the time they had made in the heavy jungle undergrowth. That all changed when they felt a slight vibration in the ground, soon escalating to a low rumble.

As the rumble grew, Romy knew this wasn't good at all. He hissed, "Heat shields on and take cover—now!"

They all made sure the switch on the side of the pouch at their belt was in the *on* position before they sprung into the heavy growth at the base of the trees. Most ducked behind trees while Jax and Romy shared a spot behind a large boulder. Around a shallow bend in the path, they saw the first large snout, highlighted by two long, curved tusks. This was the first *taradon* Romy had seen in the wild. It was two metres high at the shoulder and just as wide, supported by short, fast-moving legs. The beast snorted as it came down the path followed by a second taradon, then a third, half the size of the two adults.

Romy held his breath as the first taradon skidded to a stop on the path. Its flat snout rose in the air, sniffing from side to side. It did the same along the ground, blowing hot air from its nostrils, displacing a cloud of dirt. It repeated the process several times before it also made a decision. The beast wasn't sure something had been on its path, but if something had, it wasn't going to be bothered with it today. With a heavy stamp of its front hoof, it continued its gait down the trail and off into the distance.

Once the soldiers made their way back to the path, Jax offered, "That's strange. I must have misheard when I was told they have a great sense of smell."

Even though Jax was a head taller, Romy smacked him on the side of his helmet. "You should have spent more time reading equipment manuals. If you did, you would know our heat suppressing shields also blocks our scent."

Shrugging, Jax confessed, "I guess it's a good thing *you* did. They look much more formidable here than in the zoo."

"These ones looked like they were hungry. That's the difference," Marty replied.

Romy interrupted their banter. "We still have a long way to go. I think, as long as this path keeps heading in the right direction, we're going to *bust a move* and keep on going."

His soldiers believed in him, so without hesitating, they all nodded their agreement. They might have wished they weren't so agreeable, for it wasn't until seven long hours later when they saw the path take a definite change to a southwest direction, whereby Romy finally decided to make camp. They pressed into the fringe of the jungle to make a small clearing, then they abruptly stopped. In the lead, Rico had his fist in the air. When Romy joined the Junior, he saw why they had stopped. In front of Rico was a massive expanse of brown water, filled with ages-old, wide-trunked trees anchored in a vast, muddy quagmire.

Romy took a deep breath. They had arrived at the Swamp.

Chapter 6: The Departure

05:00 hours, 3rd day of the 1st Korian month, Haven year 0006

Villaro Outpost.

Ryder, still squatting beside the dead assassin, spoke into his wrist interlink. "I'lish, is everything okay?"

Confused, his sister's words were erratic. "Yes—things are fine—what's going…"

Ryder interrupted her, his words crisp with tension. "Where's Romy?"

"He's right here in front of me, playing a video game."

"Keep him inside the house. How many guards are on watch?"

"Three on the grounds and one in the house," I'lish answered.

"Double them—now," Ryder directed in a firm voice.

Ilish knew from Ryder's tone and short bursts of words, he was deadly serious. By now, she had figured out the cause of his concern. "There was another assassination attempt…"

"Yes, but it's worse," Ryder revealed. "The assassin is dead, but he had a picture of Romy in his possession."

"Oh, shit!" I'lish blurted. "I'll arrange the extra guards immediately. Are you coming home now?"

"Linkin and I will be boarding the jet momentarily."

"Be careful," I'lish urged, before she heard the *click* as Ryder disconnected the call.

Linkin had been searching the dead assassin's pockets, hoping to find some type of identification. The pockets, now turned inside out, indicated to Ryder he found nothing. Grasping the lapel of the assassin's shirt with his fingers, Linkin ripped it open. On the right side of the assassin's chest was a tattoo of a black, four-pointed star.

"I thought so," Linkin hissed. "He's from the *KIS*"

Ryder nodded in agreement. The Korian Intelligence Service was a secret branch of the Fyr military that, in fact, wasn't very successful at remaining secret. They were formed by the military after the fleet reached Haven, when the murmurs of dissatisfaction with the Council of Twelve began. Quite unusually, the KIS only allowed Fyr family members into their group, giving them the distinction of being the only family organization having such a limitation. It was one the people jokingly called—incestuous. There were rumours of ridiculous, blood drinking orgies, fueled by the mysterious nature of the KIS.

Ryder's thoughts of the KIS were fleeting, quickly returning to his concern for I'lish and Romy. He rose to his feet and brushed the concrete dust from his black trousers. "I'm not wasting more time with this. Let's go."

The two men took the elevator to the main level of the small terminal where they quickly came to a security checkpoint. The guard barely glanced at Linkin's identification, but his eyes bulged when he saw the name on Ryder's paperwork. He checked the identification booklet carefully even though it was an official document issued by the Explorer Corp. The stark look of surprise was the same treatment Ryder received every time someone realized, *shit, it's Ryder Gunn, the hero who became a zero.*

This time, Ryder's anxiousness overrode his usual cordial patience. "We're in a hurry. Is there a problem?"

The guard's lips tilted into a sarcastic grin. "No, Sir. Have a great trip."

The Sholite hoverjet's engines were already engaged. Ryder and Linkin jogged across the short distance to it before bounding up the stairs, two at a time. The door had barely closed when the jet lurched forward towards the runway. The hoverjet didn't have full hover mode, however, it did allow the craft short takeoff and landing capability. Additionally, once in the air, it had an impressive top-end velocity.

Ninety minutes later, the hoverjet's door opened. Ryder skipped down the stairs as he took a deep breath of air. They had arrived in Torrin House, the capital of the Sholite state on Haven. The central continent of the habitable zone had been divided roughly in half between the Korians and Sholites; the Korians were in the South and the Sholites occupied the north.

When the combined Sholite and Korian fleet arrived at Haven, there were two million Sholites to relocate from the orbiting spaceships that had been their home for their lifetime. With so many people to settle, the Sholites set out the ambitious task of not only building the capital, Torrin House, but three other Sholite cities: Drummel, at the base of a long inlet at the northern extent of Lower Shol, Balestrand, along the coastline at the northernmost reaches of Upper Shol and Malby, sitting on a crooked finger of land reaching southwards from Upper Shol.

The Sholites used a different tactic when they built their cities. With many more spaceships than the Korians had, they set about dismantling many of them, repurposing the materials to build their cities. It gave the Sholite cities, dominated by steel and glass, an ultramodern aesthetic.

Parts of the city were complete with towering skyscrapers and aerial bridges between buildings. Other areas were still under construction, none in more dishevelment than the long strips of land where underground tunnels were being excavated, so rail lines could be installed. Two primary lines were complete, with a spider web of secondary tunnels to be completed over a ten-year period.

I'lish had sent a car to the airfield, and two men in black suits waited beside it. By the thick, tree-like nature of their build, it would be easy to assume they were security personnel; and if they weren't, they probably should be.

As past president of the Sholite federation, and also the head of a wealthy mining company, I'lish was able to afford an expansive, two-story house. It was located on a peninsula of land, protruding into the *Lavish Waters*. Oddly, *lavish waters* was how the early inhabitants of Haven described the ocean encircled by New Kor, Lower Shol, Upper Shol, and to the far east, by the New Kor Islands. It was known as *lavish* because of the wealth of marine life within the 1,800-kilometre-wide body of water that provided an abundant food source for Sholite and Korian alike. Once more and more settlers relocated from the spaceships to the planet, the water's description was entrenched into the people's vocabulary, evermore to be called, *The Lavish Waters*.

Ryder had been away from Torrin House for a month. He could see the distinct differences as the city continued to be built. Forty minutes later, Ryder saw I'lish had taken his recommendation as there were three heavily-armed guards at the front gate. Even though it was Ryder, I'lish's brother, they asked the car's occupants to step out as they searched the entire vehicle. Rather than being irritated, Ryder appreciated their thoroughness.

Once they entered the house, Ryder gave I'lish a quick hello before asking where Romy was. His sister gave a nod towards a favorite room at the back of the house. It was a great-room running the entire width of the structure. The north-easterly wall facing the Lavish Waters was filled with windows, floor to ceiling and corner post to corner post. Ryder found Romy peering through the eyepiece of a small telescope, gazing out over the calm waters.

When Romy heard the familiar footsteps, he turned and ran to his father, throwing his arms around him. Ryder closed his eyes as he gave his son a great hug. It seemed too long since Ryder had been home, but it was the same after every expedition. In fact, Ryder felt guilt at his lack of time spent with his son. Fortunately, Romy was very close to his stepmother who he thought of as none other than a loving, true mother.

Then there was also Fehyr. He was Ryder's manservant who spent much of his time with Romy when Ryder was away. Ryder spent the day with his son, and it wasn't until after dinner that he excused himself from the table. Ryder's finger curled towards Fehyr, indicating he wished to speak with the older man alone.

Fehyr was well past his 70th year, still sharp of mind, but not nimble or unstressed by physical exertion. Ryder led Fehyr down the wide, central hallway to his study located in the wing of the house I'lish reserved for him. Once they were in the room, they both sat on a leather couch, Fehyr's face drawn, filled with a premonition of what was likely to come. He wasn't wrong.

"I have to leave," Ryder confided.

Fehyr could have feigned ignorance at the meaning of Ryder's words, but he had never patronized the man he loved like a son, nor would he begin now. "I understand. How many attempts on your life have there been now?"

"Over the past five years, seven," Ryder replied with a shrug of his shoulders. Then, he leaned close to Fehyr and whispered, "This time, the assassin was a KIS operative, and he carried a picture of Romy." His son's name trailed off into a choking gasp. His face was white and drawn as he continued. "For the past five years, I have been a target of the Council. I have been able to avoid their agents, but this has been due to my extensive time off planet. Things have changed. Now, it seems the kill order has been given to the KIS, an organization renowned for their ruthless practices. And it would appear, since they have been unsuccessful from keeping me away from Haven, they have expanded their scope to include Romy, likely I'lish—and even you, Fehyr."

There was an awkward silence. Fehyr knew he could not refute the facts Ryder laid out. He also had to grimly agree with Ryder's conclusion. Trying to remove some of the dread that hung in the room, Fehyr offered, "I'm old. No one would care to kill me."

Ryder's thoughts were already well ahead of the older man's. He rubbed his chin and asked, "Do you still have that family member of yours who you recommended as Romy's manservant?"

"Yes—but the man is, in fact, a woman. Her name is Valre, and we have discussed the position as Romy's woman servant. She has agreed to come when the call is sent."

"Then, make the call. I go on my next expedition in a month."

When Fehyr lifted his gaze to Ryder, he saw his eyes moist and filled with emotion. Fehyr read through the innuendos and saw the unsaid direction. *In a month, Ryder was leaving and not coming back.*

Ryder had a similar discussion with his sister and Linkin. With his dire direction set, the next month was spent with Romy. It was a most wonderful time for both of them, giving Ryder second thoughts about his decision. However, with a heavy security detail, he made two trips from the house. In each instance, he saw they were followed during the entire excursion. And each time, a kilometre down the road from the house, the same two cars were parked along a dirt sideroad. Ryder could have sent a security detail out to dispatch them, but he knew they would just be replaced, likely redoubled in strength. The scenario just confirmed that, for the safety of his family, he needed to leave.

Valre Edy arrived at the house two weeks after the call from Fehyr. She was an attractive, surprisingly young, 30-year-old woman. Any reservations Ryder had about her were quickly dispelled when he saw how well she and Romy interacted. They were an instant hit, and this helped Ryder proceed with his decision to leave.

When there were only three days left before his mission departure, Ryder sat Romy down for a serious discussion, albeit one Ryder had dreaded. Valre thought it odd when Ryder asked her to attend. They sat on the couch in his office with Romy sitting between the two adults. Romy was very bright for a twelve-year-old, likely accelerated by a young life of taunting as the son of Ryder Gunn; clever enough, in fact, to listen at closed doors and search out telling documents in his father's office when he was away. He knew about the assassination attempts, just as he learned of the danger to his own life while he listened at the door to Ryder's office when his father had the private meeting with Fehyr, almost a month ago.

He tried his best to act surprised when his father told him he was going away on another mission, that it was more dangerous than previous missions, and there was a chance he might not return. Inside, Romy was screaming, but he didn't want to make this more difficult for his father than it already was. Instead, he reached over and clasped Valre's hand. "I'll be fine, Dad."

The next three days were torturous for Ryder. He spent time with his son, leaving some time with I'lish to ensure all his affairs were in order. I'lish was more pragmatic than Ryder. She insisted that both she and Romy would see him again. There would come a time for that, she was certain.

On the day of his departure, Ryder donned his Explorer Corp, uniform: the black pants and shirt along with the faded, maroon jacket. He intentionally decided to leave early, not wanting to have a tear-jerking farewell. He wasn't altogether surprised when I'lish, Fehyr and Valre were waiting for him. There was a tearful goodbye, but, at least, it was mercifully quick.

Selfishly, Ryder was happy Romy was asleep as he wasn't sure he could maintain his composure. However, when Ryder and Linkin left the house towards the car, Ryder had a premonition. When he turned, he saw Romy's face framed in an upstairs window. For Ryder, it was a proud moment, for his son was not crying. Rather, he had a wide, ear to ear smile. Ryder returned the smile and waved. In that moment, they both knew, no matter the circumstances nor the passage of time, they would share the deep, loving bond of a father and son.

A second Sholite security vehicle, with four armed men in it, followed the vehicle occupied by Ryder and Linkin. As they passed the two KIS cars parked on the sideroad, Ryder gave them a sarcastic wave and muttered, "Fuck you."

Four of the armed security men joined Ryder and Linkin on the flight back to Villaro Outpost. There, another car with blacked-out windows was waiting, taking them directly to the shuttle that was about to depart to the *Odyssey* space station.

Linkin had been with Ryder for many years, and there was an emotional goodbye. Ryder hugged Linkin, slapping him on the back. "You are now charged with the care and protection of my son. See to it."

The direct words straightened the emotions from Linkin's face. He pulled from his friend's embrace and said in a steady voice. "You can count on me, Sir."

Second thoughts screamed through Ryder's mind. He needed to get on the shuttle—now—before he lost his nerve. He whispered, "goodbye, friend," before turning and striding up the stairs to the shuttle.

Once the area was cleared, the pilot fired up the electromagnetic drives. The craft lifted off the runway, then the nose was tilted up at a 40-degree-angle. The shuttle pilot spoke into the microphone attached to his headset. "*Haven Control 2*, this is *Shuttle flight 23*, requesting permission to proceed to *Odyssey* station."

The control station was a generally circular structure. It looked like a donut, 200 metres in diameter with a 300-metre-long shaft through the hole. It rotated on its central axis as it orbited Haven. The command deck was a round room near the top of the shaft, with thick, glass windows around its perimeter. Wryson Tor, the Control officer on watch, turned and looked at the man behind him. The aloof man, dressed in dark midnight-blue, covered with a long, black, leather overcoat, held his hands clasped behind his back. His head was shaved, yet there was a black tinge of stubble matching the shadowy stubble on his face. In response to Wryson's questioning gaze, the man gave a nod of his chin.

Wryson's face snapped back towards the microphone. "*Shuttle Flight 23*, this is *Haven Control 2*. You are clear through to *Odyssey*." He wiped a few beads of sweat from his brow. He'd heard rumours of the mysterious KIS group, but the tall man behind him was the first operative he had met.

The KIS operative said, "Keep a close eye on the *Odyssey*. I want to know the second the *Pathfinder* pulls back from the station."

"Yes, Sir," Wryson replied.

The agent cracked his knuckles, causing Wryson to almost fall off his chair. "What are the two closest military vessels to the *Odyssey*?" the mysterious man asked.

Leaning to the left, Wryson inspected the radar screen. "Two Tiger-class destroyers, the *Dauntless* and the *Reliant*, are respectively, 5,000 and 10,000 kilometres from the station."

The KIS agent leaned over the counter, his hot, wretched breath close to Wryson's ear. "Get the captains of the two destroyers on a group link."

The Captain of the *Reliant* was the first to reply to the request. "This is Rand Sny, captain of the *Reliant*."

A moment later a second, softer voice was heard. "This is the captain of the *Dauntless*, Sasha Fyr."

"This is Lieutenant Jeremy Fyr of the KIS. Please check authorization code 3214B-83. This allows me to give you direction."

After a few minutes, Sasha Fyr was the first to reply. "Yes, Sir. Code verified. What can we do for you?"

"I would like both of you to reposition your destroyers a distance of 3,000 kilometres from *Odyssey Station*."

The two captains complied and were repositioning their heavily armed vessels just as the shuttle was arriving at the *Odyssey*. Wryson knew better than to attempt small talk with the agent who seemed dry and devoid of emotion. It was a painful, uncomfortably-long two hours before a squawk came over the speaker in the command center. "*Haven Control 2*, this is

Pathfinder, docked at the *Odyssey*, requesting permission to leave the station."

Once again, Wryson turned to Jeremy Fyr, and the man, with his eyes closed, dipped his chin.

"*Pathfinder*, this is *Haven Control 2*. You're clear to leave the *Odyssey*."

From *Haven Control 2*, both Wryson and Jeremy Fyr could see the status of all the spaceships in the region as well as those docked at the *Odyssey*. Small data boxes appeared on a large screen above the observation window, detailing the status of each ship. It was no surprise when they saw the *Pathfinder*'s engines fire up before the sleek vessel backed out of its berth.

"What's that? What's going on?" The KIS agent's crooked finger pointed at a collection of flashing data boxes adjacent to the *Odyssey*.

Wryson's finger was shaking as he pressed a button on his console. Above him, a large monitor showed the *Odyssey* via one of the command center's long-range cameras. "*Odyssey* station, this is *Haven Control 2*. What the fuck is going on?" He was ready to lose it. There were seven other explorer-class, deep-space vessels parked at the station, and they were all backing out of their berths.

Jeremy Fyr wasn't stupid. He'd been watching Wryson operate his console for some time. He pressed on the side of the communication officer's chair, flinging him across the room before pressing a second button on the console. "Captain Sasha Fyr, proceed to *Odyssey* station. Any ships that leave the station are to be destroyed. Is that understood?"

The soft, female voice replied, "Yes, Sir. Destroy any ships leaving the *Odyssey*." Her voice trailed off as her microphone picked up her command to bring the *Dauntless* on a bearing to the *Odyssey*. "Wind us up to 10 per cent SOL."

Wryson Tor dared not return to his chair. Rather, he watched the panoramic screen's telling activity. The *Dauntless* was moving quickly towards the *Odyssey* where the eight Explorer ships had successfully launched from the station. The Explorer armada was winding their speed up and moving towards the *Junkyard*.

The Junkyard, as it was nicknamed, was a sort of graveyard of Sholite and Korian ships. Roughly 300 spaceships, no longer required for active duty, were parked 10,000 kilometres from Haven. A maintenance crew kept the ships electromagnetically-enhanced, nuclear engines operating at a low power level. Once a month, the crew would move all 300 ships one month ahead of the planet's path. In this manner, the ships hopscotched along, keeping up with the planet.

At some peril, Wryson pointed to the screen, his voice shaking. "I can't believe it. That's impossible!" Another data box in the Junkyard was flashing. "That's the Sholite space station, *Ryfoss.* It can't be!" Wryson toggled a second button, and another large screen came to life. With a joystick, he aimed the camera at the Junkyard, focusing on the scrapyard of metal.

The *Ryfoss* was one of seven massive cylindrical space stations the Sholites had used as their primary bases as they travelled across the universe. Once they arrived at Haven, with little need for the gigantic vessels, five were dismantled for parts and supplies, one still orbited Haven and that left the *Ryfoss* supposedly archived in the Junkyard.

Although Wryson found it difficult to believe, he saw the *Ryfoss* rotating, then begin to ascend out of the mass of ships. The communications officer reset his panel, but it wasn't a data glitch or technical error of any sort. The visual image matched the data on the radar screen.

Jeremy Fyr slammed his fist on the console when he saw the data box moving out from the cluster of ships in the Junkyard. He pressed the channel selector and hissed into the microphone, "Captain Rand Sny, intercept the *Ryfoss.* Order them to stop. If they don't, take them out."

"That's a Sholite vessel. You're going to start the war all over again!" Wryson blurted.

The KIS agent's cold eyes snapped back to bore into the communication officer. Wryson shrunk away as Jeremy instinctively reached under his coat. After a few tense seconds—seconds where Wryson held his breath, Jeremy's flared nostrils relaxed. The KIS agent pulled his hand from his coat, but the expected weapon wasn't there. Rather, the agent snapped his fingers and pointed to the chair, indicating Wryson's best course of action was to sit down and shut up.

The Korian destroyer, *Reliant,* moved towards the Junkyard. Jeremy Fyr licked his lips in anticipation. He wondered if the destroyers would use their laser cannons or missiles.

"To the captain of the *Pathfinder.* This is Captain Sasha Fyr of the Korian destroyer, *Dauntless.*" In a light-hearted, mocking tone, she said, "We've been ordered to fire upon your fleet."

A low growl emitted from Jeremy Fyr's throat. "What's the matter with you? Just fucking fire on them, you dolt," he muttered.

"Sasha Fyr, this is Captain Ryder Gunn of the *Pathfinder.* Glad you could make it. Please take up a position on our right flank. The Reliant will be coming around to take up a position on our port side."

"Yes, Captain," Sasha Fyr replied.

His jaw gapped open, Jeremy Fyr tried to speak, but all that came from his mouth was a gurgle of spittle. Behind him, Wryson had a wry grin on his face. It took all his effort for the laughter to be held back. As Jeremy, bug eyed, stared at the screen, he saw two more ships moving away from the Junkyard, following the *Ryfoss*. Wryson pointed at the screen and clarified, "That's the *Metro*, an oxygen generation ship, and the *Morning Star*, an agricultural vessel."

So, eight Explorer ships, two destroyers, a Sholite space station, an oxygen ship and an agricultural vessel were leaving with Ryder Gunn. *Good riddance,* Jeremy Fyr thought. Then, his dark brows shot up. *They're not coming back,* he realized. His fingers were clenched into fists, knuckles white and his fingernails were cutting into his palms. He watched, but there was nothing he could do.

A half hour later, the exodus of ships could barely be seen on the long-range camera. Jeremy Fyr considered his mission complete. There was nowhere for Ryder Gunn to go. He could survive perhaps a year with the ships in his fleet, but after that, as outlaws, they would die in the cold expanse of space.

Chapter 7: The Swamp

03:00 hours, 24th day of the 3rd Korian month, Haven year 0024

Somewhere in the Southern Wildes

"Sir, it's time."

Romy's eyelids slid open to see Rico, on one knee, bent over him.

"Breaking camp, time to wake up," Rico added.

Sliding to a sitting position, Romy's jaw trembled with a great yawn. He rubbed his chin and scrunched his nose. The Swamp, just beyond their camp's perimeter, had a distinct, musty smell. Reaching into his pack, he retrieved an energy bar, making short work of it. In the opposite direction from the swamp, 150 metres distant, was a narrow, fast-flowing stream. There, he leaned over beside Callum and quickly joined him in throwing the refreshing water over his face. It felt so good that Romy undressed and soon stood knee high in the stream, scrubbing every centimeter of his body.

After dressing, he joined his crew who had packed away the perimeter spikes and were ready to begin the day's hike. Romy turned to Ren as he pointed at a nearby tree close to the edge of the Swamp. "Mark it"

It was something they had done at least every 200 metres along their trek. The red paint lines would help them find the path on their return. Although their slow progress on their way to the MAT base was understandable, it was likely on their return they would be chased. It would be folly to break a new path, so they marked the already broken trail, allowing them to retrace their footsteps much more expediently.

Romy led the group to the edge of the Swamp. Between every ten to thirty metres, a hook tree had rooted into the viscid, syrupy mud that lay under a thin layer of water. The hook trees thrived in the wet ground. Many of them were over 100 years old with trunks as thick as two metres across and, typically, 70 metres high.

However, these weren't the most unusual characteristic of the hook trees. As their name might suggest, they had long twisting branches that searched outwards from the trunk. And what they searched for was a similar branch from another nearby tree. When the two branches came together, they would coil around each other, continuing to grow in length and girth.

Beck pushed to the front of the group looking up at the thick branches. "I read about this. You see, the hook trees are dioecious."

"Di-who?" Ren blurted along with a laugh.

"Dio-ec-ious," Beck repeated, with slow emphasis. "It means the trees have both female and male reproductive parts, but only with an adjoining tree, not within itself."

Rico had a twisted sarcastic look under the thick beard. "Yeah, that *would* be gross."

Romy interrupted the banter as he slapped Beck on the shoulder. "Okay, let's get going."

Since the Swamp was 200 kilometres in width, separating the Southern Wildes from the Northern Wildes, there wasn't time to go around. Early explorers had discovered it wasn't difficult to cross the Swamp, moving across the thick, intertwined branches. One might have to climb from level to level to maintain the desired direction. Many had been successful, and only a few had slipped and been swallowed by the mud.

Beck was the best climber in the group. There were no objections when he took the lead. He had been busy early in the morning, fabricating a makeshift ladder from a few smaller branches from the forest. Now, he retrieved it and angled it against the trunk of the nearest hook tree, three metres from the shoreline. Propped in place, he scurried across and removed the coiled, knotted rope from his shoulder. With an experienced throw, he threw the metal, hooked end around a limb, ten metres above him. Pulling it snug, he then snapped his fingers and pointed at Rico.

Rico, using the knots, easily made his way on top of the limb. He deftly slid around to the other side where two limbs had intertwined together, creating a half-metre-wide pathway to the next tree. With the pattern set, Beck climbed up and took the lead. The remaining eight soldiers followed, leaving the rope and ladder in place for their return trip.

Once they were all up on the intertwined branches, with great care, they proceeded with Beck in the lead, Romy second and Rico bringing up the rear. They made good headway across the branches, allowing them to continue north, although they were veering slightly west. At the sixth tree, there was an absence of branches at their level. Romy threw his coil of rope to Beck who repeated the process of slinging it over the next row of branches another ten metres above him. One by one, they all climbed to the next level and continued their trek across the upper reaches of the Swamp.

"Did you feel that?"

Romy heard Callum's voice behind him. Romy held out his hand and felt a drop of rain. *Shit*, he thought. Looking at his wrist interlink, he saw it was 4:30, a time that rarely saw rain. Their planning had them avoiding the 9:00 time frame when rain would most certainly pummel them. This was odd and a bad omen. He pointed forward, "Everyone, be careful. Let's keep going."

Fortunately, the rain was light, but still, the branches became slick, and greater care was required. Three trees later, once again, they needed to go up another ten metres, leaving them 30 metres above the mud. Romy looked down and saw bubbles in the murky water. He had seen them since they left the shoreline, assuming gas was being expelled, most likely methane.

They once again worked their way across the intertwined branches. The surface was irregular, with shallow points at the seams. They had to look each time they pressed their foot to the slick, wrinkled bark. Halfway across a thick branch, Romy was startled by a scream behind him. Instantly, he turned to see Callum jump backwards. A small, eight-legged, red lizard had jumped from a higher branch, landing directly in front of him. Callum's ankle rolled as it slid into a seam. He threw his other foot into the air, trying to recover his balance, but he rolled off the branch.

Romy dove, lunging where Callum's fingers tried to dig into the bark as he slid off the side of the branch. But by the time Romy's hands arrived there, Callum's hands were gone. Prone on the branch, Romy heard a sickening *thunk* as Callum bounced off a lower branch, followed a second later by a splash. When Romy slid his face around the trunk, he saw Callum, his neck at an unnatural angle, being absorbed by the sludge. Glancing at the branch just below him, Romy saw a splatter of blood. He hoped Callum had died before he hit the mud.

The bubbles Romy had seen during their trip now reappeared. Several lines of bubbles sped towards Callum's body. They followed him as his hand was the last part of his body to become submerged. Romy sighed. He had seen much death during the war. There was no time to get emotional, but an odd thought crossed his mind. The early explorers had lied. When someone was lost in the mud, it wasn't so calm and peaceful, after all.

When Romy rose to his feet, he saw Ren, who had been behind Callum, with an inquisitive look on her face. Romy knew what she meant, and he just shook his head in response. There was no sense trying to recover him.

Lines appeared at the corners of Romy's mouth as he pulled his lips tight. Through them, he spat the words, "Callum made a mistake. Now, he's dead. No one else be so stupid." Turning forward, he muttered to a blank-eyed Beck, "Keep fucking going."

Ironically, the rain stopped. The remainder of their trip across the Swamp was uneventful. They lowered themselves, level by level, until they were on the far shoreline, now officially in the Northern Wildes within Mat held territory. The half-kilometre trip across the tree branches had been accomplished in three hours.

They stopped for a half hour to rest and eat. No one said another word about Callum. They knew this was part of war. Selfishly, a few of them were thankful, knowing it could have just as easily been them.

Their hike for the day had just begun. The dense forest ahead looked the same as what they left behind. Rico took point with the electric wristband. As he slashed through the undergrowth, his thoughts went back to Callum. He was pissed, and it heightened his energy, whereby he made short work of the defenseless plants.

They changed the point soldier several times, and each time the soldier relished hacking the plants and branches. Romy noticed there was a distinct uphill inclination to the terrain, and it continued for seven hours until they decided to make camp.

They were once again breaking the trail by 3:00 the following morning. It was purely habitual for the Korians to call the time by morning, evening and night, since, in this world's reality and the forever twilight, there was actually no such thing.

It was the fourth day since they'd left PAT Base 4. After three hours of carving a path through the jungle, the sounds of animals, especially that of the howling monkeys, lessened and almost stopped. It was replaced by manmade sounds, so they stopped their hacking and moved forward through the trees with great care. The light level was increasing ahead. They could see what looked like a clearing, so they lowered to a prone position and shimmied forward.

Romy snapped his fingers, drawing his crew's attention. Dipping his fingers into the mud, he wiped a thin layer over the visible portion of his face below his helmet and goggles. The soldiers did the same before they continued their crawl forward. Finally, their heads pressed through a thick grouping of metre high ferns. Romy saw they were on a slight rise of land. Below them, no more than thirty metres ahead, was a wide, dirt path, and just beyond it was a two-metre-high fence topped with razor wire.

As soon as their heads had popped through the vegetation, things changed. Now, they smelled oil and the distinct smell of generated electricity. The fenced compound was filled with helocrafts, maintenance personnel, pilots and loyalist soldiers dressed in grey. They had arrived at MAT Base Firestorm.

Chapter 8: Blackmail

07:00 hours, 28th day of the 3rd Korian month, Haven year 0024

PAT Base 4, 400 kilometres east-northeast of Villaro

Something big was about to be announced. Sirens throughout PAT Base 4 sounded at 6:00, rousing every officer, soldier and support worker. Word spread that an important message would be shared on every video screen on the base at exactly 7:00. There were numerous satellite canteens equipped with video equipment throughout the base, in addition to the huge central mess hall situated just outside the officer's compound. This was where most of the base personnel now flocked.

General Brett Jezeer stood leaning against the side wall of the central mess hall with five minutes remaining before the announcement. Soldiers filled every chair in the massive room, and those continuing to enter stood in the aisles. With the excitement of *big news,* no one noticed the general's heightened state of anxiety, evident from the slight backward snap of his head as another smack was popped into his mouth.

As advertised, at exactly 7:00, the four large video screens, one on each wall, crackled into life. A piercing fanfare of trumpets came through the speakers as the blue emblem of the PAT forces appeared. After a few seconds, the emblem was replaced by the face of Murdock Parbli, the minister of communications for the patriotic movement. He said,

> *"Greetings to all patriots. As you will hear in a moment from the president himself, today is a great day for our movement. Many have died fighting for our values, including equality and representation in our governing bodies."*

The minister was 60 years old with a ring of grey hair surrounding the bald area at the top of his head. His face was pudgy, not representative of a fighting man or even one who worked hard for a living. He instantly smiled in the manner only politicians could.

> *"With no further delay, I present, President Bala Torez."*

A handsome man who, at 45 years old, many considered too young to be president, appeared on the screen. His face was highlighted by a square chin and high cheekbones under a wave of brown, flowing hair.

"People of Kor, today will be a day well documented in history books. Today will be noted as the day when the families of those who have suffered and died for our cause, will know those unselfish acts were not in vain."

The president's light-brown eyes were moist, and for a moment, his voice cracked with emotion.

"Today, the patriotic movement has reached a peace agreement with the Council of Twelve. The war is over!"

At first, there was stunned silence, but what followed was a crescendo of cheers and whoops. When the president continued, the voices hushed, and the silence in the room was once again complete.

"Citizens, a negotiating committee has been in deliberation with the Council of Twelve for several days. It was agreed that the ongoing war was resulting in nothing but the continuing deaths of our people. As in any negotiation, we had to fight hard for our issues to be resolved, but there is always some give and take.

A senate consisting of 30 members will be created. The members will be voted into those seats by the people. Every person over 18 will have a vote, no matter their family or occupation."

A roar erupted from the many voices in the mess hall. Fists were thrown in the air. As if the president knew what the reaction across New Kor would be, he paused his speech for a few moments before raising a finger in the air.

"The senate will have equal, shared power with the Council of Twelve. Each group will have veto power over bills brought forth by the opposing party. This will allow for a healthy democratic process."

This time, cheers were vacant. Rather, pervasive murmurs and grumbling spread through the men and women listening to the terms.

"I know many of you might not see that as what you expected. Many of you want the Council of Twelve abolished right now, yet that is not feasible. It will take a year to vote for and establish the Senate. During that time, the Council of Twelve will lead us with Minister Parbli and I, by their side."

The murmurs grew just as it was likely they grew in every patriotic base in the south.

"But there is always hope, and in this case, it is resolved to a certainty. Once the Senate is established, ten years forward, the Council of Twelve will be abolished, leaving only the Senate to lead the people."

Listeners throughout the lands couldn't believe their ears. *Abolished!* The people would need to wait through a ten-year transitionary period, but surely that was what they had fought and died for. Cheers erupted. Many were now crying with joy as they thought, *soon they could see their families.* Soon, families torn apart by the civil war could reunite. Brothers who, today, fought against each other, could walk across enemy lines and hug their kin.

The president continued.

> *"As of 6:00 today, a cease fire has been ordered. All active forces are to withdraw and hold their positions until further orders are issued. All forthcoming missions are cancelled, and all missions in progress are to be withdrawn."*

President Torez couldn't help the sly grin forming.

> *"There are aircraft deliveries of fruit wine on their way to all the PAT bases as I speak. Enjoy your day."*

The screens shut off. Some soldiers were on top of the tables dancing while others jumped up and down, hugging each other. General Jezeer had advance notice of the content of the announcement, so he knew a peace agreement had been reached. He didn't whoop or fist bump anyone. He just popped another smack into his mouth. After the throng of soldiers swept outside into the large, paved area in front of the mess hall, General Jezeer adjusted the dark-blue cap on his head and stepped out into the forever twilight.

He considered the soldiers under his command. Perhaps their delirious happiness would be short-lived once they realized the purpose they held for the last three years was gone. The military had given them order in a world fraught with chaos. Some would soon realize this and reinforce their commitment to remain in the military, no matter the form it would evolve into. Others, the ones the general considered naive, would struggle to find their place in a society that hadn't yet set a direction.

Music began to play through the loudspeakers. Soldiers grabbed their nearest mate, be it a man or woman, and even if they hadn't the skills to do so, they danced as best they could. General Jezeer looked through the many pairs of foolish dancers. His eyes focused on the man he was looking for. As he walked through the crowd, many soldiers slapped him on the back. When he reached the man, he tipped his head to the woman dancing with him. "Lieutenant Parbli, I'll need a few minutes of your time."

The two separated before the young man stood at attention. "Of course, Sir."

Lieutenant Stefan Parbli was young, ambitious and impressionable.

65

That's why the general liked him and, partially, the reason he selected the young man as his communications officer. His selection had also been compelled by the man's lineage. He was the grandson of Minister Murdock Parbli who was the second most powerful person in the patriotic movement. In addition, the young soldier still had strong ties to the Bli family, one of the leading matriarchal families within the Council of Twelve. It took quite some time and even more effort to finagle Lieutenant Parbli directly under his command. The young man had, with a higher level of peer pressure, more to lose than the average soldier. He was the perfect person if the shrewd general ever needed to utilize the leverage he revelled in.

The general turned to the attractive woman and offered, "He'll be back to you before the wine gets unloaded."

Lieutenant Parbli followed the general through the gates to the officer's compound, continuing to the building housing the general's office. Once they were inside, the general pointed to the chair in front of his large desk. "Have a seat, Lieutenant."

As General Jezeer took his own seat, the lieutenant blurted out. "Is this about Romy Gunn? We have to break radio silence and tell him to abort the mission."

When the general was irritated, he had a visible twitch where one eyebrow shot up and the opposite corner of his mouth drooped. It did so now. The mission was top secret. Only the general, Pilot Demoro and his two crewmen, knew about the jungle mission. He deliberately took Lieutenant Parbli into his confidence just for this moment. He leaned on his elbows over the table. "Son, there will be a message, but you're not going to send it."

The lieutenant's chin fell, and his eyes opened wide. "I don't understand."

Reaching into the drawer of his desk, the general withdrew a piece of paper. "You're an expert at communications and electronics, correct?"

The confused look hadn't left the young man's face. "Yes, top of my class, but…"

"Quiet now!" the general hissed. "Just listen." Once Lieutenant Parbli relaxed back into the chair, he continued, "On this paper is the content of the radio message you'll create. Once it's complete, you'll doctor the encryption to make it look like it was sent at—" The general looked at his wrist interlink "—11:00. Then you'll store the recording in archives as if it was sent." He pushed the paper across the desk.

The lieutenant wiped the sweat from his brow before retrieving the paper. As he read it, in a shaky voice, he mumbled, "With all due respect,

Sir, I can't do this."

Again, the twitch appeared. "Why? There are many radio conversations with Senior Romy Gunn in archives. If you're as good as you've told me numerous times, surely you can piece together the fragments and create the message."

"I don't understand!" the young man blurted. "This message clearly says for Romy to abort the mission. General Hayden Fyr is not to be assassinated."

"Exactly!"

"But then you don't want me to send it. You want me to give the *appearance* it was sent." As he finished the words, his eyes gained a glow as the confusion left his face. He was young, so it just took a bit longer for him to comprehend the general's motives. Now, he realized the general needed him, so there was an obvious question. "What's in it for me, Sir?"

"Good question," General Jezeer responded. He reached into his drawer for a second time and pulled out an envelope. He pushed it across the desk where it slid off into Lieutenant Parbli's lap.

Parbli opened the envelope, and the photos within spilled into his lap. His body visibly jolted as he saw the photos of he and the pretty young officer he had been dancing with, having sex together.

"She's very pretty," the general said in a mocking tone.

The young lieutenant's jaw was gapped open, yet no words came from him. He just looked up and down, from the pictures to the general's smug face, over and over.

"But you do know it's against regulations for soldiers to have sexual or intimate relationships of any kind?" There was still no response. "And really—in the communications room? That's not even trying to be discrete." The general, who had been doing his best, finally couldn't help but release his laughter.

"Right, back to your question, 'What's in it for me?'" The general's face turned red, and he spoke through a sinister scowl. "Right now, you're seen as an intelligent, young officer, one with a bright future ahead of him. Do as I ask of you, and that won't change. In fact, I'll write you a letter of commendation." His hand flashed up and pointed at Parbli. "Just do as I've asked, then keep your mouth shut—except—if officials ask. Then, with a great degree of sincerity, you'll explain how you sent the message, and Gunn confirmed he was to abort the mission."

"And if I don't?"

Pulling a pistol from his desk, the general pointed it at the lieutenant and removed the safety. "I should just fucking kill you now," he sneered.

The lieutenant's lips began to quiver. He hadn't seen the general in this type of agitated state before. His quivering eyes looked crazy. Having tested how far he could push the general, Parbli hoped he hadn't gone too far. "Okay, I'll do it," the lieutenant finally agreed, hoping it appeased the general. After all, Parbli didn't really give a shit about Romy Gunn. If he received a commendation, it was all good.

Putting away the gun, General Jezeer held out his hand. "Best you give me those pictures back. You don't want anyone else seeing them." The photos were placed in the general's outstretched hand as he added, "But don't screw with me. If you do, I'll send the photos to your *papa* and the Bli family matriarch. You'll be lucky to find a job mixing concrete after that."

Rising to his feet, the lieutenant gave a smart salute. "I'll get started right away." That said, he clicked his heels, turned and left the office.

The general popped another smack between his lips. He reached into his desk again, but this time into a lower drawer. The framed picture had a support in the back which he pulled out before sitting it on his desk. The photo was from a time ten years ago, before the war and before the tragedy. In it was a grand, front foyer of a large house, and in the forefront was an attractive young woman and her newlywed husband.

The general leaned his face close to it and whispered, "My sweet sister, Carla, our revenge will soon be complete." As he pulled a black marker from the drawer, he continued. "He let you die in the fire yet was somehow able to save himself. He has run from base to base, but in short order, he'll be dead. Even a peace agreement won't stop me. I've been waiting to do this for a long time." He lifted the marker to the picture and began to black out the man's face. The man had once been handsome before the fire burned half his face. With a satisfied smile, Jezeer whispered, "Goodbye. General Hayden Fyr."

Chapter 9: Mission Accomplished

09:00 hours, 28th day of the 3rd Korian month, Haven year 0024

Outskirts of MAT Base Firestorm

Two MAT soldiers in drab, grey uniforms and black boots, walked along the curved, dirt path at the corner of MAT Base Firestorm. The base was well entrenched in loyalist territory, only 400 kilometres south of Murcia, and as such, an attack was considered highly improbable. The casual atmosphere in the base was exhibited by the lackadaisical nature of the patrol soldiers with their rifles slung loosely over their shoulders.

The taller soldier tilted his face upwards, studying the eastern sky above the treetops. Seeing the dark, billowing clouds, he said, "It's going to rain."

The second soldier didn't break his wallowing stride. He was slightly ahead of the taller man, so when he rolled his eyes, his partner didn't see his irritation at the announcement of the obvious. Mumbling, he replied, "Same thing every day. We have one more round of the camp. If we're lucky, we'll make it to the main gate before the deluge comes."

As the two men continued, behind them, in the bramble of tall grass and wide-leafed ferns, on the short rise of land 30 metres to the south of the dirt track, two camouflaged helmets lifted off the ground. Prone in the undergrowth of a patch of needle-leafed trees, his elbows digging into the moist dirt, Romy lifted the binoculars to his eyes. Panning from east to west, he saw the cargo craft begin it's track down the runway. An hour earlier, he had seen at least 200 MAT soldiers board the mega craft, likely on their way to the eastern front.

"That's odd," Romy stated.

"Why so?" Jax's hushed voice replied.

"This is our third day surveying the base. Every morning a cargo plane, filled with fresh soldiers, takes off, then veers east because that's where the fighting is—on the eastern front. Yet, this one veered west." Romy explained.

"It doesn't affect our mission."

"Let me finish!" Romy hissed. He was tired, and with the rains coming every day, even when his clothes dried out, he felt the musty damp through to his bones. He put down the binoculars and took a deep breath while putting his hand on Jax's shoulder.

Jax and the rest of the squad were weathering the same jungle elements, but at least, they didn't have the responsibility of command to deal with. Romy was his best friend as well as his leader. Based on both, Romy had earned significant leeway. "Any sign of the general?" Jax whispered.

"Nothing at all. The same as yesterday—the same as the day before that." Indeed, Romy's crew had the base under surveillance for three days, searching for an opportunity to come close to General Hayden Fyr. Unfortunately, the general was a cautious man, barely coming out from his assigned quarters in the officer's compound on the west side of the camp. Romy thought it would be so much easier if the planet rotated, allowing for a dark, nighttime period. Without that, attempting to cross the 30 metres of clear ground to the fence would be suicidal, considering there were guard towers every 500 metres around the camp. Consequently, Romy's crew, in sets of two, were at each corner of the compound, watching people movements, hoping for a break in a pattern—something that would allow them access to General Fyr.

Jax picked up the binoculars and took his turn observing the base's activities. "Did you ever think, if circumstances were different, we might be in there with the loyalists?"

Having been prone on his stomach for quite some time, Romy rolled to his back and stretched. "What circumstances would those be?"

"Let's say the Council of Twelve hadn't been so hard on your father. Let's say your stepmother had remained as the vidame of the Gunn family. Let's say your father had a lead responsibility in the family." Jax rolled his neck. The slight micro-snaps of ligaments were loud to his own ears. "Under those circumstances, we might have been wearing those ugly, grey uniforms, loyally serving the matriarchal system."

Romy couldn't help a sarcastic smile from forming. He looked upwards, through the wide tree limbs, through the scattered clouds, envisioning the cold, black space beyond the atmosphere. "My father left me 18 years ago. Since he's never returned, it's not likely he's alive. That's the reality."

As Jax heard the crisp words, he replied, "As you've explained to me before, you wouldn't be alive if your father stayed—neither would your stepmother."

Thinking back to the day his father left, Romy's memory of it was as clear as if it happened yesterday. He recalled looking out his bedroom window, watching his father's smile. He remembered the odd sensation in his mind at that minute. It was like a strange connection occurred, and their minds joined. Even though his father's lips didn't move, in his mind, he heard his father's voice, *don't forget, I love you. I'll always be your father. We will meet again.*

Drops of rain fell through the limbs above, splashing into Romy's face, bringing him back to the present. He rolled back onto his stomach and snatched the binoculars from Jax. "I think you talk in hypotheticals too often."

Jax's lips curled up in a sly ear-to-ear grin. "It's fun to think of other alternatives. I've always found it extremely interesting how an event, even an insignificant one, can change the course of history."

"Like what?"

With his hand supporting the side of his head, Jax turned onto his side, leaning on his elbow. "When my leg was blown off during the Murcia Uprising, you were really upset—probably more upset than I was. Even after my leg healed, your anger just grew. That's why you joined the PAT forces, and that's why I followed you."

"You think we were wrong to join?"

"Sometimes I think if we didn't, we'd probably be in *Bellantor*. Since the city is on the most Eastern point of New Kor, it wasn't a surprise they declared themselves a neutral city, after which all the Korians sitting on the fence—and there were many of them— flooded there. We could have been right there with them," Jax continued with the hypothetical offerings.

Romy stared at Jax from under lowered eyebrows. "If you have to talk, talk about something other than *what if scenarios.*"

Romy did his best to avoid sensitive conversations about his dark history. Romy was ashamed to tell Jax that his enlistment in the PAT military had nothing to do with Jax's leg being blown off. Rather, as a Korian, even though he lived amongst them, it was not home. His own people saw him only as the son of a traitor. So, he enlisted because the dilemma he faced was, where else was he to go? Where else could he find a purpose in life?

Romy brought the binoculars back up to his eyes, continuing his surveillance. By now, the rain was falling in a torrent. It didn't stop Jax from continuing to chatter. "There's some irony here, and if we weren't here to kill someone, it would be funny."

"What are you talking about now?" Romy grumbled.

"It's ironic that we're here undertaking a covert operation against a loyalist base with the goal to kill one of the top MAT generals."

"I assume there is a point to you telling me the obvious," Romy grumbled.

"Oh yeah—the irony. Well, when we succeed, we'll have provided a disabling blow to the matriarchal system, yet you have in your possession the Gunn family ring. At over 2,000 years old, it's one of the oldest family rings in existence. It's comical that *you* have it. The Council of Twelve and even your own family don't know you have it. They would be livid if they knew what I do."

Jax was the only person who knew the secret of the family ring. It was on the one-year anniversary of Ryder Gunn's departure, when Romy was 13 years old and had held up to the loss of his father respectably, when the remembrance hit him hard. His stepmother saw he needed something to lift his spirits. She took his hand and led him to Ryder's study which had been left exactly as it was before his father left.

I'lish retrieved a small, wooden box from the hidden safe built into the wood panelling. Romy watched as she pulled the Gunn family ring from it. It was a wide band with light-blue tendrils shooting through it, giving it the appearance of lightning in a thunderstorm. The secret of the *real* ring's location was a part of the Gunn legacy that only I'lish and Ryder knew about, and now she revealed it to Romy.

Typically, the family ring was worn by the vidame of the family. When the vidame's son, the primor, became of age, the ring would be entrusted to him to be given to his wife to be, whereby she would become the next vidame. Many years ago, when I'lish was born with red blood due to remnants of human DNA, her mother knew she would not survive in a race of blue-blooded Korians. Rather than lose her all together, I'lish's mother sent I'lish away to secretly be raised by, and live with, the Sholites. As a memento, one that was to remind I'lish who she really was, I'lish's mother sent the ring with her daughter. From that point forward, I'lish's mother wore an exquisite, yet nevertheless fake, copy. In the office that day, the original two-thousand-year-old ring was what Romy had looked upon.

The rain was heavier and the pattering of the water drops on his helmet brought Romy back to the present. He brought the binoculars back up to his eyes, the bracelet on his wrist sliding down his arm. As far as he knew, no one else knew the secret of the bracelet, except Jax. Jax often looked at it with the curiosity in his eyes being hard to hide, telling Romy he recognized the pattern of light-blue tendrils within a black background.

Years ago, knowing he could never wear the ring or give it to a wife, Romy had it cut and carefully flattened. The skilled jeweller, sworn to secrecy, incorporated the flattened ring into a larger silver band, joined at the back by a matching silver chain. Although he despised the matriarchy and what his family had become, he understood the virtues of his family in Korian history. He would never modify his family name as many PAT supporters had done. He was proudly a Gunn, and the bracelet was a silent pronouncement of that.

"Something is really odd today," Romy offered.

"What are you seeing?"

"It's not that, Jax. It's what I'm *not* seeing," Romy clarified. "Where are the soldiers on the shooting range we have seen the last two days? Where are the troops in the exercise yard or on the running track?"

"Don't you see any soldiers?" Jax asked.

"Sure, lots of them. They're loitering about the compound, many of them with drinks in hand. You'd think they were having a party."

Through a chuckle, Jax replied, "Maybe they're having a day off."

"Apparently, not General Hayden Fyr," Romy muttered.

The general was a cautious man. In fact, cautious to the point of obsessiveness would be a better description. This was the third day Romy and his crew had been observing the base. It was long enough to realize the general only came out of his quarters three times a day. At exactly 6:00 and 18:00 hours, he walked from his office building to the officer's canteen where he ate breakfast and dinner. Lunch was delivered to his office, and the only other time he left his quarters was midmorning, during the short walk from his office to the general officer's building on the opposite side of the square.

It was 10:00, so it wasn't unexpected when Romy saw General Fyr come from his office building once again. Each time the general left his quarters, four security personnel formed a tight diamond formation around him. In this manner, a sniper would have difficulty hitting the target. To make matters more difficult, each security guard wore a wrist shield. When energized, the device created a one-metre-high by one-metre-wide plane of energy, capable of deflecting air charges or bullets, and unfortunately, the shields were energized whenever the general was outside.

Romy didn't know what event had caused the general to be so anal about security while being so far behind loyalist lines. Romy focused in on the general's face, almost gagging as he saw the scars from horrible burns. He reconsidered, *maybe that was enough pain to create the general's extreme level of insecurity.*

Romy and Jax remained in position for most of the day, just as three other pairs of his soldiers did the same. Marty was the fortunate one, remaining behind to watch over the makeshift camp, two kilometres within the jungle growth. When they set out to their positions each day to monitor the base, they were instructed to return to camp by 21:00 hours. Today, they followed the set protocol, but when they arrived at the camp, one person was missing. Beck had been teamed up with Rhea, one of Rico's squad, but he didn't return with her.

Romy's brows lowered, and his lips stretched tight. "Where's Beck?" he asked Rhea.

"Sir, he stayed by *Shanty Row*. He wanted to investigate something."

Taking a step closer to the brunette, Romy flung his finger in front of her nose. "I told each team not to separate!"

"Sir!" Rhea screeched. "We've been out here for three days with not a sign of an opening to the general. Beck had an idea. I could've stayed close to him, but you would've worried and come after us, putting everyone at risk." She lifted her shoulders and continued. "I made a field decision. I came back to notify you that he'll be along shortly."

Romy, who had been edging closer until he stood nose to nose with the woman, relaxed, putting his hand on her shoulder. "Okay, I got it. You did the right thing."

They dared not start a fire or even use their heat packs to warm their food. The heat signature might be seen by MAT sensors. As such, they were eating cold food from their packs when Marty jolted to her feet. On bent knees, she tilted her grenade launcher to the sound she heard—the barely audible sound of a footstep crushing a dried leaf.

A few seconds later, they heard a familiar hushed voice. "Stand down. It's me, Beck."

Lowering her weapon, Marty wiped her brow. Romy threw Beck a food pack and pointed to the spot on the fallen, moss-covered log Beck had previously claimed as his own. "Well, tell us about your adventure at Shanty Row."

Shanty Row was a stretch of 20 mobile buildings along the dirt path that circled outside the perimeter of MAT Base Firestorm. Military bases did move from time to time, dependant on the proximity to a moving military front. Shanty Row was run by opportunistic entrepreneurs who took advantage of the large population of soldiers by selling their services and wares. Within the ramshackle grouping of buildings were two restaurants delivering food into the base on a regular basis, several shops selling sundries including specialized soaps and shampoos, a laundry serving those having special needs outside of the base's own laundry service and many other shops offering products not available from military sources.

"I had an observation I wanted to follow up on," Beck began. "From my vantage point, I've noticed that a young woman from Shanty Row, carrying a neatly bound paper package, has been let into the compound at 4:00 every morning. She has had only one stop, and it's at General Fyr's quarters. She enters and, on each of the three past days leaves shortly thereafter minus the package, but now with a medium sized paper bag."

Leaning forward, Romy tilted his head even closer. He knew Beck to be a good soldier but an even smarter individual. He suspected Beck was onto something, and since they weren't even close to discovering a means to complete their mission, he listened with piqued interest.

Beck removed his helmet and pushed his fingers back through his short, brown hair. "The girl works at the laundry. I suspected what was in the bag, but I needed to verify it, so I waited until 23:00 hours when Shanty Row, but especially the laundry, closed for the day."

Romy's blue eyes widened. "Don't tell me you broke into the laundry."

Beck tilted his head and chuckled. "Okay, but once I was inside, I searched for the bag."

The soldiers in Romy's command had all stopped what they were doing, now listening to Beck. Rico said, "What then?"

Swinging his gaze towards Rico and his dirty, black beard, Beck replied, "I found the package and carefully opened it." He lifted a finger in the air. "It seems the general must have some type of issue with the base's cleaning service."

Marty interrupted, her mouth twisted sideways, her eyes playful, "Maybe the soap is irritating his sensitive, charred skin."

"Likely," Beck said with a nod. "Whatever the case, inside the package were two cleaned and pressed shirts, his name printed on the tags at the neck."

"I'm not following. What good does this do us?" Romy offered.

Tilting his glance to Marty, one eyebrow raised, Beck asked, "In your pack, don't you have an *EHK*?"

In that instant, as Romy straightened, while his eyes narrowed into shrewd slits, he knew exactly what Beck had in mind. An EHK was an *explosive homing kit*, and he knew Marty had one. She pulled the kit from her pack and handed it to Romy. Releasing the clasp, Romy peered inside, his eyes passing over the specialized bullets within. He was looking for something specific, and he let out an, "aha!" when he found it.

There were several homing beacons inside the box, each a different size, but the item catching Romy's attention was the tiny, grey button that had a microchip built into it. The button was in a small bag that he handed to Beck. Romy snapped his fingers at Rico. "You go with Beck who will place the device." Romy paused as a realization came to him. "Beck, there are two shirts. How do you know which one he'll wear?"

Beck's grinned and gave a smug response. "Shit, Boss, he'll wear the shirt without the big, dirt smudge!"

"Get going," Romy urged. "We don't know when the laundry lady starts work."

The following day, Romy was in his usual spot in the thicket of ferns underneath the needle-leafed trees. However, Jax was hidden in the branches, ten metres above his position. Similarly, he knew that at the three other corners of the compound, Ren, Rico and Beck were in elevated, concealed positions. Romy watched through the binoculars. It was 9:55 and he was waiting for General Hayden Fyr and his guards to exit his quarters.

Earlier in the morning, the team had reviewed the plan. In the front of their magazines, each of the four shooters had placed three bullets from the EHK. In the nose of each bullet was remarkable, latest-tech, microcircuitry. This included a homing sensor that would guide the bullet to the miniature button Beck had placed under the collar of the general's pressed shirt. In addition, the micro-circuitry in each specialized bullet had a disrupter charge capable of short circuiting an energy field.

Taking a quick glance at his interlink, Romy saw it was 9:58. There was a wire connected from the microphone, hinged off his helmet, to the band at his wrist. This way, Romy would give three orders: *fire one, fire two* and *fire three*. He knew this would be their only chance to complete the mission. Successful or not, in a few minutes they would all be fleeing the MAT soldiers that were bound to follow.

Romy saw the door to the general's quarters open. He shook his head, clearing his thoughts, then he focused through the binoculars. Two guards came out first, then the general, followed by the remaining two guards. The group tightened up around General Fyr, and Romy saw the familiar hazy static of their energy fields being activated. He waited for the group to make their way to a point halfway to the office building.

It was now or never. In a low but clear voice, Romy said, "Fire one."

Above him he heard the muzzled sound of Jax's rifle. Two seconds later, he said, "Fire two." He once again heard Jax's rifle fire. Immediately, he said, "Fire three."

As Romy watched the courtyard, he heard Jax scuttle down the tree, then scamper into the jungle towards their temporary camp. He knew the other shooters were doing the same.

The first group of four bullets, aimed for the homing button under the general's collar, hit the energy shields. Two shields crackled and disappeared. The next wave of bullets hit, two of which hit the two unprotected guards on their way to the target button. The other two bullets hit the remaining energy shields, disabling them. With two soldiers down and two standing above a crouched general, they didn't stand a chance. Two of the last four bullets hit the guard on one side of the general. However, there was no protection on the other side, and as Romy watched, he saw the two bullets rip into the front of the general's neck. There was a spurt of blood as the sadistic general rolled to the ground.

Romy watched for another minute as the life's blood seeped from General Hayden Fyr's body until his twitching stopped, and his eyes became glazed over and lifeless. At first, Romy sighed with regret filling his mind, but he knew the general was an evil man who had killed many of his fellow soldiers. He didn't enjoy the thought of killing people, military or otherwise, good or bad, but if this was the price to bring the civil war to an end, so be it.

Chapter 10: Betrayal

10:20 hours, 29th day of the 3rd Korian month, Haven year 0024

The Northern Wildes, south of MAT Base, Firestorm.

The rainclouds moved west, leaving small pools of water on the wide, yellow and green variegated leaves lining this part of the jungle floor. A slight breeze jostled the leaves, causing them to sway, resulting in a *drip—drip—drip* onto the rich soil. Beams of light released from the clearing sky, burrowed through the branches, lighting up insects that flew through the warming rays in an effort to dry their wings.

The serene atmosphere was broken by a *thud* as Romy's foot crashed into a puddle of murky water. At a full run, his knee hit into one of the rain-covered leaves, breaking the stem of the plant while splashing the water into a mist of droplets around him. A few moments later, he was on the barely-discernable path leading to their camp. Once there, he saw only Jax and Marty present. The others hadn't yet made their way back from their positions during the sniper fire.

Romy said to Jax. "Come with me."

Romy retraced his steps along the path with Jax following close behind. When they had backtracked 50 metres from their camp, Romy heard footsteps ahead. Instantly, he dropped to one knee with a fist in the air. Once Jax took a concealed position on the other side of the path, they both pulled their rifles to a menacing, upright position. Romy, sighting down the length of his rifle, pointed at the spot where the path was lost between two tall trees, their branches twisting up into the jungle canopy.

Seeing a booted foot press out from the shadows under the trees, Romy held his breath. When he saw Rico, soggy from the earlier rain, step from underneath the two trees, he let out a deep sigh of relief. Lavell, Rhea and Nat were close behind.

Rising to his feet, Romy waved them forward. As Rico was about to jog past, Romy put a hand on his shoulder. "Where's Beck and Ren?"

Under Rico's helmet, droplets of water mixed with sweat, dripped off his nose. "They're at the back corner of the fence. Take'em a bit longer."

"Jax and I will wait for them. The rest of you head out, and we'll catch up to you on the other side of the Swamp."

Rico nodded before continuing towards the camp.

Romy and Jax both lowered down into their concealed positions, Jax behind the thick trunk of a tree, while Romy moved into a two-metre-high thicket of goldenrod. Suppressing their anxiety, they both waited motionless.

Beck and Ren had excellent jungle survival skills. Consequently, when they finally appeared, one second the path was empty, a second later the two stragglers were there. Romy stepped out from his hidden location. In that same instant, Beck and Ren's rifles snapped towards the squad leader. Realizing who it was, they relaxed and moved towards Romy.

"You're late," Romy hissed. "Where have you been?"

Tilting his helmet back on his head, Beck wiped his wrist across his brow. "There's soldiers combing the perimeter of the camp. Most are searching the area north of the base, but we've seen one squad heading in this direction."

Grabbing the shoulder of Beck's camouflaged jacket, Romy nudged him down the path. "Follow the path back to the Swamp. Be careful, but don't dally. The others have left, and we need to catch up to them."

Their trek towards the Swamp was much easier than their initial passage since the path was still somewhat clear. Yet, there were tangles of vegetation and vines that had already begun to reclaim their territory, so the soldiers had to be aware of each footstep.

At the edge of the Swamp the knotted rope they had used a few days ago was still slung down from a thick branch overhanging the shoreline. The four soldiers scurried up onto the first, wide limb. There, Romy turned to Beck. "You'll bring up the rear. Cut down the ropes after you're finished with each one."

Having to move from level to level within the canopy, their progress had slowed. Each time a rope fell into the murky water, the bubbles that had been following them, changed to a frenzy of activity. Eight legged lizards of various lengths, up to half a metre, fought over the rope as they pulled it into the mud. Romy took a second to watch one of the ropes disappear. He now truly believed, since the rope was made of nylon, that nothing ever escaped the mud of the Swamp.

Beck heard muffled voices in the distance behind them. Imitating a bird, he let out a staccato of whistled tones. Ren, Jax and Romy, instantly dropped to a prone position on the tangled branches, while Beck hugged his back against the trunk of the hook tree. Romy shifted, letting his head drop to the side of the wood branch, looking back towards the direction Beck was pointing.

A hundred metres distant, on the shoreline of the Swamp, four loyalist soldiers knelt, considering the dangers of the deadly mud. Since they were at the same position where Romy and his crew had entered the Swamp, it was obvious the MAT squad had found their path through the jungle. They knew the assassins had come in this direction.

Romy slid his rifle off his shoulder, tilted the magnifying eyepiece into position and pointed it towards the loyalists. They were talking amongst themselves, pointing first to the Swamp and then vehemently back to their base. Their voices rose as they argued, but not to a high enough level so that Romy could understand their words or their odd behaviour. After a few minutes of observing their activity, Romy saw the men rise to their feet and retrace their steps back towards their base. While he waited a few minutes to ensure the MAT soldiers didn't return, Romy rubbed his chin, perplexed by their behaviour. Romy's confusion would have been instantly cleared if he could have heard the MAT squad leader's last words. "The war's over. We're not going to risk our lives in the Swamp. Everything will be simpler if we tell *Command,* we saw nothing."

Two hours later, Beck was the last man to climb down the last rope and step across the makeshift ladder to the south shoreline of the Swamp. Rico stepped out from the dense foliage and greeted them. He looked at each of the four stragglers and smiled. "We made it. Anyone following?"

Romy didn't answer Rico until the nine soldiers trekked through the short distance of thicker jungle and onto the familiar animal trail. He turned to his squad. "I don't think anyone is following, but they will likely be searching from the sky. Make sure your heat diffusor pack is on." Pointing to Ren, he said, "You take point." His eyes shifted to Rico. "You and Marty bring up the rear, but keep 30 metres behind us."

Romy was their leader. There were no questions. They took their positions and began their trip back to the same clearing that had been their drop off point. On their way towards the Swamp, this duration of their trip, cutting through dense jungle for much of it, had been a time consuming 32 hours. Knowing their way along the animal trail, they made excellent time during their return. There were four short delays as loyalist aircraft flew over their positions. Since the path created a break in the canopy, at these times, the soldiers took cover in the surrounding undergrowth until the aircraft cleared the area.

When they left the animal trail for the path they'd previously cut in the jungle, their progress slowed, but it was still much faster than their inbound trip. Although they were exhausted, they slept only once for four hours. As such, when Ren broke through the jungle into the tall rainbow grass of the clearing, they were a day early for their scheduled pick up.

Even though they were in the Southern Wildes and far from MAT held territory, they dared not make a fire, or even use a heat pack. Just inside the edge of the clearing, they cleared out a larger area than they normally would have. The squad took extra time to gather grass and leaves that would provide them more comfortable beds than they had since they left PAT Base 4. As usual, Beck climbed a tree on the perimeter of their camp and set up their recharging apparatus. The last task was setting up the energy spikes in the ground and on the surrounding trees, to ensure they were isolated from the dangers of the jungle.

Two soldiers at a time were sent a couple of hundred metres back along their path to watch for anyone who might follow. Marty and Lavell took first watch as the remaining seven soldiers sat on logs that had been set up in a square. They were almost out of rations, but since this was their last night in the wild, they ate what they had left.

Beck, with a mouthful of food, pointed at Romy. Romy, pulling his hands outwards from his body, had no idea what Beck had on his mind.

The food was dry and Beck did his best, rolling it around his mouth. Eventually, he swallowed and managed to say, "Your hand."

Romy brought one hand under his gaze, rolling it over, seeing nothing odd. He did the same with his left hand, and as he turned it over, he saw a long cut across the top of it. Romy thought he must have cut it while making camp. As he looked closer, it wasn't deep even though a thin line of blue blood still trickled and dripped off the top of his thumb.

As Romy wrapped a rag around his hand, he heard a mix of whispers and snickers. When he raised his eyes, he saw Rhea and Nat huddled close together with bemused smiles on their faces.

Raising an eyebrow, Romy chirped, "Is there something amusing about the cut on my hand?"

Rhea and Nat were from Rico's squad, so not as familiar with Romy as the others in Romy's primary squad. The emotion vanished from their faces, and Rhea stuttered out a response. "No—no, Sir."

Nat quickly added, "But there is something."

Rhea inhaled a deep breath and elbowed Nat in the side. "There is *nothing*, Sir."

Slapping his thigh, Romy let out a loud guffaw. It felt good to laugh after a tense week in the jungle. Now, knowing they would be back at their base tomorrow, they could relax. "Ladies, if there's a question, there would never be a better time to ask it."

Scooting forward on her log, Nat offered, "Your blood is blue. We all know the documented version of your family history, including a cross between red and blue blood. Is it all true exactly as it is written in our history?"

"Ah, you are looking for some juicy pieces of gossip."

Nat's face flushed and her eyebrows lifted. "It would only be gossip if we shared it, which we won't—but juicy will work."

Picking up the canteen of water beside him, Romy took a long swig before replying. "Your name is Nat, short for Natalie. Is that correct?"

"Yes, I'm named after Natalie Lowe."

"Let's start there," Romy said. "Natalie Lowe was my great grandmother, and she was from the planet, Earth."

By now, the other six soldiers sitting on the logs had stopped eating, not wanting to miss a single word.

"It was 89 years ago when the asteroid-world, Talus 3, was passing in close proximity to Earth," Romy started. "The Sholites and Korians, knowing the path of the asteroid, also knew, tens of years ahead of time, that the passage would be close but without risk of an impact. The Sholite war with the Korians was at a high point, and the Sholites sent teams of their people to Earth far in advance."

A group of clouds passed over the clearing, setting an eerie play of shadows across Romy's face. "The Sholites on Earth set about a well-crafted plan, utilizing scientists and engineers from Earth to help them." Raising a finger while shaking his head, Romy clarified, "If you think the friction between Korians and Sholites is difficult, think of the five or six major factions on Earth having such friction, but at a redoubled level. In that environment, the Sholites found it easy to dupe the scientists and engineers from one of these factions, having them assist in creating a huge electromagnetic weapon—one they hoped would destroy Talus 3."

Rico, who was usually one of very few words added, "Sholites can be nasty," then spat on the ground beside his boot.

"The Sholites told these scientists Talus 3 was on a collision course with Earth, and the device would nudge the asteroids path just enough to avoid the impact."

Romy took another drink of water. Even though they had all heard the story before—many times— each of them could now tell their grandchildren they had heard the story directly from a living descendant. Romy saw their anticipation, grinning as he stretched out the pause.

Finally, Nat blurted out, "Then what?"

Romy chuckled. "Then we realized, once again, Korians can be just as nasty as Sholites. Several were sent to Earth to stop the Sholite-Earth alliance from creating the electromagnetic device. My great granduncle was one of them. He was sent to convince one of the other factions—the Russians—to work with the Korians to stop the Sholites. That man's Korian name was Arlo Gunn, known on Earth as Logan Russell."

Natalie's eyes lit up. "Your great granduncle is one of the most famous men in our history!"

"Almost as famous as my great grandfather, Rowan Gunn—a man known on Earth by the name, Josh Harris," Romy added. "Rowan Gunn had an even more dangerous mission. He had covertly infiltrated the Sholite group to sabotage the mission as a last resort, if need be. He had met Natalie Lowe because Natalie's father was one of the scientists being used by the Sholites. They fell in love even though she didn't know Rowan Gunn was an alien."

Rhea interjected, "It's the love story of all love stories."

"But a tragic one," Romy clarified. "Natalie, still unaware the Sholites were prepared to kill millions of lives, and not knowing Rowan was a Korian, took matters into her own hands when the Sholite leader was about to energize the weapon. Rowan Gunn was on the verge of shooting the Sholite leader, but Natalie, thinking the Sholites were saving Earth, shot the man she loved at the same instant Rowan shot the Sholite leader."

In a hushed voice, Rhea whispered, "It's a tragic story."

"Indeed," Romy agreed. "Thankfully, the sequence of events saved Talus 3 and Earth. Natalie Lowe, having lost the man she loved, left Earth with the Korians. She became close to Arlo Gunn, eventually marrying him even though, at the time, Natalie Lowe was pregnant with my grandfather."

Rico, sensing the story was degrading into sentimental mush, nodded towards Rhea and Nat, quipping, "Get back to the blood. That's what they want."

The cut under the rag had dried. Romy uncovered it, lifting his hand towards the two women. "As you see, my blood is blue. Sholites have red blood. People from Earth, including Natalie Lowe, also have red blood. So, yes, my grandfather had mixed genetics, but his blood was blue. It seems the DNA making our blood blue was and is more dominant than that creating red blood. Consequently, as far as I know, all the descendants of Natalie Lowe had or have blue blood—with one exception."

"I'lish Mann," Rico reminded the group.

"Two years before I was born, my mother had a baby girl," Romy explained. "Unfortunately, my sister died during childbirth—at least, that's what we were told. In reality, the Earthen DNA was dominant and the baby was born with *red* blood. As I'm sure you would agree with my mother's thoughts, a baby with red blood would not survive in a civilization of blue-blooded Korians."

"But our recent history would say she did survive," Rhea said, impatient that the story wasn't moving faster.

"My mother sent the baby to live with a Sholite friend, and that's where she was raised."

"Until she became the president of the Sholite people," Nat offered through her laughter. "Then, to maintain the stability of the joint Sholite-Korian fleet, with no one knowing I'lish Mann was your father's sister, your father completed a politically motivated marriage."

With a wide ear to ear grin, Romy added, "The plan worked to perfection until the time came—and both I'lish and my father knew it would come—when they would have to confess."

"Then what," Nat asked.

"Then, I'm sitting here on a damp log with you slugs, exhausted and malnourished."

Several mouths were opened, about to protest, when a voice from behind Romy interrupted, "What the fuck is going on? Were you going to leave us out there all night?"

Romy turned to see Marty, eyes smoldering. "Is it my turn, already?" Romy asked, his light-blue eyes the picture of innocence.

Marty scowled and momentarily pressed the tip of her rifle into the energy field even though it gave her an instant jolt. A spattering of blue sparks erupted while Marty growled her impatience. Rico turned off the energy field. Romy and Jax, for their own safety, made a wide arc around Marty as they headed down the trail.

"Send Lavell back!" Marty yelled after them.

The rest of the evening through to the early morning hours, was uneventful. They continued taking two-hour shifts guarding their rear until Romy saw the dark, morning clouds gathering in the east. He called back Rhea and Nat after which the nine soldiers anxiously waited at the edge of the clearing. The pickup time wasn't exact other than it was to coincide with the morning rains.

The dark clouds billowed and lumbered closer. Sometimes the rains were light, but at times, massive thunderstorms would roll across the habitable zone. Today, the rumble foretold this would be one of those days. At first, there were random drops of rain, but they were huge. Then, the frequency increased until the noise of so many raindrops pounding into the foliage became deafening.

Romy began to wonder if Pilot Demoro would attempt their retrieval in such insane weather. However, barely audible, Romy heard a distant whine through the rumbling storm. It became louder until they saw a black shadow hovering above the clearing. As it lowered, the air vortexes created by the four sets of blades, made large swirls of mist, making the helocraft even harder to distinguish.

Taking a flashlight from a pouch on his jacket, Romy pointed it at the black swirling mass. He flashed, *long flash-long flash-short flash-long flash-long flash.*

From the helocraft a signal flashed back, *short flash-short flash-long flash-short flash-short flash.*

Seeing the correct signal, Romy rose from his kneeling position. As loud as he could, he yelled, "let's go!" while he rolled his arm forward towards the hovering craft.

As the nine soaked soldiers jogged across the clearing, Romy thought it odd the helocraft was maintaining a position a few metres above the ground. By now, they should have landed. The next sound he heard sent the hairs on the back of his neck to standing on end. It was the subtle sound of a laser cannon charging to full power. At the same time, his mind was assaulted. *Danger,* screamed in his mind's eye. They were almost at the center of the clearing when Romy yelled out, "Something's wrong! Get back to the jungle—now!"

Romy began an awkward backwards run as he watched his group. They all began to run towards the jungle except Rhea and Nat, who stood with confusion on their faces. The first laser blast from the helocraft slammed into the two women, tearing them to pieces. Jax was running towards him when Romy turned, heading for the safety of a group of large boulders on the edge of the thick, jungle vegetation.

Jax sped along behind his friend. He heard screams as another laser blast hit into the soldiers. They were almost at the rocks when Jax heard the laser cannon charging once again. A *woosh* told him the beam of energy was on its way. Oddly, in front of him, he saw Romy almost at the nearest boulder with a glowing, green field of energy surrounding his body.

That's the last thing Jax ever saw. The blast hit the ground just behind him. His body, at least most of it, flung forward, slamming into Romy.

The air was knocked from Romy's lungs. His flailing figure skipped across the boulder and into the large mud pit on the other side. Romy's consciousness kept fading in and out, but at best, he was groggy.

The mud pit was a stinking, two-foot-deep pool of rainwater captured by the formation of rocks, mixed with decomposing dead leaves and grass. Romy's body was submerged in the mud. His helmet had been blown off, so only his head, featuring a deep gash on the side, protruded from the mud.

The sound of yelling pushed through Romy's delirium. From the other side of the boulders, he heard Demoro. "Do you have all of them? We can't leave any evidence!"

Through the pounding rain, another voice answered. "I think so. It's hard to tell because, mostly, there's only pieces."

"Did you get all the *pieces*?" Demoro asked in a sarcastic tone.

"Yes, everything's bagged!"

"Check behind those boulders."

Half conscious, Romy heard the words and managed to close his fingers on a handful of mud. Pain shot through his shoulder as he lifted his arm, dragging his mud-laden hand over his face. The final movement of his damaged shoulder was more than he could bear. As he heard footsteps climbing the boulder behind him, he lost consciousness.

The gunner, menacingly holding a rifle, peered down behind the boulder. He wiped the rain that was flowing off the rim of his helmet, but still his vision was obscured. He held his hand horizontally under the rim of the helmet, giving him a momentary clear view. He panned his gaze between the rocks for a few moments, then turned and shouted, "There's nothing here—just a stinking mud pit!"

Demoro's voice answered, "Okay then, let's get the fuck out of here!"

Chapter 11: Efia Kuma

14:10 hours, 1ˢᵗ day of the 4ᵗʰ Korian month, Haven year 0024

The Southern Wildes, 110 kilometres north of PAT Base 4.

The yellow, red and blue lights playing in Romy's subconscious were magnificent. His mind's eye allowed him to float amongst them. They looked close by, but as he moved his hand towards one, he realized they were actually very far away. He felt disappointment, and as soon as the emotion came, he was dragged closer to them. He was in fear but mainly in awe of the vision his imagination created. But still, he felt an urgent desire to see more.

At that moment, the lights peeled away, then returned—at least that's what Romy's mind's eye was telling him. However, he inspected the panorama of lights from one end to the other, realizing the pattern was completely different. He wanted more, and as if his wish was answered, again the pattern of lights rolled away, then returned. Once again, the pattern was different.

His fascination grew, and as it did, the layers of light patterns changed faster and faster. It came to the point he couldn't keep up, eventually seeing only a mixed blur of yellow, red and blue. Pain exploded behind his eyes. Now, as the patterns changed, he felt as if his head would explode.

He tried to let out a scream, but his mouth was clamped shut. Then, he heard urgent words in his mind—*Wake up!* The sound broke the patterns of shifting lights into thousands of shards, like a pane of glass having been hit by a rock.

The supernatural vision was replaced by blackness and quiet, only broken by the calm chirping of birds above him. Romy tried to open his mouth, but it was still clamped shut, as were his eyes. The pain was still in his head, but it was joined by a severe strain in his shoulder even as he tried to lift his arm. It was weighed down, but Romy pushed the jarring pain to the back of his mind, forcing his hand up from the thick mud.

Scratching at his face, he realized the coating of mud had dried, creating a mask. He ripped at his chin, removing hardened chunks, bit by bit. Now freed, he flexed his jaw, then proceeded to his eyes, continuing to remove the mud. When he was finally able to pry his eyes open, he saw hazy, tall figures in the distance. As his vision cleared, he realized they were trees. He opened and closed his eyes several times and shifted his gaze down to the rocks on the other side of the muddy bog he was lying in.

There, on a boulder, sitting on her haunches, staring at him, was a woman. She was young, no older than he was, but it was difficult to tell since she had the skin colour of the Mabuza people who Romy often thought looked much younger than they really were. Most Mabuza had black skin, but ten per cent, including this woman, had a light brown pigmentation. Her face was well proportioned with a thin nose and striking lips; the lower lip was normal enough, but the upper lip was full, curling at the tips into deep dimples. In the middle, her upper lip was raised, giving her the appearance of someone who was always smiling through a pout.

The woman watched for a few moments, then rolled her eyes. "Wake up!" she shouted.

Romy tried to slide himself out of the mud, but the suction worked against his efforts. The Mabuza woman slapped her thigh and rose to her feet. As she strode around the mud pit, she mumbled words, half Korian and half in some foreign language. Romy heard her say, "Men—how do they get themselves into such a mess?"

Wriggling and pushing against the sticky mud with all his effort, while the Mabuza woman pulled on his arm, Romy managed to remove himself from the quagmire. By now, between the pain in his shoulder and that in his head having moved from behind his eyes to a point above his ear, the grogginess had lessened. He turned to the woman who squatted beside him, picking pieces of dried mud from his head. "What's your name?" Romy asked.

"Efia Kuma," she promptly replied, her voice having a melodic tone. "But most call me Efi."

Romy's body jolted as Efi continued to pick mud from him. "Shit—that hurt! Be careful," he grunted.

"Don't be so childish," she chided. She pulled down the corners of her lips, her eyes opening wider as she inspected his scalp. "You have an ugly cut. Fortunately, the mud packed against it actually helped, but it needs to be properly cleaned."

Putting her hands under his arm, she helped Romy to his feet. With his mind and vision now clear, he saw Efi stood half a head shorter than he was, but that included quite an impressive head of hair, consisting of a seemingly endless number of bunched, tightly curled spirals. At the base of each curl, the hair was dark-brown, turning lighter until the tips were bright-blonde. That said, even more captivating was the golden colour of her eyes. His gaze had been drawn there as they sparkled in the forever twilight.

It was an awkward moment made even more so as Efi realized he was admiring her. As her lips curled upwards in a smug smile, he felt a flush, thankfully covered by the dirt from the pit. Moving his focus to the rocks behind Efi, his mind came back to the events of the early morning.

"Where's my team?" Romy asked, his voice quivering.

Efi's voice was hushed, barely audible above the slight breeze. "I'm sorry. They're all dead."

Climbing up onto the boulder, Romy looked out across the long, yellow grass in the clearing. He knew the answer to his question when he asked it, but he was hoping Efi would tell him he was wrong.

Efi joined him on the rock. "We need to leave. The helocraft might come back."

Romy slid down the side of the boulder with Efi following. "I need to see for myself." He panned his gaze over the grass, looking for some evidence of his soldiers, but all he saw were charred, shallow craters fringed by scorched grass. "I don't know how the loyalist helocraft found us. We were careful," he muttered.

Slim fingers grasped Romy's elbow, turning him. Her eyes were wide, the golden pupils once again mesmerising him. Her voice had lost its melodic tone. "It wasn't a loyalist vessel. I was watching from the safety of the jungle's edge. On the side of the craft's fuselage was the emblem of the patriotic forces."

As Romy's jaw dropped, the edges of his brows above his nose, rose. "It can't be. Why…" He cut off his own words as he wiped the dirt from his wrist interlink. He pushed at it several times, but it was unresponsive. After another futile attempt, he realized it was dead. His gaze, now hardened, turned back to Efi. "You said you saw the events. Where are my soldiers?"

"The soldiers from the helocraft took what was left of them."

Still determined to see for himself, Romy turned and walked through the long grass.

Efi didn't follow. She knew Romy needed to see for himself, so he could put closure to the events of the morning. Romy walked in random circles, occasionally dropping to his knees for a closer inspection. Korian blood, when it dried, turned clear. It didn't take long for him to discover several pools of it on the ground. At one point, he saw a flash of metal. He dug into the base of the long grass and pulled out a silver, hinged mechanism, broken at each end. He gasped as he realized it was a linkage from Jax's bionic leg. He saw Efi watching in the distance and turned away, wiping the tears that were flowing down his cheeks. Allowing only a few sentimental moments, he cleared his throat before striding back towards the woman.

He lifted a finger towards her and grunted, "What circumstances find you here in the middle of nowhere?"

The tips of her eyes stretched out, causing the golden hue to become barely visible. "I was hunting. There's a Mabuza settlement 40 kilometres in that direction—" Her arm shot up, her finger pointing to the northwest "—and that's where we need to go."

Once again, Romy tried to energize his interlink as he muttered, "I need to contact my Command Group…"

Efi cut off his words. "Romy, your *Command Group* just tried to kill you. Your *Command Group* just killed your soldiers. What more is there to say?"

Romy's eyes narrowed. "How do you know my name? I never told you, so how do you know it?"

For a moment the hue of Efi's face turned a shade darker. She put her fists against her hips and leaned her upper body closer to him. "Because I found a bashed helmet on this side of the boulders. Inside it, was a torn tag. On it was the name, Romy Gunn." She leaned even closer. "I assumed the word, *asshole*, must have been the portion that tore off." She spat out the words.

Romy's mind was trying to process the jumbled pieces of information as best he could. However, this was the most time he had ever spent with a Mabuza woman. He was impressed by her spirit and hoped she was someone he could rely on. In reality, he didn't have many other options but to do so.

Even though he could see she had a slim figure under the loose clothing she wore, her exposed arms and neck, visible above the low-cut shirt, were lean and athletic. A sheath, hanging from her belt held a long knife. Two handles were visible behind her, one angled across each shoulder. Romy assumed they were some sort of jungle weapon. As he considered the woman, he thought, *she wouldn't be the worse person to be with.* "You said your village is 40 kilometres away."

"C'mon then," Efi urged before she turned and started towards the jungle's edge. She turned her head and scoffed, "And it's a settlement. Mabuza people don't live in villages."

Running a few steps to catch up, Romy growled as pain drove through his shoulder. Efi noticed and said, "Before we go anywhere, we need to get you cleaned up. There's a stream half a kilometre away. We'll go there first."

'One moment," Romy said. "I'll meet you by the jungle's edge." Without waiting for a reply, he walked back to the mud pit. Kneeling down he reached into it, searching until he felt a nylon strap. He pulled, and with difficulty, managed to pull his rifle free. It was thick with mud, and as he tried to free the magazine, he found it jammed just as if cement had sealed it. It was the same result when he tried to empty the firing chamber. Realizing the weapon was permanently damaged, he threw it back into the ooze where it slowly sank beneath the surface. Fortunately, the air pistol he carried in the holster at his side had been protected by a flap. When he inspected the gun, he found it to be fully operational.

Without a functional interlink, Romy had no way to determine the time, but as he walked towards Efi, her impatient pacing told him she was more anxious the longer they remained at the clearing. Once he arrived at her position, she told him to stand back. She reached over her shoulders and pulled at the two handles. When they slid from the double scabbard across her back, he saw two pointed, short, stabbing spears. As if that wasn't menacing enough, she pressed a tiny lever on each handle, whereby the silver blades came to life with a blue, electrical glow.

"There's an animal trail 30 metres into the jungle. It'll lead us to the stream."

Without waiting for a response, Efi turned and slashed at the vegetation. She swirled the stabbing spears expertly, and as Romy followed a safe distance behind, he thought the motions could have been part of a fluid dance. Each time the electric-blue blades cut through a branch or thick stem, a crackling static discharge could be heard. It didn't take long before they found themselves on a well-trodden path. They followed it west until it widened, finally coming to an abrupt end at a fast-running stream.

"I'm curious. We are 40 kilometers from your settlement," Romy pointed out. "Do you usually hunt this far from your home?"

"The Mabuza settlement is called, Rifa, and I never said it was my home."

Romy took note of the fact she didn't answer his question. "All the more reason to wonder, I suppose," he replied. "How did you know the animal path was here and that it would lead to this stream?"

Tilting her gaze towards him, Efi's golden eyes were not so welcoming. In the short time he was with her, this was the second time her face was filled with what appeared to be contempt. "I'm Mabuza," she began, her voice distinctly patronizing. "My people have been on this planet for 200 years. We're close to nature: the plants, the trees and the creatures that live on the surface. It's not difficult for us to make our way through a jungle we're very comfortable in."

It didn't take even average observation skills to realize Efi had something bothering her. He also realized she, once again, didn't answer his question. But in her present mood, he thought it better to let the matter rest—at least for the time being.

Seeing that Romy wasn't going to pursue the line of questioning, Efi lifted one corner of her mouth while shaking her head. They were wasting time. The further away they were from the clearing, the better it would be for the both of them. Efi squatted and put her hand in the water, then tasted it off her fingers.

"What are you doing?"

"Moran eels frequent some of the waters in this part of the jungle," Efi explained. "They wouldn't kill you if they latch on, but they can create a dangerous wound. Fortunately, this water comes from an underground spring. As such, it's too cold for them. Some of the rivers in this area also have a high sulfur content. This one doesn't."

"Great." Romy mumbled as he peeled off his muddy clothes after stepping out of his boots.

Efi hadn't turned around, but when she saw Romy's naked form pass by, then step into the stream, she shot up and turned away. "Naked! Really!"

Once Romy was waist high in the frigid water, he turned and remembered the Mabuza race weren't as sexually free as the Korians and Sholites. In the military forces, the soldiers had unisex bathrooms and showered together. By her reaction, it was obvious this wasn't the case with the Mabuza.

Romy was grinning as he washed his body, hearing Efi continue to mumble. He yelled out, "Throw me my clothes so I can wash them."

She snapped her head around and was relieved to see the water up to his waist. She glared at him as she retrieved his clothing, then threw them more at him, than to him. When the chore was complete, Romy continued to provoke her by walking out of the water without covering himself. This time, even though her face turned a few shades darker, she didn't turn away. She decided the Korian man wouldn't show her up.

Romy laid out his clothes on a rock to dry. He felt some sympathy for Efi. After all, she was here helping him, so he decided he would give her some leeway. As such, he wrung out his underpants as best he could before pulling them on.

Efi had found a comfortable patch of short grass where Romy sat down beside her. The view of the stream was intoxicating, like looking into the flames of a fire. He said, "I never said thank you. I do so now. I appreciate the help you are giving me." Her face tilted up to him. His breathing stopped for a moment as once again her golden eyes spellbound him.

She smiled and said, "I'm glad to help. In many ways, the life of a Mabuza is to help others and set things straight." As she explained, she realized she was also having trouble looking into Romy's light-blue eyes. As she turned to gaze at the fast-flowing water, she continued. "My home is in Hagaza, the capital city of the Mabuza Islands. The majority of my people live on those islands, but as you know, we do have small communities within your cities and a few remote settlements such as Rifa. I was there visiting when I decided to hunt, but maybe my purpose wasn't so deadly. Rather, I love to walk in the beauty of the jungle. The guise of hunting suited me."

Having only limited experience with Mabuza people in both Sholite and Korian cities, Romy had found them to be quiet. In fact, he always thought of them as submissive. However, Efi didn't fit that generalization. She did have a peaceful persona, but there was a fiery disposition below the surface that he had seen break through a few times now.

For a time, they sat quietly, waiting for Romy's clothes to dry. Romy's mind went back to the tragic morning. His team was killed, and as his recollection returned to him, he recalled Matt Demoro's voice giving orders in the aftermath. Romy thought it out, realizing it was unlikely the pilot made a unilateral decision to kill his team. General Brett Jezeer *must* have been behind it, but why?

An image of Jax came into his mind, and he took a deep gulp of air in an effort to avoid crying out. He needed to speak his mind. But Efi was the only person here, and he didn't know her at all. However, his gut feel told him she was a good person. "Do you know who I am, Efi?"

"I told you already. You're Romy Gunn."

"That's my name—yes. But do you know *who* I am?"

Once again, her delightful gaze was upon him. "Ah, I understand. There aren't many people who don't know who Ryder Gunn is, and yes, I know you're his son."

Romy brought his knees up and leaned his elbows on them, his hands supporting his chin. "The military was the only thing I called home. Jax was one of only a very few people who I called my friend. Now he's gone. The military is gone. In fact, it seems they tried to kill me."

Efi put her hand on Romy's shoulder. "I know this because she is also high profile, but you have a mother."

Letting out a sarcastic chuckle, Romy responded. "I am a Korian, shunned in Korian cities. My mother is a Sholite, living in a Sholite city where I have very little comfort." After an awkward pause he continued. "Don't get me wrong. I'm not looking for sympathy or pity. What I have just told you has been the case since I was 12 years old."

"You'll come to learn, although many Mabuza aren't big talkers, we're good listeners."

Romy leaned back, grinning. "Well, thank you for that."

Efi's eyes widened and lit up as she poked Romy in the arm. "But I have to warn you, I think I listen well enough, and perhaps not being one of those 'many Mabuza,' I have been uniquely gifted with the power to talk at length—too lengthy for some."

When Romy glanced at her, she playfully waggled her thin eyebrows and said, "Get dressed. We need to begin our trek. Your general might be coming back."

After rising to his feet, Romy froze and looked down at her. "How do you know about the general?"

"You're in the military. Nothing happens without a general ordering it. Isn't that the case?"

After dressing, the rest of the day involved difficult progress through the jungle. Efi led the way, cutting through the vegetation. She did indeed like to talk and gave a running commentary of what she considered, her jungle. She would point out footprints, educating Romy on which animal had made them. When a shrill cry would break the silence, Efi would tell him which bird sung it out.

To Romy, the undergrowth just seemed to repeat over and over. He realized he would have been hopelessly lost without Efi to guide him. Oddly, Efi didn't have a device of any kind to give her a direction to follow. Somehow, and Romy put it down to her Mabuza experience, she seemed to know their heading. He was surprised Efi had a knack for finding animal paths that crisscrossed the terrain. They would be walking along one, when suddenly, she would pull out her spears and begin to hack into the jungle, indicating an alternate, preferred path was a short distance away. She did this numerous times, leaving Romy scratching his head in each instance.

Romy was past the point of feeling useless when the path they were following separated into two forks. Efi continued on the western fork, and

Romy, having a need to be useful, started up the northern path. He yelled, "I'll see what's down here!"

Romy took one step down the alternate path and had his foot in the air for the next step when he heard a scream, "Freeze!"

Romy did just that, leaving his foot suspended in the air. Instantly, Efi was beside him and whispered, "Don't put your foot down." She looped her arm around his waist and, as she coaxed him backwards, said, "Very slowly—retrace your steps."

Romy had no idea what she was going on about, but her tone caused beads of sweat to break out on his brow. He didn't relax until Efi removed her hand and said, "It's okay, but don't move."

Romy didn't dare do anything but comply. She reached into the underbrush, pulling up a stout, dried-out section of a thick branch. She moved forward and inspected the area where Romy was about to step. She kneeled and brought the branch down to hover over the path. She moved it back and forth, seeming to find a preferred position, then she lowered it against the dirt. As soon as the wood hit the ground, a huge cloud of dirt was thrown into the air.

There was an eerie squeal from the wood as Efi rose. Attached to the wood was a creature much like a centipede, but much larger. Romy took a step back as Efi turned with the creature hanging from the branch.

"Don't worry. The danger is past. This is a burrow slug. They dig themselves underground along paths frequented by animals and, in some cases, people. Upside down and covered in dirt, the spike in their underbelly waits for an unsuspecting victim."

The corners of Romy's lips were curled down. He looked like he was going to vomit.

"If you would have stepped on it, the spike would have punctured your foot, irrespective of your thick boot. And if that wasn't painful enough, the slug isn't easy to remove. That's when it begins to feed, sucking the blood from the closest veins. However, in this case, the spike punctured the wood. Unfortunately, with the spike locked in place, the slug won't be able to remove itself, and it will die."

Walking a few steps to a wide tree trunk, Efi slammed the stick into it, making contact at what, to Romy, looked like the head of the slug. She mumbled a few words, then threw the dead slug and branch into the vegetation. "A quick death is better. Other insects and creatures of the land will now benefit."

"I didn't see anything. How did you know it was there?"

Efi showed neat rows of white teeth as she grinned. "I'm a Mabuza. I told you, we're one with the land." Without another word, she slapped him on the back before returning to the correct pathway.

Walking behind her, Romy's mind was churning. He believed in coincidence, but something seemed odd. As he thought about it more, he realized the events were absolutely ridiculous. Finally, he took a few fast strides and put his hand on Efi's shoulder, turning her. "Something isn't right. I need some better answers."

He couldn't believe it, but it seemed she just batted her eyelids before saying, "What answers?"

He took a deep breath and exhaled before continuing. "Let's start with the probability of you happening to be at the same clearing I was in, in the middle of no-man's-land. Then you knew my name while telling me some bullshit about reading the name in my helmet." Romy pointed in different directions as he emphasized his words. "Then, you happen to know where a path leading to a convenient stream is, even though you are 40 kilometres from a settlement that apparently isn't your home. How could you possibly know where every jungle path lies, yet you continually cut through dense sections of foliage to miraculously find them?"

"Well…"

Romy cut her off. "I'm not finished. Then somehow, on a path you've never travelled along or were able to see down, you sensed a dangerous slug hidden in the dirt. Then, you give me some mumbo-jumbo about Mabuza people being one with nature. Bullshit!"

"I'm not sure you're ready."

Romy laughed. "What—are you going to tell me you have some type of super power?"

Efi shrugged. "Actually, *psychic powers* would be the correct term."

Throwing back his head, Romy laughed. It was a defensive reaction, hiding the fact he was thinking, *could it actually be true?*

Chapter 12: No Loose Ends

10:30 hours, 1ˢᵗ day of the 4ᵗʰ Korian month, Haven year 0024

PAT Base 4.

Things certainly were different. The canteen was empty, save for General Jezeer and, across the other side of the large room, four soldiers playing a group video game. Over the last few days, after the peace treaty had been announced, 70 per cent of the soldiers—roughly 7,000 men and women—had been furloughed. Most went to their homes in Villaro or Bellantor, while some were brave enough to visit family in Murcia.

Nevertheless, the large video screen, secured to the far wall, was powered during all hours of the day. The news reporters, one after the other, gave their own perspective on the peace treaty, or interviewed dignitaries to obtain theirs. Unfortunately, the day prior, with the list of influential dignitaries exhausted, now obscure, lower-level officials gave their opinions, leaving fewer and fewer viewers with any interest.

Thankfully, the peace treaty special report concluded, leaving an attractive woman to report on general news of the day.

> *"Another transport has gone missing over the Eastern Ocean. The last contact with the air carrier, Cassandra, was 180 kilometres southeast of Bellantor. The airplane was travelling to Villaro with a full load of copper from the mines located in the Ice Shield.*
>
> *Over the last four months, this has been the third cargo transport to disappear along with one military transport. All craft were mysteriously lost within a 400-kilometer area extending east from Bellantor.*
>
> *Sea search forces have been dispatched from Bellantor to search the area, but up to the time of this report there has been no sign of survivors."*

General Jezeer slapped his palm against his open mouth, propelling the smack between his lips. The loss of ships, both on the sea and aircraft above it, had gone on for too long. Hopefully, now that a truce had been reached, additional resources would be sent to Bellantor to uncover the mystery.

The newswoman on the video screen, shifted, facing a second camera.

"Just as mysteries continue on the planet's surface, so do they abound in space. Yesterday, maintenance personnel at the Junkyard noticed the Pulsar, a mothballed scientific research vessel, had vanished. Yes, vanished was the word the maintenance crew used. The ship, 150 metres long, had been docked in the Junkyard for eight years before its sudden disappearance.

This is not the first unexplainable disappearance, and people are becoming frightened. Some have protested, thinking the Mabuza are responsible, silently conjuring up demons because we invaded their planet.

We go now, live, to Murcia where a group of 20 protestors are in front of the Council of Twelve Chambers."

The image on the screen changed. A hand holding a microphone was in the foreground. Just behind it was a man wearing a woolen hat, pulled down over his ears, barely allowing his crazy eyes to peer out from below it. Behind the round face were a small group of yelling protestors, signs in hands, indicating their displeasure with the Mabuza. The man's eyes widened as he said,

"It's the Mabuza. They're so quiet. What are they really up to? They say they're more than willing to share the habitable zone, but since we came here, our ships continue to go missing. In the last year, this is the fourth spaceship to vanish from the Junkyard, while one military frigate travelled into space, supposedly lost without a trace."

The man's eyes grew wider as his voice rose. He continued in a high pitch,

"It's the ghosts. We hear the rumours. They used to live on the planet. Now, they're angry at us. There have been sightings of black, shifting shapes slithering through space with two blood-red eyes searching for ships to feed on."

As he snatched the microphone, spittle came from the man's mouth.

"It's the Devil Raiders! They're coming for all of us! The red eyes will find you!"

The newsfeed cut away from the protest back to the newswoman in the studio. She was shuffling papers on her desk, trying to buy a few seconds for the director to cue up the next story.

The general didn't know who was funnier: the crazed protestor or the embarrassed newswoman. The amused look on his face was interrupted by a *beep* from his wrist interlink. He tilted his face down and saw it was 11:00. "Time to go," he mumbled as he rose to his feet. He lifted the military cap onto his head before striding out the double doors towards the six-wheeled, all-terrain vehicle parked just outside the officer's compound.

Even though PAT Base 4 had been established two years earlier, considering the extended distance to both Villaro and Bellantor, it made no sense to pave a road outside the encampment. Instead, there were two parallel, dirt tire tracks, riddled with holes and bumps. The green and grey camouflaged vehicle was able to maintain a reasonable speed along it for 20 minutes. After that point, what maintenance the base crews regularly performed, became nonexistent. The dual paths narrowed as fresh tree shoots sprouted up through the rock-laden dirt. Tall, yellow grass grew in a bog on either side of what little was left of the makeshift road until the two sides of the bog met. The road was no more.

The general shifted the six-wheeled-vehicle into a lower gear. Although the pace was slower, progress was steady as the angled, front bumper cut through the grass and shoots. The general kept the power lever engaged to a moderate rate until the nose dipped down into a ditch. Immediately after, the front wheels lifted high in the air, and as the general applied the brake, the vehicle came to a screeching stop, sitting across a paved roadway.

In the distance to his left, he could see the waters of an inlet where a dock, now broken and riddled with rot, once stood. It was built to transport iron ore from the mine he saw in the distance to his right. The general steered the vehicle towards the abandoned mine that had been exhausted of its minerals five years earlier.

He drove the vehicle through the broken metal gates, then around an old office building before stopping on the pockmarked and cracked parking area beyond it. As he brought the vehicle to a stop near the building, he exited and strode towards the helocraft.

Matt Demoro threw his hands in the air. His voice quivered, and his eyes were wide under his blonde hair streaked with dirt. "It's about time! I've been waiting for too long!"

General Jezeer popped a smack between his lips and replied, "Why are you so wound up? Was your mission accomplished?"

"Sure as shit it was. Romy Gunn and his squad are no more, just as planned."

Walking towards the open side door of the black and grey helocraft, General Jezeer peered inside. "Where's the bodies?"

"You told me not to leave any loose ends, so I took them to *Smoke Island.*"

Jezeer turned his face back to Pilot Demoro. He saw the younger man was nervous, shifting his weight from one foot to the other. Smoke Island was a good idea since no one goes there, but the general was worried. In the pilot's agitated state, maybe he missed something. "How did you verify you killed all ten soldiers?"

Demoro's eyes narrowed. "Have you ever seen anyone hit by a laser blast?" Before the general could answer, Demoro continued. "There's not a lot left. Nothing you'd call a body—just body parts. And we fired four laser blasts into them!"

"You bagged all the parts?"

"As planned," Demoro replied.

"You didn't keep count as you were bagging?"

"For fuck's sake—of what?" Demoro yelled.

The general's wide face turned red as it twitched. His arm snapped up, his finger almost touching the tip of Demoro's nose. "Can't you think for yourself?" he sneered. "There were ten soldiers, so there should be twenty arms or twenty feet! It's not that complicated."

"I can't handle much more of this," Demoro blurted. "The job is done. Now, you just need to keep your part of the bargain and get me that promotion."

General Jezeer placed a reassuring hand on the pilot's shoulder. "You did the job, and you'll get what you deserve. At least tell me, how many body bags were there?"

"Eleven."

General Jezeer almost jumped out of his boots as he thought, *how can there be eleven body bags for ten soldiers, even if they're in parts?* It wouldn't make sense to yell at the pilot again. The general realized he would need to verify the results for himself.

"Fire up the engines, Demoro. We're going back to Smoke Island."

Holding his breath, Demoro finally relented and let out a deep exhale. Through clenched teeth he said, "I've already flown there and back once today. In each direction it's just under three hours of flying time."

There was a step under the side door of the helocraft. With one foot on it, the general turned to Demoro. "Then, the sooner we get going, the better."

Thankfully, Demoro was a good pilot. Even though he was exhausted, he was able to maintain an altitude just above the tree tops. Smoke Island was one of three islands in *Tempest Bay* on the west edge of New Kor. There were many reasons people didn't travel there. First, the bay was directly on the leeward side of the *Snake Mountains*, a rugged mountain chain that ran down the length of the habitable zone. The winds that always came from the east, accelerated down the leeward side of the mountains, resulting in churning vortexes of wind over the bay. To make matters worse, the shifting, unpredictable winds caused whirlpools to form in the waters of the bay.

Second, Smoke Island was volcanic. There was a central vent at the top of a high hill, but for as long as the Korians had been on the planet, it did nothing more than simmer with a constant overflow of bubbling lava that moved in three winding, narrow rivers to the bay. There, the interaction was chaotic with constant columns of steam shooting into the air. In addition, the bubbling volcano had several relief vents that spouted water vapour with a high concentration of sulfur dioxide. With the constant flow of steam and smoke into the air, the island could be seen from many kilometres away.

"Check your seat belts," Demoro glumly said to the general seated beside him. "We're about to crest the mountains, and when we do, we'll take quite a buffeting from the heavy tail wind."

The pilot was correct. When the plane cleared the tips of the mountains and began to descend on the leeward side, it was as if a giant hand grabbed the helocraft and shook it. Demoro didn't flinch as he held the controls, calmly adjusting for the violent turbulence. Ahead, in the distance, the general saw the plumes of smoke that identified their destination. The general was also a pilot, having many years of flying experience, but nevertheless, he was relieved when they finally touched down on a wide shale plate away from the relief vents.

Both Demoro and the general donned environmental suits, masks and air tanks since the sulfur dioxide gas sat on the island like a heavy blanket. It wasn't deadly over the short term, but it irritated the eyes and throat and could cause serious damage to a person's respiratory system.

The island consisted primarily of volcanic rock, but there were a few areas of shale still untouched by the hot lava streams. It was under one such layered plate, where the wind had undercut a protected hollow, that Demoro had hidden the bodies. That was where General Jezeer saw the body bags piled in a neat row. Beside the black bags were two unbagged bodies in MAT military uniforms. The general had wondered what happened to Demoro's two gunners. It was no longer a mystery.

As the general peered towards Demoro, the pilot could see the questioning look through the general's mask. Demoro threw up his arms, blurting out, "You said, 'No loose ends.'"

General Jezeer wasn't sure what to make of Demoro. He knew the pilot from a time before the civil war, and still, he couldn't determine which trait was dominant: his childish demeanour or his ruthless tendencies. "Unzip the bags," the general ordered. "I'm going to have a look for myself."

Fortunately, any blood in the bags had turned clear as it oxidized, making it easier to go about the grim task of counting the wrist interlinks. The body in the first bag was a man missing his left arm. The next four bodies were in tact while the following four bags held bodies that were missing limbs. When he inspected the last two bags, the general realized Demoro and his gunners had collected all the missing limbs in these two.

In the last two bags, General Jezeer inspected closely. As he pulled the limbs from the bags, he paid particular attention to the wrists. His goal was to count all the interlinks since he was determined to account for all ten soldiers. However, his greater concern was to determine if Romy Gunn was in the bags. This was made difficult since many of the heads and faces were damaged beyond recognition.

He felt a pang of regret, but it was only momentary. These soldiers were just grunts, but he knew Romy Gunn to be clever, a leader and a survivor. As the recollection of Romy Gunn passed through his mind, he meticulously inspected the right wrists and also the inside of each bag. *Fuck,* he thought. *The bracelet isn't here.*

After the bags were resealed, both the general and Demoro boarded the helocraft. Once the engines were started and the ventilation system turned on, both men removed the environmental suits.

The general, sitting in the co-pilot's seat, said, "There were parts of eight bodies, and Romy Gunn wasn't one of them."

The pilot was surprised. They had thoroughly inspected the clearing after the attack.

It seemed the general knew the pilot was second guessing himself. "Was it raining when you attacked Romy's squad?" the general asked.

"Yes, as per the plan."

"Heavily?"

"Well—yes," the pilot stuttered.

Asshole, the general thought. "We're heading back to the clearing."

For Demoro, the three-hour trip, whereby the general didn't say a word, was excruciating. When they landed, he was never more thankful to be out of an aircraft and on firm ground.

"Walk with me," the general said.

In the years the pilot had known the general, he'd come to find these requests weren't optional. Demoro stepped out the side door and inspected the clearing just as he had after the attack. He pointed out the areas where the bodies had lain before they were bagged.

"There was a soldier with a metal leg. Where was his body?"

Demoro pointed at the scorched ground in front of a group of large boulders.

"Gunn would have been with him. Let's have a look."

The two men climbed over the boulders and came upon the mud pit. Immediately, the general saw one set of footprints around the quagmire—then a second.

The pilot saw them as well, and muttered, "That must be our two missing soldiers."

Ignoring the useless comment, General Jezeer climbed back up on the highest boulder. With both hands on his hips, he shuffled his feet, making a tight, slow circle. He lifted his hand and pointed. "There!"

He jumped down from the smooth rock and strode across the long grass with Demoro following in his footsteps. From the higher vantage point, the general had seen an irregularity in the undergrowth of the jungle on the west side of the clearing. Dropping to one knee, the general fingered the cut grass stems, then brought his fingers under his nose. His eyebrows shot up as he muttered, "Interesting—they were cut with an electrical device."

Demoro didn't dare say another word as the general rose to his full height. "You lead. Let's see where this path goes."

Demoro pushed aside a group of overhanging branches and led them into the jungle. It wasn't long before they came out on a dirt path. The two sets of footprints were once again clearly visible.

"Check those footprints again," the general ordered.

It was obvious there were two sets of prints. The pilot didn't understand what the general wanted, but he wasn't in a position to argue with him. He lowered to one knee and, stretching his finger and thumb, placed his hand down beside one print. Then he did the same beside the second set of prints. "One person had larger feet, and the other was wearing boots that were much smaller."

"What else?"

Beads of sweat fell from Demoro's forehead as he wondered what the general was insinuating. Then he saw it. "Sir, one set of boots has a heavy tread. It looks like standard military grade." He took a deep breath. "The other set—the smaller prints—don't have a tread at all."

"Would you say the second set is military issue?"

"No," Demoro said as he tilted his head up to the general. He was surprised by the charge of compressed air that burrowed into his forehead. The general stood with his sidearm held less than a metre from the pilot as he toppled to the side, blue blood quickly pooling around the pilot's head.

"No loose ends," the general whispered.

He knew Demoro's body would never be found, but he still needed to take precautions. Withdrawing his knife, it took four chops to cut through the pilot's arm just above his wrist interlink. Walking further along the dirt path, he found the perfect place to hide the limb. He threw it into the fast-running stream, knowing the fish and crabs would make short work of it.

The general didn't waste any more time. He made his way back to the helocraft and flew it back to the abandoned, iron ore mine. He left the engines idling as he moved to a computer mounted to the inside wall of the aircraft. His fingers flew over the keys as a plan formulated in his mind.

From the computer's speaker an electronic voice said, "Auto mode activated."

"Show map."

In response, a map of the habitable zone appeared on the screen.

The general pressed his finger on the map, northwest of the helocraft's position. "Magnify."

Now the general's finger pressed on a specific location on the far side of the large lake that took up a significant portion of the landscape west of their location. "Record target for landing."

The general could hear the computer's microswitches clicking as it processed the request. An obnoxious beeping emitted from the computer at the same time a red icon flashed in the top corner of the monitor. The electronic voice stated, "Unable to comply. Batteries are at 15 per cent. Insufficient power for this destination."

Striding to the opposite side of the fuselage, the general pulled open an electrical panel. Within it were three long rows of circuit breakers. With his nose almost pressed against them, he scanned down one row, then the next.

He was at the top of the third row when he read the tag he was searching for:

BATTERY POWER SAFETY CIRCUIT.

He flicked the switch to the *off* position before returning to the computer. The screen now flashed a message in orange letters.

Error Code 312. Battery Power Safety Circuit fault.

"Bypass error code 312," the general said.

Immediately, the error message disappeared, and the icon in the upper, right corner changed to green.

"Confirm target destination," the general said.

A red crosshair flashed on the monitor, identifying the location the general had previously requested. "Target location confirmed," the electronic voice said.

The general set the speed. Then, he set the collision avoidance distance to 20 metres. That would keep the helocraft low over the trees or any other obstacles. Finally, he set the timer to five minutes before pressing the *Start Countdown* icon.

After taking a long drink of water, General Jezeer leaned back against the all-terrain vehicle as the helocraft rose to its pre-set altitude. It slowly rotated, before dipping its nose, then accelerating towards the far side of the lake. Having performed the calculations, the general knew the aircraft would lose all battery power somewhere over the middle of the lake. *Another loose end eliminated.*

The only worrisome factor left was Romy Gunn. The general scratched his head as he wondered who the second set of footprints belonged to. Since, counting Romy, nine soldiers were accounted for, he assumed one of the team must have been killed during the mission.

It was likely Romy Gunn wouldn't survive in the jungle. Even if he made it to civilization, once he implemented the rest of his plan, no one would welcome the man. When the general was finished, no one would dispute the fact that the son of the treacherous, Ryder Gunn, was also nothing more than a wanted outlaw.

Chapter 13: Disclosure

20:00 hours, 1ˢᵗ day of the 4ᵗʰ Korian month, Haven year 0024

The Southern Wildes, 25 kilometres east of Rifa.

After Efi corrected Romy, in that his comment about supernatural powers was actually *psychic powers,* he threw his head back in uproarious laughter. Efi's eyes narrowed to slits before she turned and continued her trek down the dirt path. Romy thought it odd she didn't join his laughter. After all, it was a good joke.

Romy ran a few strides to catch up, but when he heard her mumbling in a language foreign to him, he felt it would be better to keep a safe distance behind. At least he thought it was a safe distance when a long sapling, conveniently pushed aside by Efi, snapped back, slashing across his face.

He didn't know what to make of the Mabuza woman. She was helping him, and he was thankful for that, but she didn't seem pleased she was doing so. In fact, Romy was beginning to feel like he was a burden. These thoughts were confused by the sight of Efi's lean figure walking ahead of him, her flowing movements accentuated her indisputable attractiveness.

Romy was so self-absorbed with his thoughts, he didn't see the animals until he and Efi popped out into the small clearing. They both froze. There were three beasts. The shoulders of the largest stood just above the height of Romy's head, but more intimidating was the long head with a protruding lower jaw highlighted by two curved tusks. They had unexpectantly come upon a female *trat* with two small calves who were feeding on the grass along the edge of the jungle.

The black, short-haired beast opened its gapping jaws, letting out a reverberating roar while it's long tail, brandishing a round protrusion of bone at the tip, swayed menacingly back and forth. Romy pulled his air pistol from is holster, but Efi placed her hand on his. "It's just trying to protect its babies. There's no need to harm it."

Romy scowled, showing his disagreement as the mother trat bellowed again while stamping its front foot into the ground.

"Stay here until I call for you," Efi said. She turned, gingerly sidestepping around the edge of the clearing.

The beast shook its head as snorts of hot breath came from its nostrils. Romy watched curiously as Efi closed her eyes, holding her palm out towards the beast. It had been looking at Romy, continuing to stamp the ground when the beast's foot froze, suspended in the air. Its long head turned with its dark eyes now focused on Efi. The beast shuffled back. Its snout lifted in the air.

Efi's hand shook and her lips were drawn back as she concentrated on the trat. After a minute, the beast calmed with its head submissively lowered. Efi opened her eyes and took small steps towards it.

Romy's body tensed as he thought of the danger Efi was putting herself in. He raised the pistol, but without looking, Efi lifted her hand towards him. "No," she whispered.

Efi shifted closer. The beast rhythmically swayed its head back and forth until Efi was directly in front of it. Holding out her hand, the trat nuzzled its snout against her. Efi smiled and rolled her hand, rubbing along the beast's head from between its nostrils up to the top of its head. After a few seconds, Efi pressed her head against the long snout, then slapped softly on the side of its head. The trat lifted its jaws, now looking like it was set in a docile smile, before it scampered off to join its calves.

With a quick wave, Efi motioned Romy to join her. They walked around the edge of the clearing and onto the continuation of the dirt path. Efi was ready to continue as if nothing had happened, when Romy grasped her arm and turned the Mabuza woman towards him. "How did you do that?"

"I told you—psychic powers."

She moved to turn, but Romy's grip tightened. With lowered eyebrows, Efi glanced down at his hand, then back up, meeting his blue eyes. "You don't want to do that," she warned.

Quickly withdrawing his hand, he said, "I'm sorry. Please explain what just happened."

"I will," she replied. "But we still have to travel a few kilometres before we rest. Walk beside me." She turned and shifted to one side of the path, allowing him to join her. Once they began walking again, she said, "I have telepathic abilities."

"You can talk to animals?"

She glanced at Romy, flashing that beautiful smile. "No, silly. Animals can't talk. I sent the trat images indicating we weren't a threat to her or her calves."

Pushing aside a branch, Romy hesitated before saying, "You understand this is difficult to believe."

"Even after you saw what I did?"

Romy shrugged. "Just as it is difficult to believe, I suppose it is impossible to refute what I saw," he admitted in a soft voice still showing vestiges of disbelief.

"Wake up! Wake up!" she shouted.

"What?"

"Wake up! Wake up!" she shouted through a giggle.

As he glanced at Efi upon the second shout out, he saw her lips weren't moving, yet the words were in his head. His mind was working hard, and the beginning of an ache was forming due to the facts he was having difficulty accepting. Then, his eyes widened as he remembered the words from earlier in the day. "Earlier, when I woke in the mud, I was dreaming. In my dream, I heard the words, 'Wake up!' That was *you*!"

Efi replied with a snicker, "What was I to do? The day was moving on, and you were sleeping it away."

The conversation was broken by an imposing sight. As they stepped out from the jungle, ten metres away, Romy saw a layered wall of natural stone, 60 metres high. Looking in one direction, then the other, he saw the wall extended until it disappeared in the distance.

Romy scratched his head. "What now?"

"This is the *Ukuta*," Efi declared. "When this planet was being formed, there was a great upheaval, and the land in front of you was thrust upwards by the forces within it."

The sheer, vertical surface was pockmarked with vegetation: a few persistent trees finding a foothold, a clump of long grass here and there, or a vine hanging down the layers of rock. Romy considered the impassable obstacle. "What now?" he asked again.

"Follow me," Efi replied. She jogged parallel to the base of the escarpment for fifty metres as her eyes searched the rock. Then she pointed upwards. "There!"

Romy peered up and saw three caves in the shadow of an overhang of stone. He gave Efi a curious look that didn't hide his bafflement.

Walking ten metres further, she strode to the wall and took two steps, seeming to levitate on the side of the sheer face. When Romy came closer, he saw there were steps cut into the surface of stone. The optical illusion wasn't revealed until one was right upon the cut stone. Romy followed in Efi's footsteps as the steps zigzagged along the stone face until they stood on the stone slab in front of the three caves.

Efi, wasting no time, strode into the second cave with Romy following close behind. Moving ten metres into the semi-darkness, they came upon a heavy, iron grate door. Romy didn't see the narrow slit in the rock beside the door until Efi pointed to it. "Pull the chain," she said.

Inside the slit was a chain made of many links of heavy, rusted steel. Grasping it with both hands, Romy expected a huge effort would be required. Instead, the door easily slid upwards, helped by an internal counterbalance. Once they were through the opening, Efi pulled on the same chain having carried over a series of pulleys, and the gate came down. Romy asked, "Why the gate?"

"There's a rest area ahead. This gate, and a similar one at the opposite end of the system of tunnels, keeps it protected from predators."

Without waiting for a response, Efi turned and walked down the tunnel, into the waning light. Just as Romy thought it was too dark to proceed, a circle of light was visible ahead of them. The light grew until they exited the tunnel out onto a short landing of stone. Even though Romy had lived most of his life on Haven, he realized there was so much he and his people didn't know. He stood on the edge of a second vertical wall, but this one was arced, continuing in a circle where both ends met on the opposite side, 200 metres away.

Efi explained, "When the planet, in its infancy, was still hot with lava, steam and gases, it is suspected a meteor crashed into the planet, creating this hole."

Gingerly stepping closer to the edge, Romy peered down. "How deep is it?"

Through a smirk, Efi replied, "Only those foolish enough to step close to the edge would know, but they didn't live to tell."

Romy pulled his head back. "Message received," he replied, but Efi wasn't there. There was an undercut of stone that left a two-metre-wide walkway around the perimeter of the hole, and she was quickly making her way along it.

By now, it had been nine hours since Romy regained consciousness in the mud pit. Adding to his weariness was the difficult trek, while the cut on his head and the bruised shoulder had worn down his stamina. He was thankful when, halfway around the hole, the path opened into a deeper undercut, providing a 20-metre-wide, protected area. Hearing the lapping of water, Romy followed the sound to the back of the cut-out, where a narrow stream of spring water flowed from an opening in the rock only to disappear into another, ten metres away.

Romy didn't realize his thirst until he saw the crystal-clear water. He dunked his entire head below the surface of it. Trails of water droplets spewed through the air when he lifted his head free. Cupping his hands, he drank several handfuls of cold water before he took notice of Efi.

Along the side wall of the cave was a neatly piled stack of wood, a few pieces of which Efi had placed into a shallow depression in the rock floor. Moments later, flames were flickering, causing shadows to dance across the stone walls. The Light revealed cast-iron utensils hanging from nails in the wall beside the wood. Efi selected a wide skillet and washed it in the cold spring water.

"What can I do?" Romy asked.

Reaching into her satchel, Efi pulled out the four large, bulbous roots she had dug up several hours earlier. She threw them to him. "Wash these thoroughly and cut each into quarters."

Romy did so, and while he was cutting them, he was surprised at the soft, meat-like texture. When he brought the pieces to Efi, she already had water simmering in the skillet. She tossed in the roots and reached into her satchel for a second time.

During their trek, alongside the path, she had recognized different fruit trees and had stopped at a few to pick the ripest selection. Now, she pulled them free and tossed them to Romy. "Wash these as well."

By the time Romy returned, a wonderful scent was filling the air around the fire. The hot skillet was placed on the stone between them, and Efi pulled two forks from her satchel. She removed the thigh-length jacket she had worn all day, revealing the short sleeved and short cut shirt underneath. Romy feigned his disinterest, but continued to glance at her as they picked the food from the skillet.

Romy's interest in Efi brought an anxious thought to his mind. He asked, "Can you read minds?"

After a swallow of food, she replied. "No, that's a completely different skill. But I'm glad you're beginning to believe me."

The fruit was sweet, and the three types gave them an excellent variety to complement the cooked roots. With Romy's stomach satisfied, he shifted his cross-legged position to face directly at the Mabuza woman. "I know there is more to this coincidental adventure we are sharing than just telepathic powers."

After wiping her fingers on her pants, Efi also shifted to sit directly across from Romy. "Yes, there's much more." She paused for a moment. The time had come. This was something she had been born and trained for—at least if the Mabuza see'ers were correct—and they most often were. "The Mabuza people are what we call a pureblood race. That means, in our DNA, we have hereditary, psychic powers."

"You mean telepathy," Romy interrupted.

Efi frowned. "No. This is important, so just listen. The Mabuza are actually a clan within a race called the Bantu. Once there were billions of us across the Athar, but now there are much fewer. The Bantu people have the ability to foresee the future."

Romy blinked in disbelief.

Efi saw the look and discredited it with a disdainful wave of her hand. "Most Bantu have very limited abilities. To most it's much like, 'Don't go through that door,' or 'Don't step there.'"

Romy recalled the burrow slug Efi had warned him of.

"But we have a few who can, with significant effort, see thousands of years into the future. Our people on this planet have a Council of See'ers. These five Bantu lead us and give us a purpose."

Romy was beginning to recognize the cryptic overtones. He needed to be careful so as not to sound foolish with an assault of questions. Instead, he took his time. "What of you? Can you foresee the future?"

"As all Bantu, I can see ahead into the shorter future. However, the see'ers tell me I have great potential, but typically, that doesn't come to fruition until one is much older." She shrugged. "At my age, with great effort, I can see a few months into the future, but it's not always easy to understand since the premonitions come to me as foggy dreams."

"So that's how you knew to find me in the mud pit earlier today."

"No, the see'ers told me you would be there."

Through a chuckle, Romy said, "Why on Haven would the Bantu see'ers care about me?"

Efi lifted her golden gaze to him and whispered, "Because *you* have psychic powers."

To Romy, the conversation was becoming out of control. People who could see the future? People who saw a future with him having psychic powers? "I can't foresee the future, otherwise I wouldn't have gotten my squad killed," he said through clenched teeth.

"There are other powers. I have seen one in you already."

Tilting his head, Romy widened his eyes and smirked, giving himself an adolescent look.

Leaning closer, Efi scolded, "Don't you wonder how your entire squad was blown to bits, yet somehow only *you* survived?"

Romy scowled at the vivid recap.

Efi continued, "I was at the jungle's edge watching as the laser cannon from the gunship gave four bursts into the middle of your soldiers. With the premonition of danger, your natural instincts kicked in. An energy shield formed around your body, protecting you."

"Really?" Romy scoffed.

"Yes, fucking really." On her last word, Efi slapped her palm into Romy's forehead. His body jolted as a canvas of yellow, red and blue exploded in his mind. Her fingers curled, gripping his mind as the collage of colour changed, leaving an expanse of focused yellow, red and blue lights. They were the same lights he had seen many times in his dreams, just, this time, they were even more vivid.

Efi snapped her hand from Romy's head, and he swooned to the side. His arm slid out, his palm supporting him on the rock as he took gasping breaths. "What—what was that?" he managed.

"That—was the *Athar*. You have seen it many times in your dreams, not really knowing what it was. The dream state is how it begins for all purebloods. With training, we learn to harness it at will and to travel through it. Soon, you will easily do the same."

Romy's head, which had been hanging low, lifted until his eyes caught hers. "Travel through it?"

"You'll have a hard time understanding this, so listen closely."

He snapped back, "Don't patronize me! I'm doing just fine, so explain away."

"Our brains are much more powerful than your scientists know, and there are specific purposes of areas in the brain they don't understand. There are actually an infinite number of planes of reality that our brains have access to. Sculls have only a limited access to one plane—the one we see right now— while purebloods, with control of these otherwise mysterious areas of our brains, have access to these other planes."

"So, they are alternate realities?"

"Not at all," she replied. "They're not alternate. They are other realities, but there's no overlap."

Rubbing his chin that by now had ten days of hairy growth on it, Romy said, "You said you can travel to these other realities?"

"There and back, but there is a draw on a person's energy reserve, so typically, it takes three to four hours of recharging between *hops*."

"Hops?" Romy said in a perplexed tone.

Efi chuckled, then stopped, remembering to not belittle Romy. "Scientifically, moving from one reality to another is called transposition, but in layman's terms, it's called a *hop*."

The information had been moving quickly, and he had to go back to pieces he didn't understand. "You mentioned the word, *scull*."

After a pause, she replied. "Obviously, not all people have psychic powers. For those that don't, scull is a slang term identifying them."

Romy saw Efi's hesitation. There was more to that answer than she revealed. For now, he decided to let it go as another fact came to the forefront. "You said you saw an energy shield around my body."

"It appears you have the power of the shield. It's a psychic manifestation some purebloods have. It's easily seen since it's green. And no, I don't know why."

The revelations were unbelievable, but Romy realized he didn't have a choice in the matter. He couldn't refute what he'd seen with his own eyes, but there was an obvious question." "How is it that I come to have psychic powers?"

Efi rose to her feet and retrieved two more short logs, placing them on the waning fire. She rolled up her jacket, punching it several times before laying on her side with her head on the makeshift pillow. "Earlier, I mentioned the powers are hereditary, passed down through our DNA, and at times, traits don't show up until generations later. When they show up, they might also have mutated."

Romy, taking the hint from Efi, rolled up his jacket and shifted to a prone position on the other side of the flames from her.

"In your family history, there was a very important pureblood—in fact, probably the most important pureblood of all time," Efi explained. "There was a prophet like legend in our history—a person called *The First Key*. You see, the purebloods were always at war, and the First Key was prophesized to, one day, bring peace."

"I'm not sure what that has to do with me."

"It has to do with you because you have an ancestor from Earth, your great grandmother, Natalie Lowe, also known as the past vidame of your family, Natalie Gunn. The First Key was thought to be a man from Earth, much like you, who didn't initially know he was a pureblood. He did discover his powers, bringing peace to the purebloods. But our see'ers always knew this man, Nolan Harrison, was *not* the First Key."

"I'm confused," Romy whispered, his eyes heavy.

"The Bantu see'ers knew it was actually Nolan Harrison's grandfather who was the First Key, and through his DNA, his psychic powers were passed down to his grandson."

"Why does this matter to me?" Romy asked.

"Nolan Harrison was the second cousin of Natalie Lowe. They shared the same grandfather—the First Key. *That's how the First Key's DNA comes to be in you.*"

Romy shook his head in an effort to clear his confusion. "Seriously, what are you saying?"

"I told you, the Bantu see'ers can see for thousands of years in the future. They have known for that long that we needed to come to this planet. We travelled here knowing the Korian-Sholite fleet would come here, but more importantly, we came here because we were waiting for *you*."

Romy's jaw dropped. He was at a loss for words.

"Just as Nolan Harrison was one of the most important and powerful purebloods in our history, one day, the same will be said of you."

Chapter 14: Cover Your Tracks

11:00 hours, 2nd day of the 4th Korian month, Haven year 0024

PAT Base 4.

When an unsolicited call comes from the president, there are always positive and negative aspects. The negative was that it was highly unlikely the president had sent for General Jezeer to tell him what a wonderful job he was doing. Likely, news of General Hayden Fyr's assassination had reached his ears from an incensed Council of Twelve, whereby harsh repercussions could be in store for the PAT general.

The positive aspects, at least in the short term, were much more appealing. The president had an urgency to his request, resulting in the president's private jet being sent to retrieve the general. At least, these were the thoughts in the general's mind as he heard the twin turbofan engines behind him increase to their takeoff RPM.

The jet was a bland grey colour, the only brightness being a small, blue PAT emblem on each of the two side doors. The general was pressed back into the comfortable seat as the aircraft surged down the runway. In the aisle across from him, Lieutenant Stefan Parbli's knuckles were white as his hands clenched the armrests of his seat.

At the last moment, the general had requested the young lieutenant come with him. It's possible the president might require the taped conversation between the lieutenant and Romy Gunn to be personally verified. It might also be convenient to have young Parbli there since it was likely his grandfather, Murdock Parbli, would also be in attendance at the meeting. His grandson's presence might diffuse the president's tension.

The jet lifted off the tarmac, then leveled off twenty metres above the ground. Once its speed increased sufficiently, the nose lifted once again, and the jet shot into the grey-blue sky. After making a sweeping turn, the jet was pointed to the southwest, speeding towards Villaro.

Inside the eight-passenger jet, Stefan Parbli wiped the sweat from his brow. "When you meet with the president, I should wait outside," he offered, his voice shaky.

"The president might need you to authenticate the tape," the general reminded his lieutenant.

Parbli leaned across the narrow aisle. "But the tape is a fraud. I might break under questioning," he whispered.

For an instant, the general's face twitched, one eyebrow raising up while the opposite corner of his mouth drooped, after which his intense gaze bored into Parbli. "Just keep your part of our bargain, and everything will work out just fine. Keep reminding yourself, if I get caught, you get caught. In that case, the best we can expect is we both go to the prison ship for the rest of our lives."

"I feel sick," the lieutenant grumbled.

The general, who had laid his head back against the headrest and closed his eyes, said, "Remember, before we left the base, I gave you the advice, 'Don't speak unless spoken to?'"

"Yes—yes."

"Well, start that now."

The rest of the flight was undertaken in silence. When the jet arrived at Villaro, it made a wide loop around the city's perimeter, so they could land into the headwind from the east. With only a slight bump, the aircraft's wheels hit the paved runway and headed straight for a small hanger well away from the main terminal building.

The jet was directed through the massive hanger doors before coming to a stop. General Jezeer led young Parbli down the stairs, where three identical vehicles—painted the same drab grey as the plane— were waiting. Security personnel, too many to count, milled about the hanger, and one, who was a senior officer, held open the door of the middle car. After the door closed, the chain of three vehicles left the hanger, headed for the main roadway that would take them into the city.

Villaro was half the size of Murcia. Its construction hadn't started in any great effort until a year after Murcia was well established. The need to build Villaro didn't have the same urgency since much of the Korian population in space had settled in and around Murcia. Consequently, Villaro was built at a slower pace, resulting in more careful planning. This allowed proven practices, adopted from the Sholites, where materials were scavenged from obsolete spaceships and repurposed into the construction process. As such, as they entered the city, General Jezeer appreciated the mix of contemporary plastered buildings, contrasted by modern, glass and steel skyscrapers.

It was at the front entrance to one of these skyscrapers where the three grey vehicles came to a stop. Another security guard, who could have been the twin of the man at the hanger, opened the door of the vehicle. General Jezeer and Stefan Parbli stepped out and were immediately shuffled into the front foyer by a team of security personnel.

When they paused at the elevator, two women broke off from the security group and led them in. With a *woosh*, the doors closed, and they felt their stomachs drop as the elevator accelerated upwards. After travelling through 35 stories, the doors opened directly into the private quarters of the president of the patriotic forces. The apartment consisted of a massive, single room. White floors and walls were broken by vibrant splashes of colour from the paintings on the walls and the flowering plants spaced throughout the room.

The general and the lieutenant left the elevator where they were immediately joined by another security guard. In a scruffy tone, he said, "Sorry gentlemen, but it's procedure. Arms out."

The general complied and was patted down by the security guard. Parbli understood the process and followed the general's lead.

The guard cracked a twist of a smile as he pointed to the double glass doors on the far wall. "They're waiting for you outside, General."

The president liked plants. Many filled the expansive patio along the inside of its one-metre-high perimeter wall. Two men were sitting at a long, wooden table at the far end of the patio. The president rose with a wide smile on his face. "General Jezeer," he said. "Come join us."

Both the general and the lieutenant seemed out of place in their dark grey camo uniforms, while the president was dressed in a white, flowing, floor-length robe. The Minister of Communications, Murdock Parbli, was better protected from the cool breeze by his more conventional black suit over a cream-coloured shirt.

When the general arrived at the table, President Bala Torez slapped him on the back. "I'm glad you made it, Brett. We have something important to discuss." Before the general could respond, the president's eyes shifted to the lieutenant. "Why, I recall you! The last time we met was at your grandfather's house when you had just come into your teen years." His eyes shifted back and forth between the younger Parbli and his grandfather, before he asked, "Why are you here?"

The general interrupted. "Sir, I assume I was called here to discuss the murder of General Hayden Fyr. Parbli has some critical information to share in regard to this concern."

Shrugging, the president said, "Very well then. Please take a seat."

Once they were comfortable, the president snapped his fingers, and immediately, a Mabuza man, skin as black as the carbon rock found in the rugged mountains north of the habitable zone, carrying a tray of drinks, and another woman carrying an even larger tray of snacks, hastily walked towards the table. The snacks and drinks were served, and when the two servants retreated towards a small outdoor kitchen, the president peered over the edge of the short wall beside him. "It hasn't been long since the peace treaty was signed. There are more people on the streets. I see their smiles and can sense their relief and happiness." His head tilted back to the general, his eyes cold. "Brett, I hope you haven't fucked that up."

The general instinctively reached into his pocket to retrieve a smack, but when Torez saw this, his face hardened, causing the general to think it wasn't a good time to be pumped with the mild hallucinogenic. "What have you heard?" the general chirped.

The president shifted forward. Hovering over the table, he took a drink from his glass. "It's not just what I heard. It's also *who* I heard it from and *how* I heard it." He pointed to his communications minister. "Three nights ago, I was awakened in the middle of the night cycle. When I rose from my bed, Murdock was in my foyer, in a panic. After asking me to put on a house coat, he ushered me into my own office, where one of his assistants was setting up a video call."

Torez paused, whereby Jezeer thought it prudent to take his own advice and not speak unless spoken to directly.

"And to my surprise, there I was in the middle of the night in my housecoat, facing the twelve vidames of the matriarchal council. How uncomfortable do you think *that* was?"

"Very, I'm sure," Jezeer curtly replied.

Leaning close to the general, the president continued in a subdued voice. "My sphincter sucked together. I wouldn't think it could've been tighter, but when they told me a PAT forces hit squad had assassinated one of their senior general's a day *after* the truce, I was wrong, because it clamped even tighter. It stayed that way for an hour as they threatened to back out of the truce." Torez's eyes darkened, and his eyebrows lowered. "I had to beg, Brett—fucking beg for them to reconsider. And they did, but only after I confirmed I would find out what happened and that the perpetrators would be handed over."

General Jezeer really needed to sneak his hand into his pocket and pop one of those smacks into his mouth.

"So, tell me Brett," the general asked in a cold voice, "Are you one of the perpetrators I need to hand over? If not, you better start naming names."

The general took a deep breath. He knew this reckoning would come one day. He knew it when he devised the scheme to be rid of his murderous ex-brother-in-law. As such, he was well prepared. "Six days ago, well before the peace treaty, we sent two squads of men far behind enemy lines to kill General Hayden Fyr. This man was the primary strategist in the loyalist forces, responsible for many PAT deaths. Consequently, he was a high priority target."

"When the truce was announced, why didn't you stop them?"

The general snapped his fingers towards his communications officer. Stefan pulled out a small recording device, then pushed it towards the general. Jezeer pushed a button on the side of the device and the recording began.

"Scout 33, this is Eagle base 4, come in."

There was a crackle, then silence.

"Scout 33, this is Eagle Base 4, come in."

"Eagle Base 4, this is Scout 33, confirmation code 367ATF."

"Scout 33, your code is confirmed. Verify reciprocal code 897KHY."

The transmission paused for a few seconds.

"Eagle Base 4, breaking communication blackout is compromising us. What's up?"

"Scout 33, I need to speak directly to Romy Gunn."

Another five seconds went by before the communication continued.

"Eagle Base 4, this is Romy Gunn."

"Romy, this is Lieutenant Stefan Parbli. I am authorized by General Brett Jezeer to deliver this message and following order. A peace treaty has been reached. You are to abort the assassination and report back to the rendezvous immediately."

"Eagle Base 4, you have to be fucking kidding. We are at the MAT base now!"

"Romy Gunn, I repeat, A peace treaty has been reached. You are to abort the assassination and report back to the rendezvous immediately."

There was only silence in response.

"Romy Gunn, I need you to repeat the order back to me as confirmation."

"Abort the assassination order. Message received. We are on our way back to the rendezvous. Scout 33 out."

The general pressed the button on the side of the device, stopping the recording. "The voice from Eagle Base 4 is Stefan Parbli's."

Shifting his gaze to the young lieutenant, the president's eyes weren't as jovial as they were earlier. "What do you have to say, young man?"

Stefan Parbli cleared his throat. "The communication was made at 14:00 hours on the 28th day of the 3rd Korian month. What you just heard is the unaltered, original communication."

Barely perceptible, the corner of the general's mouth lifted in a smile. *Good boy,* he thought.

Turning to his minister of communication, President Torez said, "Murdock, it's been a while since you had time with your grandson. Why don't you go inside and catch up while I continue this conversation with Brett?"

Once the two men left, the president hissed through clenched teeth. "I've known you for a long time—long enough to know you're always up to something. You expect me to believe this bullshit!"

Now, the general did calmly reach into his pocket and retrieve a smack. After he popped it into his mouth, he replied. "Bala, in all that time, I've never screwed you over. You're the president. Keep looking at the big picture cause you're doing a great job of it."

Slapping his hand on the table, the president snorted, "Is this Romy Gunn who I think it is?"

"Yes, the son of the traitor, Ryder Gunn."

"Why on Haven would you send him on such a mission?"

The general's grin was more visible. "He was an excellent soldier and had completed several infiltration missions successfully. But also, if something like this happened, he's an excellent fall guy. You message the Council of Twelve that it was Romy Gunn, and they won't have many more questions."

The president didn't like it, but the general's logic was correct. "Where is Romy Gunn and his squad?"

"When we realized Romy Gunn disobeyed my orders, a helocraft was sent to the rendezvous to pick them up. However, it seems the whole squad went rogue, attacking the helocraft. The aircraft fired several laser blasts into the soldiers, but it took small arms fire, disabling one of the electromagnetic drives. The pilot lost control, and the helocraft crashed into the lake with no survivors."

The president rolled his eyes. "And I assume the soldiers in the squad were all killed as well. No survivors! Isn't that convenient," he stated, sarcastically.

"I'll say it again, Bala. You look after the big picture, and I'll look after the details."

The president's face went a shade paler. "What details?"

"We believe Romy Gunn escaped. He's somewhere in the jungle, likely dead, but if he's not, he soon will be. The jungle is a harsh place."

Thrusting a finger towards General Jezeer's face, President Torez hissed, "You better find him, Brett. At this point, the Council of Twelve and I want to keep this out of the public eye and under tight, military jurisdiction."

With a nod of his chin, the general said, "You can count on me as you always have in the past."

President Torez's eyes tilted, giving his face a sinister appearance as he leaned back in his chair. He took a long drink of cold water from his glass before turning towards the general. "The Council of Twelve and I have agreed that a military integration team is needed to downsize and integrate the MAT and PAT forces. Each side will have three officials, and I have nominated you to lead our team. It comes with a promotion to Field General."

The general didn't usually show emotion, but after the president's words, he couldn't help but grin. "Thank you, Mister President."

"Don't get cocky, Brett. It's a nomination, and I can easily take it away. You find Romy Gunn. Capture him. Lock him up, and throw away the key, or kill him. I really don't care. You're smart, Brett. Even if Gunn gets to the media, I'm not sure anyone would believe a made-up story, let's say, of him as the one being duped."

The general realized he needed to be careful. The president wasn't a stupid man.

"Fuck," the president said.

General Jezeer gulped a breath of air. "What?"

"My drink's empty."

Chapter 15: The Chase

07:30 hours, 3rd day of the 4th Korian month, Haven year 0024

The Great Meteor Hole, seven kilometres southeast of Rifa.

Romy awoke and inhaled deeply. He thought he must be having another of his dreams, but the scent of fresh-baked bread lingered. He pried his eyelids open, and the stark, stone ceiling brought reality from his semi-conscious state. However, the appetizing scent still didn't fade. As he lifted himself up on one elbow, Romy saw Efi squatting by a covered skillet simmering on a hot stone beside the fire.

"Bread," Romy said through a wide yawn. "And sweet bread—how did you manage that?"

"By not sleeping the entire morning away," Efi retorted.

Instinctively, Romy pressed his wrist interlink, but when there was no response, he felt foolish at not remembering it was dead.

Giggling, she tilted her face towards him. "I guess it's still not working."

Rising to his feet, Romy stretched his arms high over his head. "You're at your sarcastic best this morning."

Without looking at him, she gave him a backhanded wave. "Go wash up. This will be ready momentarily."

"Of course, Efia," he said in a sarcastic, adolescent tone.

Her face snapped towards him, and an accusing finger came up. "No one calls me Efia except my parents. To everyone else it's Efi. To you, I'm Efi."

She had turned away by the time Romy replied, "Of course, Efi," now using the preferred name, but with no less sarcasm in his tone.

Romy pulled off his shirt as he walked to the stream of spring water at the back of the cut-out. Kneeling, he dipped his head fully into the frigid water, rubbing his hair and beard. When he pulled himself free, he continued to run his fingers back through his hair. The ragged brown locks were longer, covering his ears and tickling the back of his neck. It seemed a long time ago when he left PAT Base 4. His squad, including his best and only friend, Jax, had been killed. He had no idea why, but he couldn't help but think such an attack couldn't have occurred without the approval of

General Jezeer. He didn't understand, but he vowed that, one day, he would, and those responsible would pay the price.

He cupped his hands in the stream, splashing the water against his chest. He shivered, but his hands briskly moving over his skin made it bearable. He repeated the process several more times as he thought about his present circumstances, not here in the Southern Wildes; rather, he considered his place on this planet. His family history made him an outcast with the Korian people. He wasn't a Sholite, so living with them could never be home. The military had filled that need until it was blasted away. Now, he had nothing. He was a lone person being helped by a mysterious Mabuza woman he really knew little about.

However, he was intrigued by her tale of people with psychic powers. He knew he would be a fool to blindly believe her words indicating he had such powers—in fact, "very powerful" were her exact words. But he was desperate for a purpose. Where could he possibly go now? Efi gave him hope there was something in store for him. That's why he had no choice but to believe her, for without that, he had nothing.

"Hurry up. The sweet bread is ready." Efi's coaxing voice reached him along with the scent of the cooked bread, now more intense since the lid had been removed.

Romy pulled his shirt on and sat cross legged next to her and the fire. She handed him a wedge-shaped slice of the bread topped with crushed nuts. The slice was piping hot, causing him to pass it from hand to hand.

Romy provided a childish image, his eyes wide as he blew on the slice. Efi just shook her head, mumbling, "Men. You'd be dead by now if I wasn't here."

His hunger overtook his hesitation from the heat, and he took a large bite from the wedge of bread. He rolled it in his mouth, chewing and sucking in air to help cool the morsel before he swallowed. His lips turned sideways into a grin. "I've seen your psychic powers: the ability to foresee the future and guide us through the jungle, your ability to communicate with animals and your ability to enhance my mind's eye view of what you call the Athar. But what is most impressive is you can cook. I think I'm in love."

The words were not lost on her. There was an awkward moment as she tilted her golden eyes to his. They were intense but clouded with confusion until he let out a guffaw. She joined him, and the moment was quickly forgotten.

"Seriously, Efi, you couldn't have had the ingredients in your satchel. How did you manage this?"

"I'm an early riser," Efi explained. "There's a second tunnel leading to the Upper Savanna. I know the land well, so it wasn't hard for me to find the ingredients I needed. With the giant sweet leaves in bloom, it was easy to retrieve several pods of nectar. A patch of nut cane was also close by. Fortunately, I found two stalks that had fallen and dried. From there, it was easy to pulverise the stalk, mix it with water and the nectar. You're eating the result."

They finished the remainder of the tasty bread, broke camp and followed the narrow path around the perimeter of the meteor hole. A similar tunnel to the one they entered through, angled upwards to a second iron-grate door and another pulley system. Once they were through, they exited onto a high ridge. On one side, down a grass-covered, 30 metre incline, was the Upper Savanna. Umbrella trees dotted the plateau. On the other side, just below the ridge, were the orange-leafed trees common throughout the Wildes.

The ridge cut a northwestern path between the heavy forest and the savanna. Efi said, "Rifa is on the leeward side of the ridge, seven kilometres ahead. Once we're there, there'll be time to consider your options."

As they walked onwards, Romy remembered their previous discussion and was full of follow-ups. "Efi, you said I was a powerful pureblood, and the Mabuza people were waiting for me. How and why?"

Efi reached into her satchel and pulled out a handful of red berries. She handed half to Romy before popping one into her mouth. "Only our see'ers have those answers. For some reason, they believe me to be part of your future, so I was sent here to take care of you."

"You might not know everything, but you surely know much more than I do."

"The berries are good. Try one," Efi urged.

"What…" Romy said, then stopped his words. He was so focused on the question he forgot about the fruit. He tried one, and they were indeed sweet and juicy.

"I've told you there's a space called the Athar, consisting of an infinite number of planes of reality," Efi explained. "The Bantu race looks upon the Athar as a living entity, one that our see'ers communicate with. At times there are corrections to be made and we Bantu are tasked with being the caretakers—so to speak."

"I have no idea what that means," Romy uttered.

"It means that the Mabuza see'ers, for hundreds of years, have followed your movements and those of your ancestors," Efi elaborated. "It was done in an effort to ensure you arrived safely on this planet."

Efi had been leading. Romy now took a few long strides to come beside her. "My ancestors?"

"Of course, to ensure your arrival, that means we also needed to make sure your ancestors didn't befall a sudden death," Efi explained. "Most recently, your father's manservant took on this task."

Romy grasped Efi's arm and turned her to face him. "Fehyr?"

Her face, under the brown and blonde, tight curls, tilted. "Yes. He was an *Ionian* pureblood committed to taking care of your father. There were several people on Earth keeping an eye out for Natalie Lowe as well."

Romy held his hands up. "Wait a minute. Who are the Ionians?"

"Another pureblood race working closely with the Bantu."

Before Romy could ask another question, he was stopped by the sight of an obstacle ahead where a two-metre drop blocked their path along the ridge. Romy slung himself over the edge and dropped to his feet. As he held his hands up, Efi squatted down, then jumped into his arms. She slid down against his body, and the force was enough to topple him to his back where Efi landed prone on top of him. A *woosh* of air left his lungs, and as much as he was in some discomfort, Efi appeared amused, at least evident from the wry grin on her lips hovering just above his face.

He scowled and snapped, "That was elegant."

She playfully knocked dirt from his hair before rolling off and jumping to her feet. "We'll never get to Rifa if you keep this up."

Romy thought to respond, but so far every time he did, she came back with another smart comment. So, he just growled and continued along the ridge beside her. After a short time, he asked her another question. "Where are your parents?"

"They live in Kut, a small city within the Mabuza Islands."

"I was taught Kut was an island," Romy replied.

"I've noticed when you talk, you slow down, so either stop talking or make an effort to keep up."

Once Romy was beside her, she said, "Kut is the name of the city, but it's also the name of the island."

Letting out a guffaw, Romy blurted, "That makes no sense."

"How so?"

By now Romy's hands were moving as he talked. "Well, let's say, for argument's sake, we were on the island of Kut, and you wanted to go into the city. How would you say that?"

"We would just say, 'We're going into the city.'" Shaking her head, she said, "I'm not seeing how this is that complicated. The see'ers told me you have great potential, but, honestly, they didn't tell me you were stupid."

"I might not be as familiar with this planet as you are, but I'm not stupid," Romy retorted.

"Then don't ask stupid questions."

Efi's words were interrupted by a deep, reverberating bellow off to their right. As they turned towards the sound, a second bellow erupted from the same direction. "I hope that's not what I think it is," Efi offered as she pulled a miniature eyepiece from the inside pocket of her jacket. Putting it to her eye, she scanned the savanna below them. After half a minute, she snapped the device from her eye and said, "shit," through clenched teeth. "It's bad."

"What is it?"

"It's an armour bear," she answered.

Romy ran his fingers back through his hair. "They're one of the most feared predators on Haven." Another bellow reverberated through the air. This one wasn't as deep as the first two. "What's that?"

"It's mate," she replied. "Armour bears mate for life, so there are two of them. They're about two kilometres away, and we have six kilometres yet to travel to Rifa. They're no faster than what we can achieve at a good run, but they have endless stamina. We'll need luck on our side to escape them."

Romy hoped he wasn't asking another stupid question. "Can't we just hide, or climb a tree?"

Bringing the eyepiece back to her eye, she said, "They're together now, running this way. They have an exceptional sense of smell. That's how they discovered us." She pushed him towards the woods on their left. "They're known to be relentless. Once they key in on their prey, they run it down, no matter the distance."

Holding his ground, Romy tilted his chin in the direction of the ridge they had been following. "Rifa is that way."

"We don't have time for this," Efi snapped. "When I heard the first bellow, I had a vision of the future. Travelling in that direction does not end well."

There was another loud roar from the male armour bear. It was closer. Romy and Efi needed no further encouragement as they sped off towards the forest. Neither one of them knew exactly what they would find in that direction, but it was the direction directly away from the bear's pursuit.

As they ran side by side, Romy managed to say, "Can't you put some kind of vision in their minds to stop them—like you did to the trat."

With a few words between each heavy breath, Efi replied, "The trat is a vegetarian. The armour bears are meat-eating predators. I don't know what I could possibly put in their mind that would deter them from making a meal of us."

Another howl from the female told them the bears were closer.

"See, you're slowing us down with your infernal questions! Shut up and run!"

The running motion brought pain back to Romy's injured shoulder. He clenched his teeth and kept his legs moving.

Then, as if they hit a wall, a horrid smell of something rotting assaulted them. Romy stopped for a moment, but Efi grabbed his hand, dragging him along. They ran deeper into the smell, both of them doing their best to hold back the urge to spill the contents of their stomachs. By the time they noticed their feet splashing in water, the smell of rot hung even heavier in the air. They were in a bog, surrounded by massive, dead Tasset trees.

Tasset trees could grow for a thousand years. At some point, the land in this area settled and water took over this portion of the forest. The once grandiose trees, typically three metres in diameter at the base, now stood black and devoid of bark. They were the source of the rotting smell.

"The smell might throw off the bears," Efi offered. "We need to find somewhere to hide until they pass."

Ankle deep in water, Romy shifted his feet as he turned. "Where?"

Another bellow echoed off the dead trees. The bears were not far behind them.

"These dead trees are typically hollow and cracked. If we find an opening, we can hide inside."

"The smell is already unbearable just being near them!"

Efi, ignoring Romy, went to one tree after another, until she yelled out, "Here. This will work!"

Romy ran over and, being so close to the rotting tree, he gagged. When he saw the long, vertical slit, he drew his pistol. "I'll take my chances facing the bears here before I go in there."

"They call them armour bears because of the overlapping plates over their flesh," she clarified, trying to control the panic in her voice. "Even my spears are useless against them. Now, follow me." Holding her breath, she shimmied in through the crack.

He was frozen in place until her hand slid back out. Seeing no other option, he took it and was pulled in. He was thicker than she was, so his back and chest scraped against the moldy wood, and again, he almost retched. Once he was inside, he found the space was a little over two metres across. They shifted as far from the crack as they could, their bodies close together, their faces almost touching.

She whispered, "Don't make a sound."

Then they waited. Romy's heart was racing, and he felt as if it would break free from his chest. A mighty roar broke the silence. Efi let out a gasp as she heard the sloshy footsteps of the bears close by. Romy wrapped his arms around her as they waited. It seemed an eternity passed. Romy tilted his lips down to her ear and whispered, "I think they're gone."

At that moment, a wide snout with a black nose on the end, jammed into the crack. The beast, incensed since its head was too wide to enter the tree, opened its jaws filled with two rows of sharp teeth. It bellowed, filling the interior compartment with its hot breath. Romy and Efi, even though they were pasted to the far side of the opening, tried to move even further away. The beast pulled its snout out, then rammed it back in, resulting in a violent *thud*. A narrow chunk of deadwood was displaced, allowing the snout a few centimetres further in.

Now, as the male armour bear shoved in a paw highlighted by five long claws, Efi gasped. "We have to transposition away."

The razer-sharp claws began to work at the wood on the edge of the long crack. "You can, but I can't. You need to save yourself."

Efi's words were quick, filled with anxiety. Her hands clasped Romy's face. "You're a pureblood. There's something called a *psychic wake*. I'll focus on our destination. If you relax, you'll be sucked along behind me."

For once, Romy didn't debate her words. "What do I do?" he asked just as a large length of wood was broken free by the bear, now in a frenzy with its meal so close.

Efi pulled her spears from the scabbard on her back. On each, she rotated the pommel and two long battery packs fell to the ground. "Lose all your battery packs. Any source of energy travelling with you will damage you permanently."

The wide snout was pushed further into the crack. The hot breath assaulted them as Romy released the battery pack from his pistol, and popped the battery from his heat signature mitigator. "That's everything," he said.

"Put your hand on my shoulder," she urged. When he did so, she continued with fast-paced words. "In a moment, you'll see the Athar as you did when I put my hand on your forehead. It will not be as intense, and there'll be one light brighter than the others. If you relax, you'll be drawn towards it. If you do this, we'll leave this place."

The mighty paw crashed through, the swing of its sharp claws just missing their legs.

"Now," she said.

Romy closed his eyes, and the red, yellow and blue lights of the Athar appeared in his mind's eye. The sound of the bear faded as he felt himself being pulled towards the brightest light in the center of the panorama. He let himself go limp while he felt his stomach tumble. Feeling like he was falling forward, he fought the need to put his leg forward—at least for as long as he could. His head spun, and when he couldn't hold back any longer, he lurched forward. He felt dizzy and weak. His leg buckled, and he tumbled to the ground where he lost consciousness.

When Romy woke, it was to see a blurred image of Efi hovering over him. Her hand was on his forehead. His head was groggy as he mumbled, "I think you're beautiful."

She blushed and ignored the comment, one that was only the last of a long line of nonsensical words he had uttered in his delirium. It took another 30 minutes for Romy's mind and vision to clear. He pulled himself to an upright position with his hand held to his head.

"How do you feel after your first successful transposition?" Efi asked.

His head throbbed, but still, as if on a swivel, he turned it to inspect each corner of what appeared to be a massive cavern. There was an angled slab of stone at the far end leading to a small opening where light beamed in. At the rear of the cavern was only darkness. He didn't know how deep the cavern was until he spoke and heard his words echo off the distant wall of the recess. "I'm a bit sore, but much better now that the bear isn't snapping at us. Where are we?"

Efi knelt beside him and pressed her hand to his forehead, then looked into his eyes. Finally, she pressed two fingers to the inside of his wrist. Romy's eyes widened as he pulled his wrist away. "My wrist interlink has a battery in it—shit!" he cursed as he visually inspected his legs, then counted his fingers, making sure nothing was missing. Then, with his eyes wide, he softly pressed his hands to his face, thankful his ears, nose and lips all appeared to be unchanged by the transposition.

Through a snicker, Efi said, "Two days ago, as a precaution, I removed the battery from your interlink when you were unconscious in the mud pit."

Romy's eyebrows lowered. "You find this all very funny?"

"Not at all," she replied. "I gave us very low odds that we'd make it here, yet here we are. I removed the battery because it was important you didn't try and communicate with the PAT forces after their attack. It was just a bonus that you didn't have to fiddle with it before we hopped out."

Romy tried to clear his throat, but the dryness allowed nothing more than a ragged cough. "Is there any water?"

"You'll have to make do without water for a few hours. This is a dead planet I come to whenever I need some alone time. The people who lived here long ago called it *Denum*"

"What happened to the planet to deem it dead?"

"For millions of years, Denum had a moon. However, the path wasn't stable and followed a slowly decaying orbit. Finally, two thousand years ago, the moon crashed into the surface, and as you can imagine, it was a cataclysmic event that ended all life."

With a need to stretch his legs, Romy rose to his feet before taking slow steps around the rock floor of the cavern. "Since we have time, there is something on my mind. You said the purebloods were always at war. Why?"

Efi, seeing his steps were unsteady, rose and held his arm as she walked beside him. "I didn't tell you the full story," she admitted. "The Bantu are only one of seven pureblood races, each of which have only *one* psychic ability."

Romy stumbled and Efi slid her arm around his waist while he wrapped his hand around her to settle on her far shoulder. "But you have two powers. You're telepathic, and you can foresee the future."

"Let me explain from the beginning, then we'll get to that. "As you know, the Bantu have the power, in varying degrees, to foresee the future. The Celtae are a pureblood race having the ability to alter their internal energy into a protective shield like the one you instinctively created when the helocraft's laser blast lit up your squad."

"So, I am a Celtae?"

"Not so fast, Romy. We'll get to that. There are five other races. The *Toltec* have the power to change their internal energy into deadly spheres they can throw from their fingers. The Ionians can will matter to move, the *Kush* can use their minds to create illusions, while the *Shang* can read minds. That leaves the *Anasazi* who can teleport themselves within the same plane of reality."

Romy stumbled again and Efi muttered, "That's enough walking until you regain your energy." She moved him to a low rock outcropping where they sat next to each other.

"I thought you said all purebloods can teleport," Romy said.

"No," Efi corrected. "All purebloods have the ability to *transposition* from one plane to another. They cannot travel within a plane, except if you have Anasazi blood. That is called *teleportation.*"

"Then, back to my original question. Why all the wars?"

Letting out a sarcastic chuckle, Efi elaborated, "It's like wars everywhere. Most are caused by differences between people. In the pureblood's case, it was accentuated by the differences in their DNA." Knowing this was important, Efi turned and faced Romy. "It's normal for some purebloods from different races to intermingle, marry and have children. At first, it wasn't seen as an issue until the purebloods found, over successive generations, the descendant's powers were weakened until, eventually, there were no powers at all."

"I can see how that would irritate some."

She laughed. "To say the least! You see, it was discovered the DNA from different pureblood races would compete and destroy the other until, eventually, the powers were no more."

Romy's eyes opened wide as he came to a realization. "Sholites, Korians and people from Earth are weakened descendants of pureblood races!"

"I'm afraid so," Efi offered in an apologetic tone. "We call them sculls."

"I still don't understand why you have two powers." Romy pressed.

"The war went on for so long, with so many dead, the Ionians eventually became sick of it and the other races. More advanced than the other purebloods, they hid themselves in the depths of the Athar. There, they worked feverishly on a solution to mixed pureblood DNA. After many centuries, they came up with a solution, and the Ionians were the first race

131

to have all seven psychic powers."

"Then, why do you only have two powers?" Romy asked.

"Not all people thrive in power. In fact, most purebloods from other races didn't want the magic vaccine that would give them supreme power. Many thought their blood would be contaminated, becoming less than equal to their pureblood brethren."

Laughing, Romy said, "I see there are racists in your world, also."

"Surely," Efi agreed. "However, long ago, when I was young, the see'ers decided my future needed telepathic abilities. They asked the Ionians, who made it happen."

Romy exhaled deeply as he felt a tickle on his hand. He looked down, slapping away the small insect.

"What was that?" Efi asked.

"Just an ant of some type."

She laughed. "That's impossible. I told you, all life was killed off 2,000 years ago, including insects."

Romy felt a second insect, flicked it off, then rose and turned. He pointed to the corner of the wall where a cluster of red-backed ants were congregated at a group of holes in the rock.

Efi turned her head, then shot to her feet when she saw the nest. She scratched her head, exclaiming, "That's impossible!" Before he could reply, she strode towards the cavern's entrance with Romy close behind.

The sunlight blinded them as they stepped from the narrow fissure, but when their vision adjusted, Efi let out a loud gasp. Before them was anything but a dead planet. Rather, a forest of green and red leafed trees filled the plateau below them, leading to a mountain range in the distance where snow covered the tallest mountaintops. Below them was a large pool of water, fed from a waterfall falling from the escarpment to their left. There was a loud, shrill call from above where a group of birds were soaring past. In the distance a roar came from the depths of the forest.

Efi's face was pale as she mumbled, "This isn't possible."

Romy, who took in their surprising environment faster than Efi, pointed into the sky where the outline of a massive shape could be seen through the scattered clouds. "I thought you said the moon crashed into the planet."

Efi's hand shook as she brought her finger up towards the moon. Her eyes lit up as a realization came to her. To steady herself, she clasped Romy's hand. "The moon is there because, when we hopped here, we traveled at least 2,000 years back in time."

Now, all the blood drained from Romy's face. "Is this some other psychic power you have?"

Turning to face him, she freed her hand and pressed a finger repeatedly into his chest. "No, *you* have the power to travel in time!" She stopped the tapping and clenched the lapel of his dusty jacket. "I told you, the see'ers know you are special—a descendant of the First Key. They told me, one day, you would master the ability to travel in time as only five purebloods before you have ever done! Somehow, when I directed us through the Athar to this location, your latent abilities altered the timeline."

Barely above a whisper, he cursed, "Fuck—how do we get back?"

Efi lifted her gaze towards the moon and whispered, "I have no idea."

Chapter 16: What Now?

16:00 hours, 3rd day of the 4th Korian month, Haven year 0024

Planet Denum, Athar coordinates 86-2315-16.

Romy grasped Efi by the shoulders, roughly pulling her to a position facing him. "How can you have no idea how we get back to Haven?"

Efi's hand flashed up, the heel slamming into Romy's sternum. A grunt came from his lips as he stumbled backwards before doubling over. Her defensive action had been instinctive, but when she saw Romy gasping for breath, she rushed beside him. With the same hand now on his back, her voice carried a panicked tone. "I'm sorry. I didn't mean to do that."

After a few moments, Romy was able to raise himself to his full height. He put his hands on his hips, stretching himself backwards. As he caught his breath, he had second thoughts. Suddenly, his heart raced with the anticipation of the unknown wonders this land held. He wasn't used to the hot sun and the temperature that was at least ten degrees hotter than what he knew on Haven. There was a light breeze, the scent of which was different from his home world, as were the plants and animals. His curious daydream was broken, just as the scent of nature was displaced by the smell of rotting wood.

Efi said the words he was thinking. "We both stink." She glanced at the pool of inviting water below them and added, "We have some time before we can attempt a hop back, so let's get washed up."

Another waft of putrid air assaulted his nose. He didn't need more convincing, so he led the way down the grass-covered hillside towards the pool of water. Once there, Romy pulled off his worn and tattered jacket and, from a rock promontory, dragged it back and forth in the water. At the same time, from his squatted position, he scanned the surface of the pool. Seeing no odd disturbances, he turned to Efi and was about to say, *it was safe,* but his jaw was frozen. Thirty metres from him, Efi had removed her outer clothing, leaving only tiny underpants and a thin shirt, cut off just below her breasts.

Efi had told Romy she couldn't read minds, but when her golden eyes came up to him, quickly narrowing to an accusing gaze, she scoffed, "Get over it. We've been through enough together so that our modesty can be set aside."

Romy shrugged and pulled off his shirt, then his boots, socks and pants. In only his underwear, he dragged his clothes into the cool water with him, moving to a spot where the waters lapped at his chest. Efi was already vigorously rubbing the folds of her clothes together, also utilizing a round rock she had retrieved from the shoreline. Romy followed her lead, washing his own clothes as best he could. Even though her words had told him her modesty wasn't an issue, he was surprised when he saw her undershirt then her underpants, in her hands undergoing the same fervent cleaning process.

He did the same, watching with awe as she walked out from the water, placing her clothes on the rocks warmed by the sun. As she walked back in the water, naked, her firm breasts, narrow hips and long legs were revealed to him. He thought to look away, but her confident gaze kept his eyes locked there.

Romy broke the awkward moment as he walked past her and laid out his own clothes on the warm rocks. When he returned to her, she was swimming towards the waterfall on the far side of the pool. He followed her, his head popping up beside hers under the shelter of the falling water. He saw the smile on her face, the one that brought out the beauty of her high cheekbones. She splashed water at him, and he did the same. For a few moments, they forgot about the events of the last few days.

Romy leaned back against the rock wall under the waterfall as he considered their situation, one that he was beginning to think wasn't all that bad. On Haven, he had nothing to look forward to. His father had left him behind. The Korian people despised him, and the military had betrayed him. Now, circumstances left him on a beautiful planet with an even more beautiful woman. Maybe he didn't want to find a way back.

With only her head above the water, Efi swam towards him. He wanted to drag her into his arms, but those thoughts were interrupted as her hand moved to the top of his head, pushing him under the surface. When he surfaced, she pushed him under the waterfall, her fingers pushing through his long hair.

"Your hair needs a good scrubbing," she muttered. Her fingers moved vigorously, first through his hair, then continuing through his beard. Her fingers brushed his lips. His heart jumped. His fingers came to her shoulders—a much softer touch than the one a few minutes before. She didn't resist as he turned her until she was also under the waterfall.

At first, she had an embarrassed look on her face. It became obvious to Romy that men hadn't touched her like this very often. He shifted closer. His thigh brushed hers while his fingers worked through her tight curls. Her face relaxed, and her eyes closed. Romy took much longer than needed, enjoying the moment.

Eventually, Efi's head, that had lolled backwards, came up and her golden eyes opened. Her words, just a breath away from his lips, came to him in a purr. "Is that it?"

If there ever was a more leading question, Romy was not aware of one. One hand slid to her hip while the other rolled to the back of her head, fingers intertwining in her hair. With a slight pull and a tilt of his head, he coaxed her lips to his. He wasn't sure if he expected another hit to his sternum. Thankfully, it didn't come. Instead, he felt her hands slide around his hips, drawing his body against hers. The kiss deepened—lingering. He felt her curves press against him, just as she couldn't help but feel him against her.

By now, he was convinced he didn't ever want to leave this planet. But many good things do come to an end, just as she eventually pulled away from his lips. Her hand came up to caress his cheek. He wasn't sure because of the splashing water, but he thought a tear was travelling down her cheek.

She whispered, "It's something we both needed to get out of our system. That kiss was even better than I ever imagined it." Her eyes widened, a sadness coming over them. "But we both have a higher purpose—especially you. If we let our feelings or needs become a priority, then that purpose will not be achieved."

Romy's eyes relaxed, but his shifting pupils only indicated his confusion. He clenched his fingers on her waist. "I would rather stay here just like this."

Her face changed. Her cheeks had been flushed, her eyes wide and sensuous. But now, to his chagrin, they showed sympathy. Her hand gave his cheek one last caress before reaching down and grasping his wrist.

When she pulled him out from the waterfall, the sun was setting, reminding him of the forever twilight of Haven. His happiness in the confines of the waterfall was short lived, just as were his hopes. He had no words, much as a sulking child becomes silent, hoping someone notices their displeasure.

The romance between them vanished, although Romy did glance, more than occasionally, at her curves as she dressed into her clothes. The moment was gone, so he begrudgingly did the same. She sat beside him, putting her hand on his thigh. "For my whole life I have prepared for the day you would come. I was taught much about what to expect. It was inevitable that I would have feelings for you, just as I feel yours for me. Trust me, please. Now isn't the time. At some point, we'll have our time together."

Romy lay his hand softly on top of hers. Then, his fingers curled, pulling her hand up, laying it on her own thigh. Through sternly set lips, he mumbled, "What is more important than such a moment as we just experienced under the waterfall?"

She felt the sting in his voice. She turned away, so he would not see the tears welling up in her own eyes.

Romy felt her discomfort, and his voice moved to a softer tone. "Tell me more about the pureblood races and where I fit in."

Efi's head nodded up and down, clearing her thoughts before she answered. "I've told you of the purebloods and sculls. I also told you each race is characterized by a single psychic power. Because of our differences, an endless war was fought. The Ionians were the most advanced of the purebloods, and one day, sick of the ongoing petty war, they vanished—every single one of them."

With his pants still damp, Romy stretched out his legs better exposing them to the last vestiges of sunlight.

"The Celtae and Toltec races were the primary combatants in the war. The Anasazi were not far behind in their zeal for killing their opponents. The Bantu, Shang and Kush, with powers not as suitable for war, became extinct—or so the races thought. Three small groups of Bantu survived and were helped by the Ionians."

"Why would the Ionians help the Bantu?"

"Because the Ionians understood the delicate nature of the Athar and that the timeline needed to be maintained and sometimes massaged."

Romy's ears perked up. "Massaged?"

"'Adjusted,' might be a better word," Efi clarified through a smile. "You're aware there have always been discussions about time travel. The question has always been, if you travel back in time and change an event, do you trigger a chain reaction of changes?"

"That is the fear," Romy agreed.

"What if that isn't always the case? What if someone could go back in time and changed an event, but they weren't changing history; rather, what if they were a *part* of history?"

"That's a radical twist."

"But I think you would agree it's a possibility. In fact, I'm telling you it's a reality."

"Is there proof?"

Efi laughed. The birds in the surrounding trees took a cue and joined her with their chirping songs. "Look where we are. We've gone back in time. What more proof would you need?"

Romy was silent as he looked up at the darkening sky, the large moon now prominent in it.

"The Ionians knew the Bantu were the keepers of events in the Athar—what we simply call *keepers of the way*. Knowing their importance, they helped the last few tribes of Bantu hide and survive. My people, the Mabuza, are one of those tribes."

It didn't take a remarkable mind for Romy to understand the Bantu, thinking he was a time traveller, would use him to fulfill their purpose. "What if I say, no?"

Turning to Romy, her eyes were round and sad. "Even if the see'ers couldn't see the future and your part in it, anyone with sense can see you don't have a purpose. I can see you searching for that. You search for a meaning to your existence—" Her face blushed "—something more than just a woman."

He knew she was right. As much as the touch of her flesh gave him a need to stay here with her, he knew it would only fill a short-term need. He needed more, and the possibility he could make a difference, not only to his people, but to people throughout this existence he now knew as the Athar, had his heart racing. "I can't say I'm not intrigued."

"You're in a special position," Efi offered. "There have only been five other time travellers in known existence. All have worked with the Bantu to maintain the way in the Athar."

Romy felt a sudden weight on his shoulder. He wanted the adventure ahead, but not necessarily the responsibility. Needing a diversion, he said, "So, how do we get back to Haven?"

"I directed us to this location, but you shifted the timeframe. What were you thinking of when we hopped away?"

Taking a few moments before he responded, he scrunched his nose as he remembered the moldy stench of the trees. "The armour bears were almost upon us. My mind thought back to my younger days in school."

"We're much further back in time than your childhood," Efi said as she pointed to the moon.

"I was thinking that in school, I recalled reading a book about Kor, our home world. Two thousand years ago, before the asteroid Talus 3 left Kor, there were similar bears on that world. That's the last thing I remember before waking up here."

Efi nodded, but it wasn't very reassuring to Romy. "Two thousand years makes sense. We need to perform the same process in reverse. I can get us back to Haven, but you need to think of the armour bears in the moldy tree."

"No," Romy exclaimed. "I'm not going back there!"

She placed her hand on Romy's thigh. "I can direct us to Hagaza, our capital. You think of the bears, and it should put us in the correct timeframe." Her eyebrows lifted hopefully.

He put his hand on the rock, about to push himself up, when Efi's hand shifted to his shoulder. "We both need to have all our energy when we attempt this. We need to eat."

"You think you can find some roots or berries?" Romy said with a wink.

Efi's eyes narrowed as she pulled one of her stabbing spears from the scabbard on her back. "We do eat meat—Korian."

Romy grinned, seeing Efi back to her sarcastic self. "Yes, *Efia*, he replied."

She rolled her eyes. "Try not to get yourself killed while I'm gone," she chirped before turning and striding towards the forest.

By the time Efi returned with a large rodent hanging from the shaft of her spear, Romy had a fire roaring beside the pool of water. Silently, she skinned and cleaned the animal that provided an excellent meal for the two of them.

Romy lay down on his jacket. His eyes were half shut when Efi prodded him with her toe. "Get up. We need to go, now."

"Maybe in the morning," Romy slurred through his yawn.

Kicking him harder, she insisted, "It's dark now, you idiot. As your stomach just realized, there are prey animals on this planet. That means there are also predators, and by the size of the footprints I saw in the forest, my spears alone won't deter them."

The vision of him being eaten by a bear or large cat was enough to cause Romy to jump to his feet.

"Make sure you collect everything you brought with you. We can't leave anything behind," she directed.

After they both scoured the area, and Romy kicked the fire out, Efi led the way back up to her cavern. Once inside, with only a sliver of moonlight entering through the narrow entrance, they were ready to attempt their return trip to Haven. Facing him, Efi put her hand on his shoulder. "Ready?"

Romy wasn't sure they would make it. He put his hands on her waist and pulled her close against him. "Yeah, I'm ready," he whispered.

She tilted her head and fought off the urge to kiss him again. "Think of the armour bear and the moldy trees. The Athar will appear in your mind's eye. Focus on the brightest light."

Nodding, Romy closed his eyes and thought back to the bears. The Athar exploded into his mind, highlighted by the bright light in the center of his mind's eye view. He focused there while also thinking of the armour bear. His mind went back and forth until he felt his stomach tumble and the feeling of weightlessness. He was falling. His fingers clenched, but Efi wasn't there.

He kept his focus on the armour bear and the bright light in the Athar, and was about to lose consciousness when he stumbled forward. He was falling. His foot hit firm ground as he tumbled over. His head was dizzy, but when it cleared sufficiently, he recognized the forever twilight of Haven, but not his surroundings. He was in a small courtyard, 30 metres square surrounded by five-story-high, grey stone walls. On each side were several arched windows covered by cobwebs and a thick layer of dust. Overhead, the courtyard was covered by a dome of glass reinforced with curved, steel beams.

On one knee, he shook his head and mumbled, "Efi."

There was no response.

As he staggered to his feet, he turned his head but didn't see Efi close by. His heart rate increased as he squinted his eyes, searching in the shadows at the base of the walls. Instinctively, he said her name again, but this time with all the breath available in his lungs. "Efi!"

Again—no response, only the chatter of the wind across the glass plates of the overhead dome. Efi was nowhere to be seen.

Chapter 17: Bellantor

18:00 hours, 3rd day of the 4th Korian month, Haven year 0024

The city of Bellantor

Once the settlement of Murcia and Villaro was well under way, the early Korian planners realized they would need at least one additional city for the Korians remaining within the confines of the armada of spaceships. By then, the Korian explorers knew there were vast mineral deposits under the perpetual ice field covering the dark side of the planet. From those discoveries, the decision to build a city on the eastern tip of the New Kor continent, provided the most logical location.

The coastal location selected for Bellantor was surrounded by high hills, providing the optimum terrain for the multitude of wind turbines and the vast array of solar panels. With more than enough electrical power, Korian corporations pushed their operations to their maximum rate. With the experience the Krl and Tor family run, construction and manufacturing companies gained from their progress in Murcia and Villaro, Bellantor was built at a greatly accelerated pace. As such, the city quickly became a crucial stop-off port for both the oceangoing cargo ships and the massive air carriers, bringing tons of minerals from the mines having been set up over the ice fields.

The city was growing faster than expected, but the builders were prepared. A small nuclear power plant was constructed, integrated into the 100-metre-high, rock face marking the northern tip of Bellantor Bay.

It was shortly after that when the catastrophes began. One large oceangoing ship just disappeared off radar. One second it was there—the next it was gone. It was tragic, but given very little thought considering there were many carriers moving back and forth across the Eastern Ocean on a weekly basis.

Two month's later, another massive ship, fully loaded with copper and nickel, was lost. This time, an investigation was undertaken, but still without urgency. The interest piqued when, two weeks later, a third ship vanished under similar, mysterious circumstances.

However, this time, there were survivors who made it to an escape pod. They provided a recollection of a massive wave that curled up from an absolutely still sea. The rogue wave had accelerated towards the ship. The five survivors, with only seconds to spare, made it to the pod, releasing it down it's chute just as the wave hit.

As a result of the repetitive catastrophes, ocean faring ships were banned. All loads from the ice fields were to be transported via air transports. Scientists rushed to Bellantor and, using smaller research vessels, scoured the ocean for the source of the rogue waves. Baffled, eventually they left.

For some time, all was well, and when ocean going transportation was about to be reinstated, a heavily-laden, low-flying transport disappeared off radar. Erring on the side of caution, the Korian officials decided to abandon the reinstatement and implemented a minimum flying altitude for aircraft over the volatile, unpredictable Eastern Ocean.

That's when rogue waves began to slam into the shoreline at Bellantor Bay. They didn't occur often—initially one or two a month, and they weren't that large. But they were certainly a nuisance as they flooded the first few streets hugging the curved shoreline of the bay.

So, the Korians built a seawall in two halves. The northern wall, three metres above the water line, extended in an arc from the northern cliffs to a high rock pinnacle jutting out from the ocean. The southern wall continued the arc from the pinnacle and ended at the southern hills.

No sooner was it completed, when the rogue waves increased in height. The seawall was effective, but if the waves should grow much higher, the city would be awash once again. So, the wall was increased in height. The waves became even higher. The Krl builders tried to keep ahead of the unpredictable ocean, until today, the seawall, built of five-metre-wide stone slabs, sheathed in metal plates, stood an imposing 30 metres above the water line.

As the city had continued to grow over the years, the city builders enlarged the nuclear plant from one to three reactors. However, three years prior, just as the additional reactors were about to be put on line, the civil war began. The MAT government prudently delayed the commissioning of the new reactors. They were worried if that occurred, the PAT forces would see the action as a major threat and, in turn, attack the facility. One reactor was better than none, the MAT officials concluded.

When the truce was announced, a significant number of Korian passivists left Bellantor, returning to Murcia or Villaro. Although this reduced the strain on the electrical power grid, the reprieve was only momentary as decommissioned military personnel flocked to Bellantor in droves. Fortunately, the city builders had the two additional reactors prepped, and with the flick of a switch, the problem was solved.

However, it seemed the city was cursed. Every time one catastrophe was averted, another reared its head. The massive waves, higher than they had ever been, once again pounded the seawall.

Chu Kline stood in the three-metre-wide roadway recessed into the top of the wall. He looked through one of the observation ports, cut into the one-metre-high safety barrier at the top of the southern seawall. He didn't dare stand on the northern seawall. There, the waves crashed into the metal plates. It was difficult to consider them as rogue waves since they came constantly; the only unpredictability was the height.

Chu was a 40-year-old Mabuza and leader of the 2,000 Mabuza living in Bellantor. That in itself was not a career. Consequently, he spent his days working as a custodian at the upgraded nuclear plant. From behind him, he heard a voice call out, "Chu!"

Chu turned, expecting to see Faro Zaf. He couldn't hide the disappointment on his face when he saw Faro's nephew, Rowan Zaf. Chu, as leader of the Mabuza in Bellantor, had some clout, but apparently, the leader of the powerful Zaf family thought it demeaning to come to a meeting requested by someone he considered nothing more than a glorified janitor.

Chu yelled over the crashing waves. "Rowan, I was expecting your uncle."

Rowan was a junior engineer at the nuclear plant and had known Chu for many years. He considered Chu a colleague and friend. As Rowan walked closer to Chu, he chuckled. "Yeah, right. I'm sure you thought he would really come."

Chu shrugged. "I hoped."

Rowan pulled the collar of his raincoat tighter. "Why on Haven would you want to meet here? The mist and dampness are seeping into my bones."

"Think yourself lucky we're not on the northern wall," Chu scoffed. "Look," he said as he pointed north. A rolling wave was swelling up with white caps forming on the leading edge. The white caps rolled over just before they exploded into the wall. The two men could hear the metal plates groan as a geyser of water shot 40 metres into the air.

"Just waves," Rowan said.

Chu's eyes narrowed. "Since I came to Bellantor, I've come to this seawall and observed the sea once a week. For the last month, since these rogue waves increased in frequency, I've come here every day, and every day the waves are higher with increased frequency."

"Just waves," Rowan repeated, this time with a shrug.

"Everyone wants to ignore these waves. They are a threat to the entire city!"

Rowan put his hand on Chu's shoulder. "My friend, you're surely exaggerating. Look at our seawall. It's stronger than it ever was. There must be a storm out in the ocean, pushing these random waves to our shoreline."

Turning to face Rowan, Chu looked directly into his eyes. His voice was filled with dread. "If you look north of the rock cliffs, there are no waves. You can't be so naïve not to notice there are no waves hitting here on the southern wall. The waves, although they have different heights and come at varying frequencies, only hit the north seawall. That is anything but random."

Chapter 18: Hagaza

23:00 hours, 3rd day of the 4th Korian month, Haven year 0024

Hagaza, Capital city of the Mabuza Islands

Romy's heart was racing. Efi hadn't completed the hop to Hagaza. He pressed his fingers through his sweat-soaked hair. *Perhaps she was close by.* The small, 30-metre square courtyard was empty, surrounded by sturdy stone walls, soaring five stories up to the overhead, glass dome. In the center of the black, stone surface where he had stumbled from his transposition, was a three-metre diameter, red circle. It was faded and chipped from an overabundance of traffic, albeit not recent, since on top of the target he could easily see his footprints in the thick layer of dust.

A steel double-door, recessed into a protruding stone surround, was positioned in the center of each sidewall. It was only now that he saw the flashing red light at the top of the door on his left. A moment later, the doors were flung open, and five men sprung from the dark opening. It was immediately obvious to Romy, based on their movements, the men were military. They all brandished assault rifles. Three spread out on one knee in a wide front row while the two men in the rear held their rifle butts against their shoulders, their eyes sighting down the length of the barrel towards Romy.

"Get down on the ground!" one of the standing soldiers yelled.

In midnight-blue uniforms, Romy wouldn't have thought the men to be Mabuza, but they were clearly identifiable by their pitch-black skin colour. "I came with Efi…" His words were interrupted by a frown as he realized he had forgotten Efi's last name.

The same soldier, obviously the leader, ordered again in a deeper tone, "Get down on the ground."

All five soldiers were now on their feet, shuffling towards Romy, their fingers on their triggers, ready to apply pressure if Romy made even a slightly suspicious movement. Knowing the drill, Romy intertwined his fingers on his head and slowly lowered onto his knees, crossing one ankle over the other behind him. Spreading further apart, the men made a circle around Romy before closing in. From behind, one of the soldiers put his large hand overtop of Romy's while his other hand slid up and down Romy's body. When the search was complete, having removed Romy's sidearm, he gave a nod to the man who had so far been giving directions.

The squad leader, facing Romy, lowered his weapon. His eyebrows were raised in a curious gaze as he considered the man in front of him wearing a PAT forces uniform, albeit soiled and tattered. "Who are you?" the leader asked.

Having no reason to be evasive, the reply was instant. "Romy Gunn."

Romy's tone was calm, so the leader motioned for his fellow soldiers to lower their weapons. "This is a restricted area of Hagaza. How did you get here?"

Romy had been beginning to suspect he wasn't in Hagaza at all. However, the guard's confirmation of their location along with the flag he now noticed on the wall above the flashing, red light, corrected his notion. The flag had a dark-blue background, and in its center was a white, almond shaped eye. In its center was a light-blue iris. It was the flag of the Mabuza people Efi had previously described to him. Satisfied he was at the correct location, he answered, "I hopped here."

Two of the soldiers chuckled at the same time the squad leader held his amusement to a wide smile. He leaned on one leg with his hand on his hip. "Korians can't hop, so best you reconsider your story."

Romy had a habit, especially when he was pressured, of talking with his hands, and now, one hand slipped off his head as he stressed, "I came here with Efi."

One of the soldiers brought his weapon back up to bear on Romy when he shifted his hand, but the leader snapped his fingers, signaling his fellow soldier to stand down. In a low voice he said, "Yes, you've said that twice now."

There was an awkward pause as the leader considered Romy, interrupted by an odd sight—at least to Romy. In his search around the courtyard, he had shifted off center, and now, on the painted red circle at the center of the compound, the air began to shimmer with radiating ripples. The ripples formed an oval, increasing in frequency until Romy couldn't see through it. Oddly, it resembled the surface of a pool after a stone is thrown into the middle of it. He had no idea what was happening until he saw Efi step out of the ring of ripples.

Efi stumbled, but caught herself when she saw Romy on his knees surrounded by the Mabuza guards. "Don't worry, Grodin. He's with me."

Apparently, Grodin was the squad leader who now reached down, placing one hand under Romy's arm before pulling him to his feet. Grodin whispered, "Why didn't you tell me it was Efi Kuma?" With a hand motion, Grodin signalled his soldiers to hang back before he and Romy strode towards Efi.

When they were close to Efi, she asked, "How long have you been here?"

"About five minutes," Romy replied. "What happened…"

Efi interrupted his question. "There must have been a time shift."

Grodin had known Efi since their childhood, knew of her purpose as set out by the see'ers, and now, with the mention of a time shift, he whispered, "He's the *drifter?*" The words came as Grodin's eyes widened and his finger came up to point at Romy.

Efi shifted, putting Grodin's large physique between her and his men. To be sure his men couldn't see, she covered her mouth with her hand. "There'll be no further mention of the drifter, Grodin. This needs to be kept absolutely secret. Is that understood?"

Grodin's features, just as was the case for most Mabuza, provided for a chiseled, handsome appearance, but his silly gaze with his slack jaw and wide eyes, made him look child-like.

Keeping her voice low, but with a raspy tone, Efi repeated, "Is that understood?"

Grodin came to his senses. "Yes, Efi. It will be so."

Efi saw Grodin was uncomfortable, so she put her hand on the squad leader's shoulder and said in a softer tone, "Release your men. Then, please lead us to the Office of the Advisors."

"Right away," Grodin replied before turning, then striding towards his men.

Once the soldiers left, Grodin led Efi and Romy into the building through the same doorway he burst through a few minutes before. The hallway was as dusty as the courtyard behind them. The handles on some of the doors they passed were rusty from what appeared to be a lack of use over many years. The walls were painted a dark green, but they were cracked and peeling. It didn't give Romy a good first impression of Hagaza, and he said so.

Efi slowed her stride so she and Romy fell to a good twenty metres behind Grodin, and, barely above a whisper, she said, "The courtyard we hopped into is an old one, no longer used by my people. The See'ers council have secretly kept it available for the day when you would come to the city."

The hallway they walked along seemed endless, and it gave them a few moments to talk. "Grodin called me a drifter. What's that about?"

"There's a name for the time travellers we have an oath to help. There have been five, and you are now the sixth that, in our ancient language, are called the *msafiri*. It translates to, *time drifter.* That is how people will know you."

When Efi came to a specific door, she called ahead for Grodin to wait. She twisted the door handle and put her shoulder to the wood surface. The door creaked, then popped inwards. The room was empty except for a chest sitting on the floor. Efi pointed to it. "There's a change of clothes in there." Without waiting for a response, she added, "I'll wait for you outside."

When Romy returned to the hallway, he wore a pair of black, ankle-high boots similar to the ones Grodin wore. Now rid of the tattered military clothing he had worn for over a week, he felt revived in the dark-blue slacks, a dark-yellow button-down shirt and a black leather jacket.

Efi gave him a wry smile and a wink. "You clean up pretty well."

Efi and Romy's banter was interrupted by a soft but shrill whistle from further up the hallway. When they looked to the source, they saw Grodin, hands in the air, with a questioning look on his face. When Efi caught his meaning, she blushed, then moved in his direction, followed by Romy.

Grodin disappeared down a side hallway leading to stairs zigzagging down three flights. The short hallway at the bottom led out onto a long, underground train platform. Benches were knocked over, the paint on the walls was cracked with age, but Romy noticed the steel center rail was shiny, indicating trains regularly travelled along it.

Grodin moved to a small electrical box hanging on a tile covered column, opened it and pressed a green button within. Five minutes later, Romy felt the press of air pushed ahead of an oncoming train. A few seconds after that, the sleek silver train, five cars long, appeared in the tunnel on their left. He recognized the electrical whine of magnetic brakes and the train came to a stop in front of them. They were about to enter through the side door that opened when Efi said, "Grodin, Code 11."

The car they entered was empty, and when they sat in the forward-facing chairs, Romy saw there were a handful of passengers in the car in front of theirs. As they accelerated away from the station, Romy saw Grodin communicating with someone through a wide band on his wrist. Two kilometres later, when the train came to a stop at the next station, before the doors opened, a message came over the trains speaker system just as it simultaneously came over the speakers in the station.

"Everyone will need to deboard the train at this station. This train requires emergency maintenance and is out of service. The next train is five minutes away."

As Romy looked out the window of the train, he noticed a distinct difference in the Mabuza people here, versus those he had observed in the cities of New Kor. Here, the people were well dressed in fashionable clothes made of fine fabrics. The men generally had shoulder length, straight, black hair, while the women had hair, that was black, or black tinged with blonde or red highlights, and almost all the women's hair were tightly pulled back in elaborate braids. It was distinctively different from the Mabuza in New Kor who, for lack of a better word, had a *rustic* appearance.

Once the unhappy travellers deboarded, the doors closed, leaving Grodin, Romy and Efi as the only passengers. They passed through the next station without slowing, and by now, Romy saw the stations were no longer abandoned or disheveled; Rather, the walls were covered with beautiful, colourful tiles set in appealing, mosaic patterns. As they continued on, Romy realized, since their boarding, the monorail had been and continued to be completely straight. There were no curves—not even the slightest of bends.

Eight kilometres later, the train slowed and came to a stop. Grodin led them from the train and the few travellers on the platform. Romy had lost track of time, other than generally knowing it was late in the evening. They travelled up two escalator flights into a large atrium area highlighted by polished, stone floors and bright-green and yellow indoor plants. There were very few people in the train terminal at the late hour, but Efi seemed worried these few might be curious, so she made an irregular path around them to the exit doors.

Once outside, Romy saw they were in a beautiful courtyard, bound on one side by the building they just exited, and on the other side by a similar structure. Both buildings were identical with a grey, stone facing along the first floor, then black bricks making up the additional four stories. As they exited, to his left Romy saw the two buildings continue until they were lost in the distance. Every two or three hundred metres, arched, aerial bridges spanned the 80 metres between the long buildings. In the opposite direction, two hundred metres from their position, was a stone and wrought iron, two-metre-high fence. Beyond it and running parallel to the fence was another long, black building. In between the structures, the courtyard itself was adorned with a series of crisscrossed, stone pathways separated by flowering bushes and tall, slim trees, each highlighted by a burst of wide, palm leaves at the top.

Romy spun on his heel as he muttered, "Wow. This is amazing."

Seeing Grodin was already well ahead of them along one of the pathways, Efi put her hand on Romy's elbow and pulled him along. She explained, "Hagaza is comprised of nine long buildings similar to the ones you see here. They're all identical to these two, except for the central building. It's reserved for industrial, agricultural and retail purposes, so it's twice the width of the other eight."

"Why the fence?" Romy asked as they walked towards it.

"Not many foreigners are allowed into Hagaza Prime. The transposition pad we landed on is in an area strictly off limits to any but a Mabuza citizen. As you will see, there are many such areas. This area we're in now has limited access to foreigners who have a pass approved by the Advisory Council."

"And there?" Romy asked again, pointing to the building on the other side of the wrought iron fence.

"The far building contains several hotels and shops. Beyond it is our coastline," Efi explained. "Korian and Sholite visitors, who have a visa from the same Advisory Council, can vacation there along with Mabuza citizens, of course."

Grodin walked ahead as the pathway they were on curved, leading them to a stone and glass façade protruding in an arc from the black, brick building. The stone was pink, polished granite, attractively complimenting the blacked-out glass that split the stone every other level.

"This is the center of the Mabuza government, housing the See'ers Council and also the Advisory Council," Efi elaborated.

As they walked in through the automatic glass doors into a five-story-high atrium, Romy's eyebrows rose. "I'm not sure I'm ready to meet the see'ers so soon."

Through a chuckle, Efi replied, "No one just walks in unannounced and meets the see'ers. There are ten senior advisors to the see'ers council, at least one of whom is always on duty. That's where we're going."

Romy sighed in response. Whatever they needed to do, he wanted it done quickly. After the short walk, he suddenly felt the weariness from an extremely long day. He realized, in the last 20 hours, they had run from two armour bears, hopped to another world in a different time, then hopped back to Haven. *No wonder his legs felt stiff and cramped.*

Grodin led them to a series of elevators guarded by four uniformed Mabuza. The two armed women looked just as capable as the two men who were in discussion with Grodin. Several times, they glanced over at Romy, but after Efi joined them, the senior guard waved Romy forward. He was frisked by the man before allowing them to proceed into the elevator.

On the third floor the doors opened where, once again, two guards questioned Efi while glancing suspiciously at Romy. This discussion was only momentary before the guard waved Romy forward. Grodin led Efi and Romy down the carpeted hallway to a glass double-door. He stopped outside it, stating, "I'll wait for you here."

Efi glanced at Romy. "For the moment, you'll wait out here with Grodin until I call for you."

Romy nodded as a sarcastic, twisted smile crossed his lips. *Where else could I possibly go?* he thought as a feeling that had been simmering in him began to grow—one of foreboding where he was nothing more than a pawn in someone's larger plan.

Inside the outer office, an attendant sat behind a large desk, rising to her feet as Efi entered. She looked confused as she glanced at the time on her computer monitor. Before the woman could say a word, Efi said, "I'm invoking a Code 11, verification code 32A12BC. Verify the code."

The woman sat down, and her fingers slid efficiently over the keyboard. Her face was still angled towards the monitor when her gaze lifted over top of it towards Efi. "Verification code confirmed."

"Who is the advisor here right now?" Efi asked.

"Shard Soman," she replied as she pointed to one of the ten doors around the perimeter of the large outer office.

Putting both hands on the edge of the attendant's desk, Efi leaned towards her. "I need you to go into Shard's office. Tell him Efi Kuma is here and you've verified her Code 11 request. Tell him to call Ruut Nkosi in immediately. We'll be waiting in his office."

The woman nodded and rose to her feet. As she walked past Efi, Efi added, "Oh, and this visit is classified. In fact, I was never here—that classified. You'll wait in Shard's office with him until Ruut is here and gives you clearance to come out."

Once the woman scurried away and Shard's office door closed behind her, Efi hurried to the glass doors. She waved Romy in as she poked her head out. "Grodin, don't let anyone pass except Ruut Nkosi."

Romy was impressed. When he met Efi, he thought her a simple woman wandering in the jungle, enjoying the simple happiness a connection with nature offers. But in the last hour, he quickly learned Efi was a shrewd woman with leadership skills. She was at least respected—maybe even feared by the few people they had come across. So far, he knew her purpose was to help him, but he was beginning to wonder if it just wasn't that simple.

Efi led Romy through the third door on the far wall of the outer office. Romy was relieved when he saw the couch along the wall, and he dropped himself onto it. Efi sat at the opposite end. Romy realized they were waiting for someone, but he didn't care. He was so tired, his eyes closed. He fell asleep, but Romy had a military background, one that allowed him to sleep lightly. He jumped to his feet when he heard the metallic click of the door handle. His training had him in a position ready to pounce until he felt Efi's hand on his forearm, whispering, "Relax. It's Ruut."

Indeed, a tall man, roughly 40 years old, walked through the door. He was lean with immaculately-kept, black hair covering the tops of his ears and flowing back to his shoulders. He had high cheekbones, a narrow nose and narrow lips that made him easy to look at. Although Romy had been impressed by the clothing worn by the few Mabuza he had met, the admiration was overshadowed by the fine fabrics adorning the senior advisor to the council of see'ers. The satin pants were dark-green, matching the same colour knee-length shirt highlighted by an intricately sewn pattern of yellow and pink around the neckline and the cuffs of the long sleeves.

Ruut turned to Efi, and a wide smile erupted. The perfectly aligned white teeth enhanced his handsome appearance. "Efi! Thankfully it's you. I was called in on an emergency and thought the worse." Ruut's demeanour became more formal; his lips closed, and his heels pushed together. He gave a noticeable nod to the woman.

Efi took up a similar posture and gave a formal nod in return. "Advisor Nkosi, it's an honour to see you once again."

Ruut waved away the comment. "That's enough formalities, young woman." His gaze turned to Romy as his eyes widened. "Is this…"

"Yes, this is Romy Gunn," Efi interrupted as she held her hand out, presenting the young Korian.

"The drifter," Ruut whispered before he once again took up a formal stance and nodded.

Romy was a quick learner. He took up a similar stance and nodded in return. At the same time, he thought, *the only place he wanted to drift to, was a bed.*

Ruut strode to his massive wooden desk, pointing to the two arm chairs in front of it before moving to a bookcase on the other side of it. As Efi and Romy sat, Ruut pressed a hidden button on a shelf, allowing a row of books to slide sideways, revealing a safe. He pressed a series of numbers on a keypad, and a door swung outwards. He pulled out a narrow, leather case and returned to his desk, lowering into his own plush chair.

Unzipping the case, he pulled out a sheaf of documents. "During your stay in Hagaza, you'll be known as Soren Pym—a space water farmer from the outskirts of Villaro." He pushed the case and the documents across to Romy. "Included is a New Kor identity card and a foreign visitor visa to Hagaza. There's also a certified letter from me, only to be used if you find yourself in an impossible situation." Romy spied a key card, but Ruut pushed it across to Efi. "Room 304 at the Coastal View Hotel. That's where the two of you will be staying until you're called for."

"Of course," she replied.

Ruut returned his gaze to Romy. "For the time being, forget about being the drifter. For now, you are nothing but a Korian vacationer with a Mabuza girlfriend. It's not unheard of."

Under his thick beard, Romy blushed.

Leaning back in his chair, Ruut continued, "Go now. The guard at the elevator—his name is Badal. Show him the certified letter, and he will take you to the underground tunnel leading to the coastal area."

Once Efi and Romy left Ruut's office, the advisor let out a sigh as he lifted his wrist and the communicator on it. Pressing miniature keys, he scrolled his contact numbers. He came to the name he was looking for and connected the transmission.

An electronic voice said, "Security code required."

Ruut entered the four-digit code and a beeping began.

A moment later, a gruff voice came over the communicator. "it's late. What's so important?"

Ruut's face wasn't so handsome now; it was drawn with furrows of worry running across his brow. No one was in his office or in the outer office, yet still, his voice was barely above a whisper. "He has arrived."

Chapter 19: Trust

15:00 hours, 4ᵗʰ day of the 4ᵗʰ Korian month, Haven year 0024

Hagaza, Capital city of the Mabuza Islands

The Coastal View Hotel stood at the south end of the long building separating the coastal area of Hagaza from Hagaza Prime behind it. The hotel was slightly angled to the rest of the four-kilometre-long building. It was perched on the top of the southern cliffs, overlooking the ocean where the waves crashed against the rocks below. Romy stood in front of the picture window in room 304, looking down the coastline where the grade lowered to a wide, sand-covered beach. In the distance, whitecaps crashed over the coral reef, then reduced to shallow waves rhythmically pushing up over the beaches curved edge.

A narrow roadway, made of large, square stones, hugged the back of the beach, and on the other side of it, shops, restaurants and a few expensive, living accommodations, filled the long five-story building. However, the elegant, stone and black facades of the buildings in the restricted area of Hagaza Prime were replaced here by bright colours: light-green, blue matching the colour of the ocean shallows, yellow, and even pink. The area was meant as an area for visitors to play games, enjoy recreation and water sports while liberally spending their tokens in the shops and fine restaurants.

Romy and Efi hadn't arrived at their assigned hotel room until after 3:00 in the morning. As hungry as they were, their weariness had them fast asleep in the two bedrooms of the large, villa-style apartment. It was the first time Romy had slept in a bed for weeks. The many nights of sleeping on the ground, or not sleeping at all, caught up with him. As such, it wasn't until 14:00 hours when Efi, still rubbing the sleep from her eyes, shook Romy awake.

Immediately, as he turned to face her, his stomach let out a mighty growl. His stomach was empty since the last time they ate was on Denum. Romy rose to his feet, yawned, rubbed his stomach, then walked past Efi.

Efi grasped his wrist, stopping him in his tracks. "Where are you going?"

"There has to be some food in the cupboards," he replied. As he tried to move away, Efi tugged on his arm, pulling him back. She didn't mean to pull him so hard, but he stumbled and pressed against her, his arm instinctively wrapping around her waist. Her golden eyes gazed up at his face, smiling warmly. Romy took a deep breath and sighed. He understood the look. It was one that a sister gives to a brother, a look that stayed his desire to throw her on the bed and treat her as anything but a sibling.

It seemed, Efi understood his need and disappointment. Surprising him, her hand came up and caressed his cheek, followed by her lips softly pressing against his. He gave an understanding smile. The moment lingered and became awkward, broken by Efi as her lips parted into a wide smile. "We're going to find the best restaurant along Hagaza's coast."

Although Romy facetiously suggested they shower together, Efi's stern gaze told him she wasn't amused. After his shower, he was surprised to see a closet full of Korian style clothes, and he was even more surprised as he put the slacks and shirts up against his frame. They were all the correct size.

Now, as he stood in front of the picture window, Romy waited for Efi to finish her shower. When he heard her voice ask if he was ready to go, he turned and froze. Efi looked quite different out of her jungle-travelling attire. She was wearing a yellow and light-green, patterned dress, cut mid thigh. The top portion narrowed to two straps tied behind her neck, leaving her back uncovered. She wore white sandals, and across her arm was a like coloured shawl. She wore the slightest amount of makeup that widened her eyes and accentuated her lips.

As Romy walked towards her in his forest-green, button-down shirt and light brown slacks, he thought, *they gave the appearance of the young couple they were expected to portray.*

They left the hotel and walked down the inclined, stone sidewalk. As they moved closer to the core of the resort area, music drifted to them just as the scent of grilled food wafted on the slight breeze.

At the bottom of the hill supporting the hotel, the shops began. Efi had seen them before, but Romy hadn't. Holding her hand, he set the slow pace past the shops, at every one of which he had to gaze into the picture windows. One of them was a men's grooming shop, and Romy stopped her in front of it.

"I'm getting a haircut and a quick shave," he announced.

Shaking her head, she grumbled, "No, no. I'm starving."

He started to pull her towards the door as he said, "It will only take a few minutes."

Finally, she relented but said, "Only a trim. Leave your hair long, and keep the beard and moustache."

"But this looks nothing like me."

"Exactly," she emphasized the word. Her eyes shifted from side to side before she whispered, "Remember, you're *not* Romy Gunn. You *don't* want to look like Romy Gunn. You are Soren Pym, and Soren Pym has longer hair and a nicely trimmed beard." With a wink, she handed him a few tokens and pointed to the entrance. "Go on. I'll wait for you out here."

Romy didn't have to wait long before one of the women in the shop called him to her chair. He explained the trim he wanted, and she went right to work. He glanced at the shop surroundings that looked similar to what he would see in Murcia, or even Talus for that matter. But that was the point, he realized. The area catered primarily to Korians and Sholites.

Eventually, he glanced towards the picture window and Efi who was sitting on a bench across the roadway. A man sat on the bench beside her. He squinted his eyes and saw the man and Efi were having a discreet conversation.

A few minutes later, after he was satisfied with his improved image visualized in the small mirror the stylist held in front of him, he crossed the road towards Efi. The man was gone, and Romy sat down beside her. "Was that Grodin sitting beside you?"

"Yes."

"He was out of uniform."

Efi rose and pulled him up beside her. As they continued their walk along the main beach road, she said, "I requested Grodin be assigned to us. I've known him since childhood, and he's completely trustworthy. He has the hotel room opposite to ours, and he'll shadow us at a discrete distance."

"What are you worried about? The Korians must think me dead, and as you said, I am Soren Pym, not Romy Gunn."

"I'm not worried about the Korians."

Raising an eyebrow, Romy said, "Really? Then who?"

"Our government is not unlike many governments," Efi explained. "By that, I mean not all Mabuza are on the same page. The See'ers Council leads us, and their mission and the mission of our people is to maintain the way in the Athar."

"I hear a 'but' coming."

Efi chuckled. "But—there are sacrifices along this path. Our see'ers search the past, and they can see into the future, but it's not our way to be distracted."

"By what?"

Efi raised her hand, palm up, and swept it across the store fronts. "Look around you. This is nice, but not overly expensive or elaborate. If the see'ers wanted it to be, it would. Seeing into the future means they could easily come across vast wealth in tokens, jewels, metals—the possibilities are endless."

"To not be distracted takes great discipline, but what does all this have to do with Grodin being out of uniform?"

They were in front of a woman's clothing store. Efi grasped the lapels of Romy's shirt and pulled him close, feigning a romantic moment. She whispered, "There are Mabuza rebels in Hagaza. They are a radical faction that does not agree with our passive direction. They believe the see'ers powers should be used to make the Mabuza wealthy beyond imagination."

Even though having Efi's scent so close distracted him, he immediately came to the correct conclusion. "If I am, in fact, the drifter, the rebels would see me as a threat."

Efi gave a slow nod. "That's why Grodin is somewhere out there keeping an eye on us."

It was another awkward moment. Romy enjoyed being close to Efi, but the scent of grilled meat from the restaurant next door overwhelmed him. Romy's stomach grumbled once again, and as much as he enjoyed her being close, he needed food.

He grasped her hand and pulled her towards the entrance. "Let's eat here."

She pulled his hand even harder, dragging him further down the sidewalk "Five shops ahead is the restaurant we want. The one you selected is Korian and for tourists." Her free hand pointed ahead. "That one serves traditional Mabuza food, and I really want you to try it."

The Mabuza restaurant didn't look like much. It did have a small, patio area with simple, wooden tables and wicker chairs. However, the aroma of cooked food was overwhelming. A portly waiter, dressed in black with a black apron tied around his waist, came to them. After a brief discussion, Efi ordered the same meal for Romy and herself.

When the waiter left, Romy admitted, "I really don't like fish stew."

She laughed. "But you've never had Mabuza, traditional fish stew."

When the waiter returned with two fruit drinks, two large bowls of fish stew along with a plate of different fresh-baked breads, Romy wasn't overly concerned with the fish; the priority was to fill his growling stomach. When he brought the first spoonful of stew to his mouth, he groaned in appreciation. The thick stew of ocean fish, vegetables and spices was amazing!

It didn't take them long to finish every drop of the delicious stew. The waiter returned, refilled their glasses and left a plate of cookies after removing the used dishes. Romy sat back, patting his stomach. He confessed, "You were absolutely right. The stew was outstanding."

She smirked. "Maybe you should listen to me more often."

"With that in mind, what did Grodin have to say?"

Once again, Efi glanced left and right to ensure they were alone before she leaned close to Romy. "Ruut is coming to visit us tonight. He'll be bringing a visitor who has information we'll be interested in."

"What about the see'ers? When will I meet them?"

"When they're ready. Ruut might know."

Romy growled, "That's not a lot to go on. I hope information starts coming soon because I do not like being left this uninformed."

Efi slapped five tokens on the table. "Let's walk off the meal."

Her smile had a way of changing his mood. His demeanour instantly mellowed, and he rose to his feet. She led him down a short flight of stairs, where she removed her sandals before sinking her toes into the white sand. Romy followed her lead, then intertwined his fingers through hers. Her eyes flicked upwards, clearly sending a warning.

"Relax," he said as he pulled her towards the water's edge. "We are supposed to be a couple, so act the part."

She didn't resist as they walked through the sand, each wave washing the cool water over their feet. They didn't say much as they were deep in their own thoughts. Romy had never seen a sunset or a night sky filled with stars until the previous night on Denum. He missed it, wishing it was here now to enhance their privacy.

The beach came to an end at a series of large, flat rocks. They sat down on the edge of one with their toes still awash by the waves. Romy hadn't let go of her hand, and she hadn't pulled away. The breeze coming off the water was cool, so Romy slid his hand around Efi, coming to rest on her far shoulder.

She wriggled out, jumping to her feet. "This won't work like this! We can't get close. We need to stay focused on your training."

In response, Romy also rose to his full height, facing her. "I don't like it this way." He lifted her chin with his finger and looked into her eyes. "I have feelings for you. If you don't feel the same, then tell me so, and I will not press the issue further."

Efi twisted her neck, snapping her chin away, then slapped his chest. Her eyes were different—fiery. "Of course, I have feelings for you—you dolt. Since I was a child, I've been told of your coming, been educated in all knowledge of you and your family and trained to support you, knowing my life would be dedicated to defending you with my life, if need be." She slapped his chest again, but it was soft, and her hand lingered there as tears filled her eyes. "You big dolt," she whispered again.

At a loss for words, Romy shifted away.

Efi's fingers clenched in his shirt. "No," she said. Her other hand slid behind his neck, dragging him downwards. "The last time, for now," she whispered just before their lips touched. It was a long kiss, their bodies sliding against each other until they knew, if it became more passionate, they would surely run away from all their responsibilities.

When they walked back up the beach, they were close together with their shoulder's touching, but they dare not hold hands. Romy broke the silence when he asked, "Do you know what is amazing in all this?"

"What?"

"Well, if the rebels were checking us out, they would have seen us walk down the beach, have an argument, followed by the most passionate make-up kiss. They would think of us as nothing but a typically-erratic, young couple," Romy concluded with a wry smile.

Just before 21:00 hours, a mix of songs—Korian, Sholite and Mabuza—were playing on the sound system in the hotel room, when the door chime sounded. Efi went to the door, pressing a button on the video screen beside it. The camera in the hallway showed the face of Ruut Nkosi along with a woman unknown to Efi.

Efi led them into the living area, where Romy rose to his feet and formally nodded. Ruut, more casually dressed than the night before, in faded, grey pants and a nondescript, white shirt, chuckled. "No formalities here, my friend. We only do that nodding shit back in the office." His words concluded with another boisterous laugh. When it subsided, he added, "My apologies. Where are my manners?" He pointed at the middle-aged woman beside him. "Romy Gunn, Efi Kuma, this is Shonty Aman."

There were two couches facing each other in the living area. Efi and Romy sat on one, while Ruut and Shonty lowered onto the other. For some reason, Shonty's gaze remained on Romy while visibly leaning away from him.

Ruut crossed one leg over the other. "Shonty works as a servant in the house of President Bala Torez in Villaro. She has some information you both need to hear."

Shonty had black hair tied back in a single braid and a nose that seemed too large for her face. Other than that, her appearance, including her clothes, would not differentiate her in any way from the other Mabuza who lived amongst the Korians and Sholites. She leaned forward and said, "Two days ago, the president had a luncheon with three men. One was Minister Parbli, who spends a lot of time in the president's residence. The other two visitors were General Brett Jezeer and one of his subordinates."

A chill went down the length of Romy's spine as he heard the general's name. He leaned forward, his interest piqued.

Shonty now avoided Romy's gaze, only giving furtive glances in his direction. "The general provided a recording of a military communication between the subordinate officer and Romy Gunn." Now, Shonty's eyes glared accusingly at Romy. "Apparently, there was a mission to assassinate a prominent, loyalist general. The communication confirmed that Romy Gunn was to abort the mission because a truce was recently in place. At the end of the communication, Romy confirmed he understood the order to stand down."

"That never happened!" Romy blurted

"It sounded like your voice, Sir," Shonty feebly replied.

"Well, it wasn't," Romy hissed.

Ruut interjected, "Are you sure?"

As his fiery gaze snapped towards the advisor, Romy snarled, "Of course, I'm fucking sure!"

Ruut raised both hands, palm down, stretched out in front of himself. "Okay. I get it. Calm down." He turned to Shonty. "Is there anything else?"

"When the helocraft came to pick you up in the jungle, the general said you attacked it. Your squad was killed, and they know you escaped. They also know someone was helping you." Shonty glanced at Efi as she finished her words. "The general has orders to capture you, but if he can't, then he is to kill you. That is everything I know."

"Thank you, Shonty," Ruut said. "Grodin is just outside the door. He'll see you back to Hagaza Prime."

Once the woman left, Romy ran his fingers through his hair. "So, I'm an outlaw with a price on my head."

"For the time being, you're safe here. Remember, you're Soren, not Romy. I don't think even your mother would recognize you."

Guilt rushed through him as he thought of his mother. "My mother must be worried sick. I need to talk to her!"

Ruut turned to Efi. "Have you told him about…"

Efi cut off his words. "Yes, he knows."

"Hey! I'm in the room, sitting right beside you!" Romy blurted.

Ruut explained, "Valre has kept your mother informed about your circumstances and your location. Your mother understands the secrecy required and because of it that you can't call her right now."

"Valre—how could Valre possibly know?" Romy asked, his eyes wide, clouded with confusion.

"Valre is one of us. Well, not Bantu, but she is an Ionian as was Fehyr before her," Efi explained. "We work hand in hand with the Ionians to maintain the way in the Athar."

"Fuckin conspiracies, one within the other," Romy cursed. "What else is being kept from me?" His eyes rose accusingly towards the advisor.

"You now know everything of importance."

"I doubt that," Romy sneered. He pointed his finger at the advisor. "I'm getting fed up with being led around by my nose. I won't take much more of it!"

"I understand," Ruut replied, trying his best not to sound patronizing.

"Good. Now, where do we go from here?"

"You will find out tomorrow," Ruut replied as he rose to his feet. He strode towards the door, gripped the handle, then turned back to face Romy. "You have a meeting with the see'ers at 14:00 hours. Don't be late."

Once the advisor left, Romy sat quietly on the couch. Yet, his mind was still smouldering with the knowledge that he was being led around with very little apparent choice. As the minutes went by, he thought of a plan, and it reduced his angst along with his heart rate. "Shonty is a spy—is that correct?" he asked.

"'Spy,' is a tough word, but I suppose the answer is, yes," Efi admitted. "I think, by now, you have seen the Mabuza here are much different from those who live amongst the Korians and Sholites. That was always intended. You think of us as simple and harmless, thereby paying us no attention. Yet, we work in your government offices and the homes of your political, military and business leaders. As a result, there isn't much that happens on this world that we don't know about."

Romy shook his head and mumbled, "Just more deceit and lies." He sighed and let out a snicker.

Efi, who had been sitting quietly beside him, sensed his increasingly sour demeanour. "You okay?"

"Yes—" then he shrugged "—but not really." His hand, palm up, rocked up and down, emphasizing his words. "My people despise me. My father abandoned me. My best friend was killed, and now, I am an outlaw."

"I'm your friend," Efi whispered.

Romy closed his eyes, lolling his head back on the cushion. "Yes, but I want you as more than just a friend."

An awkward silence filled the room for a few seconds until it was broken by a sniffle. Romy tilted his head to the side, glancing at Efi and the tears running down her cheek.

"I'm sorry," Romy blurted. "I appreciate your friendship more than you know."

Efi, the finger of one hand under her nose, raised a finger from her other hand into the air. "No, I deserved that. Tomorrow, the see'ers will tell you more, and hopefully you'll understand your greater purpose."

Her eyes rose to him, golden and soft. His negative feelings seeped away. He could not feel badly about this woman.

In a soft voice, Efi said, "My hope is that one day, when you are trained, safe and on your destined path, if you still have a need to touch me, then we will be together."

Romy smiled. "Fair enough." The mixed emotions, first from the words of Shonty, then Efi's words, had exhausted him. "I think it's time to get some sleep. Tomorrow sounds like it will be a big day."

Chapter 20: A City Awash

13:00 hours, 5th day of the 4th Korian month, Haven year 0024

The City of Bellantor

The wave began to form a kilometre out from the shoreline. As the mass of water pushed upwards, it continued to grow until whitecaps topped the wall of water. Today, the waves were larger than they had ever been, and the coming wave was no different. The top of the wave was a few metres higher than the seawall. A great geyser of white and green liquid shot into the air as it hit, but the top of the wave crashed over the edge of the wall. Although the ocean water's momentum was greatly reduced, it surged towards the shoreline and beyond, seeping up the streets facing the shoreline.

Faro Zaf and his nephew, Rowan, ran along the southern seawall, followed by a group of city officials and engineers. Before they came to the central spire bisecting the seawall, they slid to a stop. An arched tunnel had been cut through the spire many years ago, and now a half metre of water spilled out onto the southern roadway.

With his back pasted to the stone surface of the spire, Chu Kline watched the water pool well above his feet, distracting him from noticing the group of city officials forty metres down the roadway—until one of them yelled.

"Chu! Get away from there! It's not safe!" Rowan shouted.

Chu had been watching the frightful waves for some time and knew the flow of water through the tunnel would lessen, at least until the next mighty wave hit. When the water lowered to the height of his ankles, he made a run towards the group. Through eyes narrowed to slits, he glared accusingly at the officials—especially Faro Zaf. "It's about time you showed up!" He pointed towards the north seawall. "You have waited too long. The catastrophe is upon us!"

Faro replied, "We still have time. The first kilometre along the entire shoreline has been evacuated. Further evacuations can be undertaken at a moment's notice."

Rowan interrupted, "Chu, you seem to have a kinship with the ocean. You come here every day. I suspect there is something you know that we do not. We're pleading for you to tell us what to do."

There was a thunderous roar as another wave crashed into the north seawall. "I don't know much more," Chu admitted as he looked from one official to the other. "I do know what you also know but have failed to acknowledge. In any ecosystem nature is in a precarious balance. It's no different here. There is something happening in the northern part of the city that has upset the balance."

As another rush of water streamed past his feet, Faro implored, "There must be something you can recommend. Your people have been here for hundreds of years, maintaining this balance, as you call it!"

"I don't have the required knowledge," Chu replied.

"Then the city is lost," Rowan said, eyes downcast.

"There is some hope," Chu offered. "There is someone who *does* have the knowledge we need."

"They should already be here!" Faro blurted.

The corners of Chu's mouth curled down, and the tip of his tongue licked against his lips in an effort to hide his feelings of disgust. The city officials looked the other way for too long; they delayed, and now their city was at risk. Chu wiped the back of his hand across his mouth. He knew it wouldn't help to counter Faro's accusing tone. Rather, he said in a monotone but direct tone. "Help is on the way. They'll be here tomorrow."

Chapter 21: The See'ers Council

8:00 hours, 5th day of the 4th Korian month, Haven year 0024

Hagaza, Capital city of the Mabuza Islands

The morning was an odd one. Without really giving a thought to it, Romy went through his morning rituals, first emptying his bladder, then stepping under a hot shower. With his eyes still half closed, he brushed his teeth using the thick mouthwash common in the New Kor cities and available here as a hotel hospitality item. He then took to scrubbing his hair after applying a drop of shampoo, while his mind was filled with thoughts of the day to come.

He was finally going to meet the see'ers, the Mabuza leaders who he knew very little about. Efi had only ever mentioned there were five of them, and that was the only fact Romy knew. In his mind, he expected ancient, wrinkled men who spoke few words while muttering incantations as they were lost in their own thoughts.

There was a knock on the bathroom door. Efi's words brought him back to reality. "Hurry up! I'm hungry!"

Romy rinsed off the lather before tying a towel around his waist. Once he left the bathroom, through the open door from the bedroom to the living area, he saw Efi impatiently tapping her foot. She pointed to her wrist communicator. The implied message was clear—*hurry up!*

Flipping through the clothes in the closet, Romy searched for an appropriate outfit for the day. He didn't want to appear flashy; rather, he wanted to give an aura of confidence and class. With that in mind, he selected a dark blue suit consisting of slacks and a loose-fitting jacket. A plain white, long-sleeved shirt completed the clean appearance he was looking for.

Once again, from the living area, he heard Efi's words. "Hurry up!"

As he passed her on his way to the kitchen area, he replied, "Typical woman—no patience."

She grinned. "I'm guilty of that only when I'm hungry," she qualified.

Retrieving a glass from the cupboard, then the fruit drink container from the refrigerator, he poured the red fluid into the glass. He saw Efi roll her eyes, but before she could badger him again, he downed the cold drink and said, "Let's go."

Outside the door, Grodin was waiting in the hallway. He led them down to the main level and out the hotel door where Romy stopped in his tracks. He glanced at his wrist, then turned quickly to Efi. I forgot my bracelet. I'll only be a minute," he said as he turned and took a step towards the hotel door.

Grodin grasped his wrist. "Hold on. You don't go anywhere without me."

Romy twisted free. "I'll only be one minute, so relax and wait here with Efi."

Without waiting for a response, Romy turned and was through the hotel door before Grodin could object any further. Not wanting to wait for the elevator, he took the stairs up to the third floor and placed the key-card against the sensor at their room. There was a barely audible click before he turned the handle and entered the room. He scratched his head, wondering where he left his bracelet. After all, if he was going to meet the leaders of the Mabuza, he couldn't do so without having the Gunn family ring, now integrated into the bracelet.

He decided to retrace his steps and that took him towards the kitchen. Immediately, he saw the silver, blue and black bracelet on the counter. He must have put it down when he retrieved the glass from the cupboard. As he clipped the clasp together, he mumbled, "Never would have forgotten it if Efi hadn't been in such a rush. Now, when I go back down, she is going to complain even more—nag, nag, nag."

His hushed words were interrupted by a noise from his bedroom. His eyebrows lowered while his ears perked up. As he walked through the door, he felt a cool gust of air. His face turned towards the far wall where the sliding balcony door was wide open. *That's odd*, he thought. I don't remember leaving it open, or even opening it in the first place. He took one step towards it when he heard a noise for a second time; this time it was from the bathroom.

This was more than odd, he thought. He took quiet, careful steps towards the bathroom door on the other side of which the noises continued to emanate. His steps were carefully placed until he leaned forward and peered into the bathroom. Unfortunately, the front of his shoe scraped the door trim.

A woman, dressed in black, snapped her face towards the sound. In one hand she held the mouthwash Romy has used earlier in the morning. The cap was removed, and in her other hand she held a syringe, the contents of which had been injected into the thick fluid. As soon as she saw Romy, she dropped the empty syringe and threw the bottle at him. Romy ducked and as soon as he lifted his chin, it was met by the woman's fist.

Romy fell and rolled backwards. With his military training, he popped right back up onto his feet, facing the woman who now wielded a long knife. She lunged at him, pressing the business end of the blade towards his neck. Romy sidestepped the thrust as the woman slid past him. Before she could turn, he clamped his fingers on the woman's braided ponytail while his other fist slammed into the side of her jaw.

Other than a grunt, the punch seemed to have little affect as the woman's free hand slid around and backhanded into Romy's cheek. He saw the knife blade just in time as he leaned back, allowing the razor-sharp edge to zip past. Romy's fist came around and hit hard into her kidney area. His other fist was already on its way to her jaw, when she ducked out of the way.

Now, the woman, seeing she needed to finish this quickly, sent a flurry of kicks and punches towards Romy. Most Romy blocked, but with his focus on the knife, he had to absorb some of the blows. The attacker became impatient, hurrying her thrusts and punches. That's when she made a mistake. She brought the knife around in a roundhouse towards his neck. Romy was able to clasp onto her wrist and drove his other elbow into her jaw, leaving her dazed. Romy turned her and flung her against the wall with a jarring thud.

The knife had fallen to the floor, and when she saw Romy pick it up, she ran towards the bed. As her nimble steps took her across it, an opaque circle began to form. Her figure began to lengthen as her steps took her off the bed towards the open patio door. By the time the woman planted her foot on the outside railing, Romy couldn't see through the rippling waves moving with her. Her body blurred as she thrust off the railing, throwing herself out into the air.

Romy ran to the edge of the balcony. With both hands gripping the wrought iron, he looked down, but there was nothing. The woman had successfully hopped away before she hit the ground.

Off to his right and below him, Romy heard a yell. "What the fuck is going on?"

He gazed down at Efi and Grodin and was debating who had the most shock implanted on their face. "You better come back up," Romy replied. "There's been an incident."

By the time Romy had walked back into the living area, the front door burst open. Efi led Grodin into the room. Seeing a trickle of blood at the corner of Romy's lips, she ran to him, while Grodin sped into the bedroom. When Grodin returned, it was to see Efi running her hands up and down Romy's body, inspecting for damage. Whenever she brushed an impacted area where bruises were already forming, Romy would let out a, "yeah, there," or he would just wince. Finally, sick of the babying, he took two steps back. "Enough already! I'm fine."

"Tell us exactly what happened," Grodin urged.

Romy recounted the events of the last few minutes. As Grodin headed to the bathroom, Efi asked for a description of the woman. Romy shrugged. "Black pants and jacket with a red shirt. She had a single, long braid."

"Anything else?"

"She was pretty."

Efi pressed her fists into her waist. "Really? You're in a fight for your life, and you notice your attacker is pretty?"

Tilting his head, through a sly grin, Romy offered, "I think you're jealous."

Her words were curt. "Don't be ridiculous." Then, she quickly waggled a finger in front of him. "That's the wrong phrase. I should say, 'Don't be more ridiculous than you and your male testosterone already have been.'"

"We need to go." The words came from Grodin as he returned to the living area. In his one hand he carried the bottle of tainted mouthwash; in the other he held a small plastic bag holding the syringe. "We need to get this tested, but I'm sure the results will indicate the mouthwash is contaminated."

"How could they know I'm here? We've been very careful," Romy said.

Efi rubbed her jaw. "I have no idea," she said as, in her mind, she calculated who was in the small circle of possibilities.

"We need to go now!" Grodin insisted. "They could come back."

They quickly left the hotel with food the furthest thing from a priority. Showing their credentials, the guards at the tunnel leading from the coastal area into Hagaza Prime, let them through. Feeling safer, nonetheless, they hurried to the building housing the See'ers Council. Once inside, they urged the guard stationed there to quickly call Ruut Nkosi down to their location.

The guard called a second guard over and explained the situation, whereby he rushed up to the office of the advisors. A few minutes later, the guard returned with Ruut close behind him.

"What's happened? You're not due to be here for a few hours," Ruut said.

"There was an assassination attempt at the hotel," Efi explained.

"I don't know how General Jezeer found you here. We were very careful," Ruut apologetically explained as he turned his concerned gaze to Romy.

"It could also be the Mabuza rebels. They have an interest in seeing Romy Gunn dead," Efi interjected.

"Soren Pym."

"What," Efi said as she looked at Romy.

"My name is Soren Pym," he replied.

"Don't worry about that now. For the most part, your cover is already blown," Ruut admitted. As he rubbed his chin, he said, "You can't go back to the hotel. In fact, I can't allow you to leave these premises until the see'ers decide what's to be done next. We need their guidance."

A grumble sounded from Romy's stomach. Ruut heard it and said, "There are guest quarters on the fifth floor." He pointed to the guard who had fetched him. "Take them to room 510. Make sure there are two guards on the door, and do not allow anyone in except those authorized by me."

Once Ruut saw the guard nod his understanding, he turned back to Grodin, Romy and Efi. "I'll have some food and drinks sent up from the kitchen."

Room 510 was as massive as it was luxurious. Reserved for visiting dignitaries, it had couches covered with the finest materials, and there were exquisite pieces of art, both hanging on the walls as well as amazing carvings within display cases. The lunch delivered was worthy of the room, and Romy, Efi and Grodin filled their stomachs. As Grodin moved from the dining table and was about to lower himself into an armchair, Efi said, "Grodin, I appreciate everything you've done to help us, but we'll be safe here. You can go back to your regular duties within the Mabuza guard."

An inkling of surprise crossed the guard's eyes, but only for an instant. He was indeed an experienced military man. That meant quick changes in direction were not new to him, as was the knowledge that the fewer the questions asked, the better.

"Do you think that was necessary?" Romy asked after Grodin closed the door behind his departure.

Efi sighed. "I've known Grodin for a long time. He's a good man and loyal—as far as I know. But with the events of this morning, the fewer people who know where we are and, more importantly, where we're going—the better."

Slowly shaking his head from side to side, Romy replied, "You sound like a lawyer."

Efi burst out in laughter. "I can dumb it up a bit for you, if that's your preference."

The banter was broken by a knock on the door. Ruut entered and strode to a position beside where they were both seated. His face held a grim countenance. "We analyzed the residue in the syringe and the mouthwash. A deadly poison called *stenolin* was detected in both. If the chemical had touched your throat, you would have been dead within seconds."

There was an awkward silence finally broken by Ruut. "Come down to the council chambers in 20 minutes." He gazed at Romy. "That's when you'll meet the see'ers."

Once Ruut left, Romy turned towards Efi. "Poisoning sounds like something the general would do."

Efi shook her head. "It might, but that's not the case. Stenolin is a poison not found naturally on this planet. It was brought with us when the Mabuza arrived on Haven. The general wouldn't know about it."

"So, the culprits are your rebels," Romy concluded.

"It would appear so," Efi agreed. She saw Romy taking deep breaths, trying to keep himself calm. "In a few minutes, we'll meet the see'ers. They'll tell us what we need to do."

When Romy stood in the hallway before the large wooden doors leading to the See'ers Council, he saw security had been increased. There were five guards in the main entry, and there were two guards at each end of every hallway they had passed.

Ruut arrived in the wide hallway shortly after Romy and Efi. With him were the other nine advisors to the council, each of whom were introduced to Romy Gunn. A few more dignitaries arrived until, finally, a high-pitched *beep* sounded along with an audible *click* from the ornate door handles mounted on the massive doors.

One of the senior advisors, a large man named Malakay, opened the door, inviting the guests to enter. Romy, urged on by Ruut, led the group into the expansive room. It was not at all what Romy expected. Rather than a formal council chamber, the room looked much like the living area they just left on the fifth floor. The ceiling was three metres high with criss-crossed wood beams matching the colour of the lacquered, wood planks covering the floor. There were smaller area carpets throughout the room highlighted by shallow alcoves where private conversations could be held. The room lacked a conference table. Instead, spaced throughout the room were couches, smaller tables and arm chairs, set in informal groupings.

As Romy made his way through the maze of furniture, at the far side of the room on a raised single step platform, stood five people. The see'ers were also not at all what he expected. First, three of them were women. Second, they all looked young for their senior positions. Finally, rather than the stoic welcome he expected, they all had wide smiles on their faces. One of the women even clapped her hands in glee at the sight of Romy Gunn.

This woman skipped off the stage and strode to Romy. She clasped his hand and said, "Finally, you're here. We've been expecting you." The smile on her face became even wider as her gaze inspected him in an unembarrassed fashion.

The other four see'ers came to a position beside the first woman who said, "My name is Elki." She pointed to the two women beside her. One was very tall with a lean face. Her black hair was straight and well past her waist. "This is Mist." The next woman, shorter and with a traditional, braided ponytail, was introduced as Jalli. The two male see'ers were introduced next. The first, with a shaved head that seemed too big for his body, was Kory, while the other, who could easily have been Ruut's brother, was Arinol.

After the introductions, a bell was rung, signalling five waiters who made their way through the guests with trays of food and drinks. Elki took Romy by the arm and led him away from the other see'ers with Efi following close behind. In one of the alcoves was a wide couch behind a short, glass table. One of the waiters put three glasses of red fruit drink on the table as Elki let go of Romy. She turned to Efi and wrapped her arms around her. Efi returned the hug, kissing the older woman on the cheek.

"I'm glad you made it safely," Elki whispered.

Efi eased back from the see'er before replying. "There were some dangers along the way."

Lines of worry appeared on Elki's brow under a thick afro of white hair. "Yes, I understand there was an incident this morning." She pointed to the ends of the couch behind her before lowering onto the middle of it.

Once Efi and Romy were seated on either side of the older woman, Efi continued. "It would appear it was the rebels."

"I agree," Elki replied. "Our plans will need to be adjusted." She glanced at Romy and saw he wasn't entirely comfortable. As a waiter passed by, she snapped her fingers, then pointed to the table in front of Romy. The waiter turned and placed another glass in front of the young Korian. However, this one was tall and thin with golden fluid filling it. "That one has alcohol in it," she said with a wink.

Grinning, Romy asked, "Is it that obvious I need it?"

Leaning forward, Elki picked up the glass by the stem and handed it to Romy. "There's much to be done. Fortunately, or unfortunately, depending on your outlook, you've been thrust into this position as the msafiri."

"The drifter," Romy mumbled before bringing the wine to his lips.

Chuckling, the see'er said, "I never really liked that word because drifting about within different time frames in the Athar doesn't sound very professional. In fact, it sounds very random, and our purpose in time is anything but random."

Mist, holding a drink in her hand, had an elegant stride Romy noticed as she walked towards them. "How is Romy doing?" she asked as she looked towards Elki.

Romy waved his hand in the air. "I'm right here, and I'm doing fine."

For a second, Mist had a curious look on her face, but it was swept away by a wide smile. "Of course," she said in a tone hardly hiding the patronizing tone.

"He's doing fine," Elki added. "At least he hasn't run from the room in a panic—yet." The last word was emphasized with another wink from the woman who seemed to be the leader of the see'ers.

Romy's assumption was confirmed when Elki rose to her feet and clapped her hands together. When the room came to silence, in a loud voice surprising for a small woman, she said, "We'll now retire to our private chamber." She pointed across the room. "Ruut, Malakay, you'll join us. The rest of you can stay here until the food and drinks are depleted," she offered through a laugh.

Elki rose to her feet. Efi wasn't sure if she should follow until the see'er turned and muttered, "Come along girl. Don't dally." Elki led them to the far end of the room, up onto the platform and through the door on the far wall. The other four see'ers, Ruut and Malakay were already waiting in the short hallway beyond it. Another door five metres down the hallway was opened by Ruut, whereby they entered a room much like the one they left, just it was much smaller.

The five see'ers sat down in a line of wide armchairs with Elki in the middle. Romy and Efi were instructed to take two similar armchairs facing the see'ers. Ruut and Malakay, as senior advisors, sat in armchairs facing inwards and at right angles to the others.

Elki clapped her hands together. "Well, it seems we need this privacy because someone close to this group is a spy for the rebels. That's why I have not allowed other officials entry." She glanced at Ruut, then Malakay. "This is the inner circle I trust."

Both Ruut and Malakay gave a respectful nod of acknowledgment.

Slapping both hands on her thighs, Elki continued. "So, Romy Gunn—I know Efi has given you some information about why we feel you are important. I could give a very bad, in fact, agonizing speech—" She winked at Efi "—But the best way for you to understand is for you to ask the questions and for us to answer them as best we can."

Romy cleared his throat. He already knew the answers to basic questions, so he decided not to waste the time he had with those. "Why are there five of you?"

Several see'ers eyebrows rose, impressed with the question. Elki formulated the answer. "Because four or six could result in a tie if we have to deliberate a direction. Five seems reasonable."

"My understanding is you can see the future and also interpret the past. With those skills, why would there be a need for deliberation?"

"Ah," Elki said. "I see you need a better understanding of how our powers work. There are an infinite number of planes of reality in the Athar. In each reality, there are billions of events occurring at any one time, not to even imagine the quantity over an extended period. We five see'ers could never contemplate all those possibilities, just as 100 or 1,000 could never do so. As see'ers, thoughts come to us, often in our dreams. We might share a specific thought and then contemplate on it over a day or two. The dream, which is really a peek into the future or into our past, is shared between us with a notion of whether or not we need to take some action." She raised a finger in the air. "Oh, yes—back to the deliberation. There are three possible outcomes from our dreams. Either we all have the same perspective and agree, or the majority has the same perspective, or only the minority has the same perspective."

"So, the dreams only give you a confidence level, rather than a certainty." Romy interjected.

"Correct, young man," Mist said. "If all five have the same dream with the same outcome, we are 100 per cent certain we must take an action. Even if four out of five have continuity, there's an overwhelming probability. However, less than that means great care must be taken as an incorrect action can have dire consequences. The preferred timeline could be altered."

"Like the future could be changed for the worse."

Elki put a hand on Mist's thigh and replied to Romy, "The Athar is very much a living entity. You might call it spiritual, or it could have scientific origins beyond our comprehension. We don't know. What we do know is our dreams, in a very crude manner, are communications with the Athar. However, we know the Athar shows us the way—the correct way. It does its best to tell us to fix the timeline, if need be."

Romy shook his head. He wasn't sure if he was ready to believe what sounded to him like more and more nonsense. But at the same time, Efi had shown him her powers, and they had already hopped to another planet in a different plane in a different time. That was irrefutable. "What's next?" Romy asked.

Elki nodded towards Ruut who reached into his pocket, retrieving a small bag. He took two steps towards Romy, giving him the bag before returning to his seat. Elki explained, "There are red pills in the bag. You need to take one every morning."

"Why?"

"You have powers beyond your comprehension," Elki stated. "If you have a spike you cannot control, be it in a dream state or wide awake, the consequences could be catastrophic. These pills numb your latent powers so wild outbursts will not be possible. You need to take one now."

Romy opened the bag and peered inside at the little red pills. If he was ever going to turn back, it was now. He tilted his gaze to Efi who recognized his hesitation and whispered, "It's okay. Take one." He shrugged, then popped a pill into his mouth.

"It will take several months of intense training before you can control your powers," Elki clarified. "Efi will guide you. We hoped it would be here, but it seems our own rebels would make that risky—even more risk than that provided by your own General Jezeer."

"It sounds like we'll be travelling," Romy replied. "Can I pack some of the nice clothes from the hotel?"

Elki wrinkled her nose at the suggestion. "The hotel isn't safe. You'll spend the night here under tight security. A bag is being packed for you and

Efi."

"Where are we going?"

Elki leaned forward as her eyes darted back and forth, and the tone of her voice lowered. "Efi, do you remember the safe house we have about 30 kilometres east of Joyville?"

"You mean, the ranch?" Efi replied.

Elki nodded. "The two of you will be flown there tomorrow, but on the way, you need to make a stop in Bellantor."

Efi asked, "What's going on?"

"The seas have risen with massive waves battering the break wall. I'm afraid the wall will soon fail, resulting in the entire city being washed away. Go there and see what you can do."

Romy's jaw dropped as his gaze bored into Elki. He blurted, "What the fuck is she going to do about an ocean that has been unpredictable for years?"

Elki rose and stepped beside Romy. She squatted and took his hand in hers. "Give us a chance, Romy. Even though it's difficult, have some faith in us."

Glancing down at the small woman, Romy couldn't help but squeeze her soft hand. In a low voice he said, "I'm trying, but it seems I'm putting my life in your hands."

Elki whispered back, "Actually, our lives are all in your hands." She rose to her feet, returning to her armchair. There was a firmness to her voice. "Tomorrow—Bellantor. Are we all in agreement?"

There was complete silence until Romy broke it. "I have one last thing to say—a request really."

Mist replied, "Please enlighten us."

"It seems this council has a plan for my life. Since you can see the future, I'm sure you know I will accept, but I do have a condition."

There was an awkward pause before Elki said, "Please continue."

"If I am understanding you correctly, this council will give me corrections to make in the past in an effort to keep the way in the Athar correct. I will do so, but I will decide my first mission."

"When?" Mist asked.

"Right now," Romy said as he leaned forward, his eyes cold and piercing.

"Many years ago, the asteroid known as Talus 3 was sabotaged. It blew up, killing six million of my people. After I am trained and no longer in need of these pills, I will go back in time and prevent the catastrophe."

A loud gasp escaped Malakay before he spit out the words, "This is preposterous! No one comes here and gives direction to the council!"

Elki's hand snapped into the air, stopping her advisor from adding to his tirade. "Actually, I understand," she said in a low voice. "Tonight, we'll give your idea consideration. Each of us will dream on it." She looked to each of her fellow see'ers, watching as each gave a nod of confirmation. "In the morning, we'll give you an answer."

Romy tried to hide the surprise on his face. He never expected the council to give in so easily. Maybe it was a ruse. All he knew was the quick, conciliatory response confused him.

Elki rose to her feet and clapped her hands. "Let's remember what a great day this is." Her face was aglow as she looked at each person in the room. "Our msafiri is here. Our true destiny has begun."

A moment later, the room was filled with smiles and laughter. Elki came to Romy first, clasping his hand. The look in her eyes was similar to one from a loving mother to a son. Then, she put her arm around Efi's shoulder. "Now, you keep him out of trouble. Is that understood?" Before Efi could answer, Elki gave the younger woman a huge kiss on her cheek.

The last thing Romy recalled, was being shooed out of the inner council chamber. In the background, they heard Elki nattering about Romy's care until Romy and Efi were finally out of earshot.

An hour later, Ruut was in his office. He had a button under his desk, and when pressed, it engaged a heavy, dead bolt lock in his door. Once he heard it *click*, he opened the lower drawer of his desk. Pulling a wire free, he connected his wrist communicator to the encryption device hidden in the drawer. The small LED light began to flash green, and he whispered a sequence of numbers into the communicator.

After a few seconds, he heard an electronic *click*, followed by a gruff voice. "What is it?"

Ruut tried to remain calm but failed as his face contorted into a sneer. "What is it? Your woman failed miserably this morning. She was almost caught by the drifter!"

"But she wasn't," the voice calmly responded.

"You idiot! If she had been caught, she just might have given the authorities all our names."

There were a few seconds when only heavy breathing could be heard from the other end of the connection. "Be careful, Mister Nkosi. You and I are leading the rebel cause even though our individual goals are not coincident. You want political power. My motivation is simply monetary. But insult me again, and I will ensure they will be your last words."

Ruut gulped and the mouthful of air went down the wrong way, causing him to let out a spasmic cough. "I'm sorry. My apologies."

The gruff voice said, "Just tell me where they will be tomorrow, and I will not make the same mistake twice. He will be terminated."

"With all due respect," Ruut offered. "I have an idea that will have the same result without risk."

"I'm listening."

"My plan is already in motion. I have a messenger already on their way to someone who wants Romy Gunn out of the way, possibly more than we do. His name is, General Brett Jezeer."

Chapter 22: Decisions

7:00 hours, 6ᵗʰ day of the 4ᵗʰ Korian month, Haven year 0024

Hagaza, Capital city of the Mabuza Islands

Romy had just finished dressing when there was a sharp rap on the door. Hearing the sound, Efi rushed from the bedroom, curious about who would be knocking so early in the morning. Romy arrived at the door first, and with Efi peering over his shoulder, he opened it. They were surprised by the smiling face of Elki, and behind her were the other four see'ers, Ruut and Malakay. The senior see'er pressed a hand to Romy's chest, and another on Efi's as she said, "Make way. Make way."

As the contingent passed by Romy and Efi, who had stunned looks on their faces, they were followed by three carts of food pushed along by hotel waiters.

Elki snapped her fingers and pointed as she gave directions in a curt voice. "Put the food carts against the wall. Put a clean table cloth on the table by the kitchen. Bring that other table from the living area, and place it here." She went on and on until the breakfast the see'ers had brought with them was ready. With a wave of her hand, Elki shooed the waiters from the room. "You can wait outside with the guards."

"Wow," Romy said as he lifted a few of the tray covers, smelling the scent of smoked meat, cheese, fruit and fresh-baked breads.

Elki's afro shook as she laughed. "You have a lot on your plate today, so we thought breakfast here would be the best way to start."

Elki picked up a plate and began to fill it with food from the trays as the remaining people fell in line behind her. Holding his own plate as he waited behind Efi, Romy was already deep in thought with a frown on his face. *What did Elki know that he didn't when she said, "He had a lot on his plate?"* Romy felt a protective wall rise as he perceived, once again, that his life was not his own. Everything was being set out for him without his input, right down to what, when and where he ate breakfast.

A prod from behind him brought Romy back to reality. "I'm hungry," Ruut said as he pointed to the trays of food waiting in front of Romy.

"Sorry," Romy replied as he filled his plate, then saw an open seat between Efi and Elki. He rolled his eyes. "Led around like a pet on a leash," he muttered.

Turning her head, Efi said, "What did you say?"

"Nothing important," Romy replied. "How is the food?" he asked through the best smile he could manage.

With a forkful of food in her mouth, Efi's bright eyes smiled at Romy as she nodded her head up and down. For a few minutes, there was some light banter until Elki pushed her empty plate away from her. She wiped her fingers on a napkin and cleared her throat. "Romy, we came here early to answer your question about travelling back to before the destruction of Talus 3. Last night, we dreamt on the possible outcomes and discussed it amongst ourselves earlier this morning."

Swallowing a mouthful of food, Romy glanced at the see'er. "And?"

"I'll let each see'er give their own recollection," Elki said as she pointed to Arinol.

The handsome see'er nodded. "I had several visions about a future without the destruction of Talus 3. The outcomes were all generally very positive."

Jalli, sitting beside Arinol, spoke next. "I had similar positive visions. I would not hesitate recommending the saving of the Korian asteroid world."

"I cannot say I had the same results," Kory said. He rubbed his hand across his bald head. "I had several visions, but they were all negative. The change you propose would result in much pain and suffering."

"More than the death of six million Korians?" Romy interjected.

Stone-faced, Kory shrugged. "Very possibly."

"I agree," Mist said. "In fact, I had several dreams that showed horrible events arising throughout the Athar from the proposed change in the way."

Elki nodded and then turned to Romy. "Like Arinol and Jalli, I also had dreams about the proposed change in the timeline, and I can say they were not negative. However, nothing I saw was a positive change, but I certainly didn't see added despair and suffering."

"So, if six million lives can be saved without added despair and suffering, we should proceed, should we not?" Romy added, the excitement in his voice quite evident.

In a softer voice, Elki said, "Slow down, Romy. Our overall recommendation works on a consensus, and obviously, we don't have that.

We also put a lot of weight in what Mist sees. She is the most clairvoyant of us, and it worries us that she saw horrors in her visions."

Romy let out a sigh. He didn't want to seem overly persistent or aggressive. The see'ers and the Mabuza were not people he wanted as enemies. Consequently, he did not push it further. "Maybe it can be given more thought later."

Elki put her hand on top of Romy's and gave it a reassuring nudge. "I like your sensibilities, young man. It will take several months of training before you are ready to hop between planes, especially to a different timeline, so we have time to review this further. We will dream on it again and provide an update when the timing is pertinent."

What the fuck does that mean—when the timing is pertinent? Romy thought. He was about to ask when Efi gave him a nudge with her elbow. "We better get going, Romy. There's a lot to do today."

With his eyes darting from side to side, Romy was about to object, but the opportunity was lost in the sound of chairs being pushed back on the floor. Goodbyes and well wishes had already begun.

A few minutes later, Romy and Efi were left alone in the apartment, where they took the opportunity to check the contents of their travel bags. Satisfied, they left the room and took the elevator to the main floor of the building. Once there, as Romy moved towards the exit doors on the far side of the atrium, Efi pulled on his arm. "This way," she urged.

Romy was led down a wide hallway, then a narrower one. At the end of it was a series of elevators. There were two guards in front of them, and these guards looked different from the ones he had previously seen wandering Hagaza Prime and the coastal resort area. They wore different uniforms, black and dark-grey camouflage patterned with a crest sewn on their chests. The crest was the same as the flag he saw in the landing area upon his arrival in Hagaza.

The guards seemed to be familiar with Efi and let the two of them pass into the elevator. Before Romy could ask, Efi said, "There's a large military facility below the city."

Romy expected a small hanger, but when the doors opened with a *woosh*, he was speechless, left gawking at the sight before him. They were in a massive, underground, cement-fortified bunker. There were smaller, sleek, light-blue aircraft parked in a metal racking system on their left. There had to be at least fifty of them. In front of the sleek jets, several large cargo planes were parked on the wide, concrete floor of the bunker. In a similar metal racking system on the opposite wall to the light-blue jets, were 50 slightly larger, black craft. With shorter wings, they looked very different from the light-blue aircraft.

As Romy and Efi walked down the bunker's length, Romy asked, "What's the difference between the two types of aircraft?"

Without missing a stride, Efi pointed to the right. "Light-blue are military fighter jets." She then pointed to her left. "Black are military fighters for use in space."

"In space!" Romy blurted. "I've never seen a Mabuza spacecraft."

As they approached a smaller, light-blue, cargo plane, Efi said, "Good. That was and is the plan."

Once they were aboard the jet and belted in, the engines roared to life. They sped down the runway towards the slit of light at the far end of the bunker. As they came closer, the slit became wider until the jet screamed out from the opening. The jet immediately made a sharp left turn.

Romy looked out the window back at the underground bunker's opening, but it wasn't there—only the rock face of the high cliff above the inlet south of Hagaza. "I don't get it. What happened to the bunker?"

"The opening is concealed by an electronic hologram," Efi confided.

As the jet adjusted its course towards Bellantor, Efi nodded off, giving Romy time to think. There was much more to the Mabuza people than was generally known. It seemed the Mabuza had played the Korians and Sholites for many years, giving the impression they were a simple, quiet people with limited technology. Yet, in a short period of time, Romy had learned they were vastly more sophisticated than the Korians or Sholites. By appearing simple, the Mabuza lulled the Korians and Sholites into complacency—a mood that allowed the Mabuza to innocently infiltrate all levels of the Korian government. By the time the wheels of the jet hit the tarmac at Bellantor, Romy was confused, wondering if the Mabuza people really gave a shit about him, at all.

Romy was surprised at the sight before him at the Bellantor airport. There was a line of large, passenger aircraft by the main terminal and a flood of people waiting to board them. In the distance, from the furthest reaches of the city, he could hear sirens blaring. As they exited their aircraft, a security vehicle, with it's blue strobe light flashing, was waiting for them. They were quickly ushered into it before it sped towards the city.

The distant sirens became louder, and now, there were intermittent crashes. As they travelled through the city and approached the beach area, the crash of waves became louder. When they arrived at the base of the southern seawall, where it met the high hills, a guard led them to an elevator that took them to the top of the metal-plated structure. When the doors opened, they were met by two more guards who urged them out onto the roadway atop the wall.

Neither Romy nor Efi could hear the guard due to the waves battering the seawall on the north side of the central spire. There was a group of people half way down the roadway, and Efi saw one of them wave, urging Efi onwards. Once the two newcomers arrived, Chu introduced Faro and Rowan Zaf, and Lalima Sny, the interim city leader designated by the PAT government.

Efi nodded, introduced herself, then said, "This is Soren Pym," as she pointed at her companion.

The Bellantorians weren't really interested in their names. Chu had said someone was coming from Hagaza who could help their dire situation. They didn't even care if it was Efi or Soren. Such was their panic as they pointed to the massive wave about to crash over the northern seawall. The wall broke the wave, but the surge of water overflowed well into the city.

"I will need a few minutes," Efi yelled, trying to be heard over the thunderous waves. She walked towards the spire as calls from behind her told her it wasn't safe. With water pooling around her ankles, she wasn't deterred, nor was Soren who followed close behind. When she was close to the spire, she turned to the ocean, placing her hands on top of the stone wall. She looked down at the sheer drop ending in the churning water. "Don't stand too close," she warned Soren just before her eyes closed.

She stayed like that for a few minutes. Her eyes twitched from time to time, and there were beads of sweat on her brow mixing with the mist droplets on her face. Eventually, as Efi lifted her hands off the wall, the ocean settled. A massive wave that was speeding towards the north wall suddenly slowed and swirled.

To Soren's surprise, he saw the swirl of water shift and, with a two-metre head on it, move towards the southern wall. The odd wave circled after it brushed the seawall directly below Efi. Soren's eyes went wide when he saw the water begin to seemingly climb up the metal plates. He leaned forward to pull Efi away, but she lifted a finger, staying his urge to save her.

The thick wall of water rose in a cylinder until the top of it was at a height just above Efi. Water rose up the core of it and fell down the side, while there were light-green tendrils of light shooting throughout its volume.

Soren mouthed a silent, *what the fuck,* when he was struck by an even more surreal sight. Out in the ocean that had settled into a calm surface, rose at least 50 similar cylinders of water. He watched in awe as Efi's eyes glazed over while using her telepathic abilities to communicate with the water. By that time, with the ocean settled, Chu and the other city officials had warily shuffled towards the raised water cylinder.

Efi gave a nod towards the cylinder and muttered, "I understand."

She turned towards Soren and smiled. "Don't worry about what is about to happen. It will not hurt me." She turned her gaze to the officials and continued. "What you see before you is what the Mabuza call, in our old tongue, the *maji kitu*. It has inhabited this world for millions of years."

Faro Zaf asked, "Why do you call it, *it?* There are many of them."

"No, they're all connected into one entity and are far advanced over our species."

Faro was about to ask another question, when Efi waved it away. "Rather than the communication continuing in this manner, the maji kitu will communicate with you directly."

"How can it do that?" Rowan asked.

"It will use me as a vessel," Efi replied. Before Soren could stop her, she stabbed her arm into the moving water. A green tendril shifted, wrapping around Efi's wrist Her body jolted, and Soren was about to pull her away when her free hand flashed up, stopping him. When her face lifted, her eyes were wide open and completely white. Her gaze panned from one official to the other. Her mouth opened, and a voice emitted, but it wasn't Efi's. It was deeper, and the words leaving Efi's mouth vibrated.

"Who among you is the leader?" the maji kitu asked.

Both Faro and Lalima raised their hands.

Efi's face, now controlled by the sea creature, was devoid of emotion or expression as her chin nodded. "It might take some time for us to become accustomed to this shell. It has been hundreds of thousands of years since we shed the need for such an encumbrance."

"Why are you attacking our city?" Faro asked.

Efi's feet shifted as she turned to face the Korian leader. "It is not an attack. If that was our purpose, we could have destroyed you mercifully, in an instant."

"Aren't you creating the waves?" Lalima asked.

"Yes, but our intent was to only attract your attention. You have—what is the correct word—irritated—yes, irritated us." There was silence as the maji kitu recognized the confusion on the officials faces. "The power plant you have built has waste water seeping into the ocean. It irritates us."

Rowan Zaf, as a junior engineer at the power plant, decided to speak up. "Do you know what exact compound is irritating you?"

"Tritium," the sea creature replied. "To inferior species like yourselves who have a casing, the tritium has minimal affect. But we do not have a casing, so the levels of tritium are harmful."

"So then, what are we to do?" Rowan asked.

"It is not what *you* can do," the maji kitu stated. "It is what *we* can do for you."

"What would that be?"

"We will give you the solution. Come closer," the vibrating voice of the maji kitu said.

Rowan shuffled forward until he was close to Efi. Her hand came up, her fingers clamping on the side of the young engineer's head. His body jolted just as Efi's had a few minutes before. His eyes also went white for a few moments. Faro grew worried for his nephew and was about to speak up when Efi's hand released his nephew.

Rowan took a deep gasp of air, but when he looked at the city officials, his eyes were wide and filled with life. He laughed. "Of course! It's so simple. The lithium in the cooling water, when subjected to radiation, creates helium and tritium. We just need to replace the lithium. It's so simple."

"How long will it take?" the maji kitu asked through Efi.

Rowan closed one eye as he performed some mental calculations. "No longer than ten days."

"That will suffice. But be warned, we can coexist on this planet together, but what you call the Eastern Ocean is ours. Smaller crafts can ply the surface, but your larger ships are forbidden. Your aircraft will also maintain higher altitudes. You have seen what will happen to vessels that invade our territory."

Lalima and Faro both nodded. "It will be so," Lalima added.

Efi's lips curled up as the maji kitu tried to smile. "That is acceptable." Efi's shell was turned towards Soren. "I sense inside her that you are the one. I have drained her energy, and she will be unconscious for several hours until she recovers. Catch her when she falls."

Efi's arm fell to her side and Soren rushed in, catching her falling body. At the same time, the cylinders of water all crashed into the surface of the ocean.

There were furrows of concern creasing Soren's brow. "We need to take her to a hospital and have her checked."

Chu agreed and led the group down the roadway to the elevator. By the time they arrived at ground level, an ambulance and two other vehicles were waiting. Chu and Soren jumped into the ambulance with the unconscious figure of Efi. Rowan took a second vehicle to the nuclear plant to begin the changes to the cooling water formulation. Faro and Lalima took the remaining vehicle to their civic headquarters to update the remaining members of the city council.

When the ambulance arrived at the hospital, Efi was rushed into an evaluation room. When Soren tried to follow, a large nurse put a hand on his chest and told he and Chu they would need to stay in the waiting area. With some time available, Chu told Soren he would need to update the Mabuza council in Hagaza, and he walked into a neighbouring, empty room.

Soren's mouth was dry, so he searched an adjoining hallway until he found a water fountain. He leaned over and took a long drink. When he rose, he felt a hand aggressively grip his shoulder. He whirled, about to defend himself, when he saw a second uniformed Korian soldier pointing an air pistol at him.

With a flick of his wrist, the soldier holding the gun said, "This way, Mister Gunn."

Fuck, Romy thought. His cover was blown. He was led down the hallway into a side room where a man sat on a couch, one leg casually crossed over the other.

General Jezeer said, "You two can wait outside." His gaze turned to Romy. "I wouldn't have recognized you with the longer hair and the beard. Well done."

Romy sat in an armchair opposite the general and sneered, "I'm lucky to be alive, no thanks to you."

"I'm…"

Romy cut him off. "What you are, is a fucking murderer!"

The general's words remained calm and even paced. "I hope you'll believe me when I tell you it wasn't me."

"Then who?"

"I do have some blame," the general confessed. "I consider myself a good judge of people. I saw when you first met Matt Demoro that there was some friction there. I'm not sure why he saw you as a threat, but by the time I recognized it, it was too late. I'm just glad you're alive."

Romy's eyes narrowed to suspicious slits. "Why should I believe anything you say?"

"Because you and I are both Korians. You and I have fought on the same side of a war that we won. We've both lost friends and family. I would think that gives us a special bond."

"I don't see you as my friend," Romy scoffed. "A Mabuza woman saved me, and the Mabuza council has given me hope for a new life with them."

The general laughed. "A new life? The girl and her council betrayed you."

"They wouldn't do that," Romy replied as he slammed a fist on the arm of the chair.

A sly grin came over Jezeer's face. In a low voice he whispered, "What, did she tell you she loved you?" When he saw the look of despair in Romy's eyes, it told him the truth. "Ah, I see. She didn't offer you her love. Maybe it was just a promise of better times to come."

Romy was angry with himself as the general seemed to know too much about his situation. He repeated, "They wouldn't betray me. Both Efi, the council and their advisors have helped me."

"Is Ruut Nkosi one of those advisors?"

"Yes—yes. How do you know the name?"

"Who do you think told me you would be here? I received the message personally from Ruut yesterday. He isn't your friend. I'm the one you should trust."

Romy felt as if he had just been hit by a brick. His life, already in shambles, was crumbling even further. He didn't know who to believe, but Ruut was one of the very few people who knew he was coming to Bellantor. That was fact. Tilting his head, he said, "Why exactly are you here, General, other than to tell me how fucked up I am?"

"I feel things didn't go well for you. The loyalist government is pissed about their general you killed." General Jezeer waved his hand in the air. "I know. I know. You were following my orders, but it doesn't change the fact you pulled the trigger. They won't stop until they have a piece of your flesh."

"Your lack of optimism is depressing, General. It just tells me I should go back to Hagaza."

"You could," the general admitted. "When the girl wakes up, you can go with her if you like. I won't stop you. But you will be an outlaw in New Kor, likely in Shol as well. Your mother will be told you're an outlaw, and life will be more difficult for her as well."

"Stop fucking around, and tell me what's on your mind."

"So far, the general's death and your part in it have been kept out of the public eye. If you come back with me and face a military court, the MAT officials have accepted that we give you a six-month sentence to be served in a minimum-security facility. Then, once you're released, your record will be expunged, and you'll continue your life as if none of this ever happened."

Romy was beginning to realize General Jezeer's words made more and more sense, especially since he agreed, Ruut must have given him up. "Why would the MAT officials accept that?"

Seeing he was beginning to win Romy over, the general smiled. "It seems they never really liked General Hayden Fyr. He was a great tactician but had no personality. Second, the fact you were able to travel through supposedly impassable terrain and catch the general with his pants down, so to speak— well, the entire situation is more than embarrassing for them."

Romy's mind was swimming with thoughts. He wasn't exactly sure what to do, but then he thought of his stepmother and his father. One was a Sholite and the other a Korian, and both were heroes in his mind. They both had made significant sacrifices for the concept of—*doing the right thing*. It sounded simple, however, it was something many people never achieved. It was that concept of honour and being able to hold his chin high, that made his choice for him. Realizing he could not live as an outlaw, he gave the general his answer. "I'll come with you."

Chapter 23: Betrayal

10:00 hours, 11th day of the 4th Korian month, Haven year 0024

Hamar Minimum-Security Detention Facility

The Hamar Detention Center had the atmosphere of a hotel. The three long buildings, set in a *U* shape, were at the end of a long, winding road in the middle of a beautiful, wide-leafed forest.

Romy walked along a cobblestone sidewalk in the wide, central courtyard, wearing the grey coveralls worn by all inmates at the facility. There were no fences, making an escape seem quite plausible, but there were two deterrents. First, several times, as he extended his walks to the outskirts of the manicured lawn, through the trees, he could see armed guards patrolling the forest. Second, it seemed he warranted extra attention with two guards never too far from his location. Even now, they were 50 metres behind him as he passed a grouping of benches between colourful, flower beds.

Years earlier, Romy had heard of this facility made for those criminals guilty of crimes thought of as unique. The MAT officials, although they found any crime abhorrent, at the same time were impressed by the ingenious plans laid out by these dubious Korian citizens. Rather than throw them into the midst of a prison filled with hardened criminals, they were sent to this facility in the hope that once they were rehabilitated, the government could use these same unique skills in the service of the government. In many cases, the government tasks weren't any less despicable or immoral, but sanctioned by the Council of Twelve, they were legal.

As he walked through the courtyard, Romy's mind was filled with Efi. The general had sent him a message indicating she had fully recovered and returned to Hagaza. When Romy asked if there was further news or a message from Efi, he was disappointed to hear there was none. In his mind, it helped justify the reasoning he used in deciding to leave Bellantor with the general.

Romy stopped in the cobblestoned square at the center of the courtyard. There was a tree in each corner of the square, each highlighted by black branches covered with a thick canopy of auburn-coloured needles. He stood in the shade of one of the trees as a man in bright-orange overalls, about 30 metres from the central square, caught his attention. Romy watched as the man handled a motorized cutter with a long, rotating blade along its length, trimming the side of a hedge.

As the cutter blades made short work of the overgrowth, he glanced at Romy. The gardener quickly looked away, but the glimpse of the man's face caused Romy to search his memory. *The man was familiar,* he thought. He had seen the thick, dark brows under a mop of dirty-blonde hair, before. Romy put his hand to his chin as the gardener glanced in his direction for a second time. Now, sure he had met the man at some point in his past, Romy was about to walk towards him when he was interrupted by a shout from the opposite side of the courtyard.

A facility attendant, dressed in a sharp, dark-blue suit, scurried along the pathway from the opposite wing of the facility. By the time he was next to Romy, he was out of breath. Between short gasps, he said, "Mister Gunn, you have a visitor. He's in waiting room three just off the main lobby."

"Thank you, Martin. I'll be right there."

Martin clicked his heels together before turning and retracing his steps to the door he left moments before. Romy followed, entering the south wing. He proceeded into the central building where a large, glass-walled atrium, one rivalling any atrium in any high-end hotel, was the jewel of the facility.

Romy found room three and entered. One of his personal guards poked his head in the door and, seeing the visitor lounging on the couch, said, "We'll be just outside the door if you need anything."

General Jezeer nodded just before the door was closed. With a raised eyebrow, he said, "I see you have kept the longer hairstyle and beard."

Romy sat on the couch on the opposite side of a wooden table from the general. "I think it suits me." In fact, the beard and longer hair moved Romy further away from the Romy who was part of the military. Some would suspect he was hiding behind a concealment. "Is there news from Efi?"

Romy's eyes stretched slightly wider as the general reached into his pocket. However, any excitement he had was squashed as General Jezeer tossed him a small bottle of red pills. "Efi sent a message saying you would need these. I was told it's some type of vitamin supplement."

Romy sighed as he tried to hide his disappointment. He didn't want the general to know how he felt about the Mabuza woman, so he put her from his mind. When he entered the waiting room, he had noticed the general was wearing a different uniform. It was light-brown with royal-blue accents on the collar and cuffs of the shirt. The jacket, lying on the couch beside the general, was also light-brown with blue buttons and lapels. The general's shirt had a raised band on top of each shoulder, and on each were five silver buttons—the sign of a *field general*. Romy smiled. It wasn't warm. The general had removed the jacket solely to ensure Romy was aware of the promotion. "Something new?" Romy asked.

The field general popped a smack into his mouth. "The difficult task of integrating the two military forces is underway. Six generals have been assigned to coordinate the job. I'm one of them."

"Congratulations," Romy offered in a tone he hoped didn't reveal his sarcasm. "I take it you are here with an update."

"Yes, good news, in fact. Your trial has been scheduled for the day after tomorrow in Murcia."

"Why Murcia? I'm not comfortable with that."

Field General Jezeer pointed to the five silver buttons on his shoulder. "You see these? They mean I have the resources to get things done at my discretion."

"Ah, so you have the power."

"Yup, I have the power." The field general winked as he tapped the buttons again.

"What do I have to do?"

Jezeer leaned forward, popping a smack. "It's simple. You need to sign a confession. I'll vouch for you, explaining the extenuating circumstances. You'll be found guilty and brought back here for the next six months. After that, you'll be a free man with a clean start."

Lowering an eyebrow, Romy asked. "That's it? What about Matt Demoro? Is he confessing to his part?"

The field general rubbed his chin. "Yeah. That would be a problem."

"Why?"

"Because Demoro's dead. When we heard he attacked your squad, we went after him. He was determined to elude us, so he was shot down. He and his two gunners were killed."

"He deserved that," Romy muttered as he thought back on Jax, Rico and the rest of his squad.

"Back to the confession," Jezeer said. "I figured you wouldn't agree to a murder charge."

"Fuckin right!" Romy blurted.

"So, we have some options: manslaughter, involuntary manslaughter, criminal negligence causing death, accidental death…"

"Accidental death—I'll take that charge."

Jezeer shrugged. "It will be a bit tougher to push through, but then…" He pointed to his five silver buttons.

As Romy shook his head, the field general continued. "As I told you before, you'll have a military trial. Just prior to the trial, you, your defender, the prosecutor and I, will meet, where you'll sign the confession. I've already talked to the general who will be adjudicating your case. It's a done deal."

"Who is he?"

"It's not a *he*. It's a *she*. Field General Shelby Fyr has agreed to everything we've discussed. She wants nothing more than to satisfy the Council of Twelve who are demanding some punishment, while making the entire situation go away quickly."

"You're sure?"

Again, Jezeer winked and pointed to his silver buttons.

Romy rolled his eyes and muttered, "I know. You have the power."

The field general rose to his feet and pulled on his jacket. "I'll see you in Murcia."

Two days later, Romy dressed into a dark-blue suit that had been sent by the field general. The awaiting security vehicle was large enough to hold both he and his two guards along with the driver. It was a pleasant 90-minute drive along the highway sweeping through the colourful forest. Thankfully, the windows had a dark tint, so when they entered the city, the secrecy of Romy's trial was maintained. In fact, fortunately, the Murcia news people were occupied with the events of the night before. Two more mining spaceships had vanished from the Junkyard. Once again, Devil Raider conspiracy theories were rekindled when accounts of serpent-like, black, shadowy figures with bright, red eyes, were the talk of the day.

Consequently, when Romy left the car and entered the back entrance of the military's high-command building in Murcia, it was without fanfare. He was whisked into a first-floor room where Jezeer and two other men were waiting for him. The mandatory handcuffs were removed as the field general introduced Tally Mal, the military prosecutor, and Jarvis Mallen, his defender.

The prosecutor pulled a sheaf of papers from a folder and placed them on the table in front of Romy. "This is the confession you have agreed to. You need to sign it here—" The man pointed to the paper "—and here."

Romy sat in the chair in front of the table and read the document. He read the first page quickly, seeing the charge he was confessing to as, *criminal activity causing accidental death*. The second and third page took more time to read through. "The first page is simple enough, but what does all this mean?" he asked as he pointed to the added pages.

"Not to worry," the prosecutor offered. "It's a standard confession contract."

His defender added, "That's true, Romy. It's all part of the plan."

Romy tilted his head up and looked his defender squarely in the eyes. "If I sign this, will I receive a six-month sentence?"

Romy's defender replied, "I was at a meeting yesterday, attended by these men and Field General Fyr. She has agreed to this."

Romy's gaze shifted to Jezeer, who winked and pointed to his five silver buttons. As Romy signed the document, under his breath, he muttered, "Yeah, you have the power."

An hour later, the same two guards who had been with Romy throughout the trip, led him into a large courtroom. On a platform at the front was a wide, wooden desk. Three metres away, facing them, were two smaller desks, and further behind these were many benches on the inclined floor extending up to the back of the room.

Romy saw the prosecutor and defender, but was surprised to see a small group of people sitting on the benches. Romy had expected there to be no observers, but then again, it shouldn't have been a surprise for the top family vidames to send representatives to verify, first hand, this ugly end to their civil war.

Once Romy took a seat beside his defender, Field General Shelby Fyr entered the room. She was thin, and the many creases on her face told anyone looking at her that she had a life filled with stress. She carried a folder with her, opening it once she was seated. She perused the document, then turned to the group facing her. "Romy Gunn, please identify yourself."

Rising to his feet, Romy replied, "I'm Romy Gunn."

Without lifting her head, Field General Fyr's gaze tilted up. "Romy Gunn, the son of Ryder Gunn and I'lish Mann?"

"Stepson of I'lish Mann," Romy corrected. "But I'm not sure how that's relevant…"

"Of course," Shelby Fyr interrupted. "Just confirming your identity. I see you've signed this confession admitting your guilt. Please verify you did so willingly, without coercion."

Still on his feet, Romy said, "Yes, I did so willingly."

Field General Fyr lifted the papers and tapped the edges on the desktop. "Very well. Then, all that is to be determined is your sentence."

The prosecutor, Tally Mal, rose to his feet. "Field General Fyr, there has been some new evidence you should hear before sentencing."

"At this stage, that would be completely inappropriate," Shelby Fyr said.

"With all due respect, I make the request with support from Field General Grant Bli. His son, Stefan Parbli has brought forward critical information."

Grant Bli was one of four high-ranking field generals leading the integration team along with Brett Jezeer and Shelby Fyr. That in itself was sufficient motivation to at least hear the information. But Shelby Fyr had heard the name, Stefan Parbli, before. "Prosecutor, is Stefan Parbli the same man who is related to Murdock Parbli, advisor to the president of the MAT government?"

"Indeed, it's his grandson," came the reply.

Shelby Fyr was in quite a predicament. The information shouldn't be allowed, but significant influence from powerful men within the MAT and PAT governments could come down to bear on her. An empty chair was on the floor beside Field General Fyr's desk. She pointed to it, saying, "Bring forth Mister Parbli."

Romy's eyes narrowed in anger as he poked his defender. Through clenched teeth, he snarled, "Say something, you idiot."

Jarvis Mallen turned. There was sweat on his brow, and his lower lip was quivering. But the young defender wasn't looking at Romy; rather, he was looking over Romy's shoulder. Romy snapped his head around and saw Jarvis was looking towards Field General Jezeer who was sitting on the end of one of the benches along the central aisle.

"You have to be kidding," Romy blurted.

"I'm sorry," Jarvis whispered before he turned, placing his elbows on the desk with his fingers intertwined tightly together.

A young man entered from the double doors at the back of the courtroom. He walked down the central aisle and sat in the chair beside the field general's wide desk. He turned and said to Shelby Fyr, "I have an audio tape to present."

After Shelby Fyr nodded her approval, the prosecutor snapped his fingers towards the communications room behind the window at the back of the room. First, there was a crackling noise, then a conversation between two voices. It was the same audio tape Stefan Parbli had provided to General Jezeer, documenting the direction to abort the assassination mission once the truce had been announced.

Once Romy realized where the audio tape was leading, and once he heard his voice acknowledging he would stand down, he sprang to his feet. "That never happened!" he cried. "It's a fake!"

The audio tape concluded. Shelby Fyr turned to Stefan Parbli. "Please provide the source of the tape."

The young man nodded. "Once the truce was announced, General Jezeer ordered me to break radio silence and contact Romy Gunn. The message, as you heard, was for him to abort. He repeated back the order, confirming it." The young Parbli had practiced his words, and they were convincing. "This is an accurate account of what happened. I have no reason to lie."

Again, Romy blurted out his words. "It's *all* a lie!"

"You can leave the witness chair," Field General Fyr said to Stefan. Once he did so, she returned her focus to Romy Gunn. "With all due respect, Mister Gunn, Stefan Parbli is the son of a field general and the grandson of a government minister. As such, I don't question his integrity."

Romy recognized the wry look on Shelby Fyr's face. It was the same one he had seen all his life. Without words, the message was clear. *You're the son of the traitor, Ryder Gunn.*

The courtroom was silent as Field General Fyr wrote notes on the documents in front of her. She looked up and once again tapped the edges of the papers against the desk. "Mister Gunn, you have confessed to the crime of criminal activity causing an accidental death, but I have now added the pertinent, aggravating factors to your file. Considering this, I sentence you to life in prison, to be served in the Delrit Maximum-Security Penal Station. A shuttle will be arranged, and you will be transported there immediately." Shelby Fyr's face twisted into a sarcastic smirk. "Enjoy your time in space."

Once again, Romy jumped to his feet, but his arms were caught by the two guards who had silently moved to a position behind him. He was quickly handcuffed and jostled towards the central aisle. Even though Romy's face was covered by a beard, Brett Jezeer along with the other observers, could see Romy's face was red with anger.

When Romy was pushed down the aisle, passing Field General Jezeer, the general winked and pointed to the five silver buttons on his shoulder. Without emitting a sound, Jezeer's lips moved slightly. It was enough for Romy to understand his words, *I have the power.*

Chapter 24: Escape

13:00 hours, 13th day of the 4th Korian month, Haven year 0024

The Hilltop Hotel, 12 kilometres south of Murcia.

Efi stood on a small, third-floor veranda of the Hilltop Hotel. The building was situated on a wooded rise of land, east of the Kriton Fyr Space Field. As her gaze peered down the manicured lawn between the white, brick hotel and the fence defining the edge of the complex, she heard a voice beside her.

Valre, Romy's long-time attendant, pointed. "There—the white, extended-length van with one black and orange vehicle in front of it, and another behind."

Efi raised her magnifying eyepiece. Her gaze followed the vehicles as they moved across the tarmac to an isolated hanger on the far side of the spaceport. The terminal on their left, with a mix of space shuttles and cargo craft in front of it, was only half of the massive complex. Beyond the spaceport, in the distance, was another even larger terminal. This was the Rowan Gunn Airport terminal where local planetary flights to and from Murcia were coordinated.

Valre brushed her white bangs from her forehead. "The vehicles have stopped. Do you see him?"

Adjusting the magnification on the eyepiece, Efi focused on the scene in front of the hanger. The caravan of vehicles had stopped, and several guards left the escort vehicles. Once they surrounded the van, its door was opened, and another guard jumped out followed by a man in bright, orange coveralls. "I see him," Efi muttered.

"Let me see," Valre said.

Efi placed the eyepiece into Valre's hand. She put it to her eye and saw the man in the orange coveralls was shuffling towards the hanger with one guard gripping each of his arms. She took an audible, troubled breath. "It's Romy. They have him handcuffed and shackled—as if that's really necessary."

Valre glanced at Efi for a moment before returning the eyepiece to her eye. Her brain finally caught up with her actions as she lowered the eyepiece.

Her gaze, once again, fell on Efi. Her face was drawn and her lips were trembling. Valre whispered, "I didn't see that coming. You love him."

Efi had known Valre for a long time. Both their parts in Romy's future had been set long ago. As such, Valre was one of only a few people Efi would confide in. "Is it that obvious?" Efi whispered.

Smiling warmly, Valre wrapped her arms around the younger, Mabuza woman. "To me it is."

After a few seconds, Efi pulled away. "It must not interfere with the path before him. My feelings for him are secondary, and I have told him so."

"Does he love you?"

"He has feelings for me," Efi confessed. "I have pushed him away, so far, but it's difficult."

Valre brushed her fingers down Efi's cheek. "The see'ers have predicted our future. If it is accurate, in time, all will be well."

Efi lifted her chin and gave her head a shake before lifting the eyepiece. "A prison shuttle has arrived in front of the hanger." A minute later, she added. "Romy just boarded."

Placing the eyepiece back in its sleeve, she and Valre watched the shuttle move down the paved taxiway. Once it reached the far end of the spaceport, it turned, pointing its nose down the runway.

The prison shuttle pilot spoke into the microphone attached to his helmet. "Murcia Tower, this is *Delrit Station shuttle 33* on runway 1 dash 4, requesting permission to depart."

In the observation room at the top of the five-story tower, the day controller checked the monitor directly in front of him. Seeing there were no incoming spacecraft, he shifted his gaze to the second monitor, checking the status of local air traffic. He pressed the button at the bottom of his microphone stand. "*Delrit 33*, this is Murcia Tower. You have clearance for takeoff. Once you're airborne, veer left on heading 85 northwest to avoid incoming air traffic."

The pilot said, "Murcia Tower, understood. Follow heading 85 northwest." As the pilot replied, he already had the two throttle levers pressed fully forward.

The small shuttle screamed down the runway until rotational velocity was achieved. The pilot pulled back on the central pressure stick. The nose lifted. Once the shuttle was 100 metres off the ground, it levelled off until it achieved a speed of 350 kilometers per hour. At that point, the pilot pulled the stick back hard and to the left. The landing gear automatically retracted as the shuttle rose at a 45-degree angle while rolling to the northwest. The afterburners kicked in, leaving a grey, quickly-receding smoke trail behind it.

Once the Delrit shuttle achieved an altitude of 40 kilometres, the pilot disengaged the afterburners, leaving only the twin electromagnetic drives to power the vehicle to the station.

"*Delrit 33*, this is Murcia Tower. We're switching you over to *Haven Control 2*. Have a good flight."

"Murcia Tower, this is *Delrit 33*. Thanks for your help." There was an electronic click as the pilot switched frequencies. "*Haven Control 2*, this is *Delrit 33*, requesting permission to continue to *Delrit Station*."

"*Delrit 33*, this is *Haven Control 2*. Welcome back to space. Maintain your speed at 7,000 kph once you achieve 80 kilometres altitude." The voice belonged to Wryson Tor, an experienced controller who had worked at the space control tower for 20 years. Over that time, the circular, rotating station hadn't changed much, at least as far as the visible eye could determine. However, the electronics had been updated five years earlier, providing advanced imaging and radar capabilities.

"*Haven Control 2*, this is *Delrit 33* confirming speed of 7,000 kilometres per hour once we achieve 80k."

"*Delrit 33*, this is *Haven Control 2*. At 80k change your vector to true position 130, 45, 120. There's a mining vessel 10,000 kilometres in front of you. You wouldn't want to sneak up on it."

The pilot grinned, thinking, *Yeah, that could get ugly.*

Haven Control 2's command room was round, with thick, plate-glass windows around its circumference. Wryson Tor squinted, peering out the one in front of him. Delrit Maximum-Security Penal Station was a large cylindrical structure, but being 8,000 kilometres distant, it was seen only as a speck in Haven's orbit. He toggled a switch, adding *Delrit Station* to the control frequency. "*Delrit Station*, this is *Haven Control 2*. *Delrit 33* is inbound, ETA, 90 minutes."

"*Haven Control 2*, this is *Delrit Station*. Understood, shuttle 33 ETA 90 minutes."

A different voice came over the radio. "*Delrit 33*, this is Warden Benjamin Fyr. Is Romy Gunn aboard the shuttle?"

"Warden Fyr, this is *Delrit 33*. Yes, Romy Gunn is aboard."

Warden Fyr's eyes lit up. This was a moment he had waited for. Eighteen years ago, he was an up-and-coming agent in the KIS. He had been assigned to Haven Control 2 when Ryder Gunn was leaving on his now infamous last expedition with the Exploratory Corp. Benjamin Fyr's mission had been to ensure Ryder Gunn didn't make it out of Haven's orbit alive. Unfortunately, Ryder Gunn escaped along with an armada of ships. Benjamin Fyr, having been made a fool of, was demoted and left to linger in the lower ranks of the KIS. Eventually, Benjamin Fyr felt he had no option but to resign. He joined *Delrit Station* as a guard and worked his way through the ranks until now, he held the position of Station Warden.

Looking out the observation port of the station's control bubble, Warden Fyr rubbed his hands together. After his escape, he had made efforts to find Ryder Gunn, but the man never returned from his expedition. He was likely dead, leaving Warden Fyr's need for revenge unfulfilled. But now, his son was coming to his penal facility. A wide sneer formed on the warden's lips as he thought of the horrors he would inflict on the young man.

"*Haven Control 2*, this is Maintenance vessel 24 in the *Junkyard*. We have some unauthorized activity here. The *Arcadia*, an oxygen miner, is powering up."

Wryson Tor's fingers danced across his keyboard. One of the high-power camera's targeted the Junkyard, and the magnified view appeared on the large monitor to his left. Indeed, a vessel in the middle of the fleet of decommissioned ships was lit up.

"*Salvation* command, this is *Haven Control 2,* requesting your assistance."

The *Salvation* was a military frigate, 3,000 kilometres from the Junkyard. "*Haven Control 2*, this is *Salvation* command. What can we do for you?"

"*Salvation* Command, we have unauthorized activity at the Junkyard. A ship is powering up."

"*Haven Control 2*, we're on our way to investigate."

Warden Fyr scratched his head as he looked at the radar monitor in front of him. The shuttle with Romy Gunn aboard was still 4,000 kilometres from the station. The *Salvation*, that had been requested to be in the vicinity as a precaution for a high-profile prisoner transfer, was now on a course *away* from the penal station. "Something doesn't feel right," the warden mumbled.

Wryson Tor watched out the observation windows as the Delrit shuttle passed by Haven station at a distance of 100 kilometers. It was speeding towards the penal station when the stars behind the shuttle disappeared. A black mass of small surfaces, shifting and rolling, followed the shuttle. The morphing mass gave Wryson the sense there was something wrong with his vision. He rubbed his eyes, but when he tried to focus on the object, things got worse. He found his vision was fine, but unfortunately, the shifting black surfaces vanished, leaving a sleek spaceship in its place. The space vessel was still black, but its sleek, long shape was well defined, with two red circles of light at its nose.

"Devil Raiders!" Wryson yelled.

As Wryson fumbled with his microphone and frantically called for assistance from the *Salvation*, a narrow laser beam shot out from one of the red circles. The beam was targeted perfectly, disabling the shuttle's engines. No sooner had the shuttle begun to roll when the Devil Raider was above it. Wryson looked on in shock as, what he suspected was a magnetic field, drew the shuttle to its belly.

Warden Benjamin Fyr watched the events unfold on his monitor. His face was white, his eyes wide, and his jaw was gapped open. His words began as a whisper. "Not again. This can't be happening again." He saw the shuttle drawn up and connect with the belly of the mysterious, black spaceship. His voice grew louder. "No. No. No!" Now, he was yelling hysterically with all the breath in his lungs. "Not again!"

Five soldiers, all dressed in claret-coloured space suits, waited in the Devil Raider's access hatch. When they heard the *clang*, the leader of the group looked at the control panel mounted to the wall. When the light turned green, he pressed a palm button, and a wide panel, in the center of the access hatch below them, opened.

With the top of the shuttle now visible, one of the men placed a firing mechanism against the access hatch of the shuttle. Pulling the trigger, with a loud *bang*, the gas cartridge lodged into the hatch, expelling gas into the shuttle's cabin. The leader looked at his wrist interlink, and after ten seconds passed, nodded to one of his men.

The locking mechanism was rotated and the hatch popped open. With only their gravity boots to help them, one soldier after the other floated down through the hatch into the shuttle. The leader held a pistol at arms length as he whirled, inspecting the cabin. There were three men in the shuttle's passenger compartment. They were asleep. He walked to the cockpit and verified the pilot and co-pilot were also unconscious.

The leader returned to his men. His voice was muffled through the gas mask he wore. "That's him in the orange jumpsuit. He's coming with us." He looked at his wrist interlink. He knew the affects of the gas was temporary as he reminded his men, "Let's move. We have two minutes before they wake up."

Valre and Efi had been standing on the veranda of the hotel for some time. Valre looked up into the sky. "It's done. He's safely aboard."

Efi nodded, but she was distracted by something at the airport in the distance. She lifted her eyepiece and gazed across the airfield. In front of a remote hanger was a helocraft, painted black and grey.

"What are you looking at?" Valre asked.

She pointed at the airfield. "It's a PAT helocraft. They haven't had time to repaint it to the new colours." She continued to examine the helocraft through the eyepiece, then smiled. "There he is."

"Who?"

"Field General Jezeer."

"Murcia Tower, this is *Villaro 322*, requesting permission to depart Murcia field," Jezeer said into his microphone.

"*Villaro 322*, this is Murcia Tower. Permission to depart granted, however maintain a ceiling of no more than 100 metres. There's some type of commotion going on in space."

After a textbook takeoff, Jezeer tilted the helocraft north, and the craft headed towards the bay on the far side of Murcia. It was standard practice to head north, then sweep east to southwest targeting Villaro, 450 kilometres away.

Efi and Valre watched the helocraft climb. Efi placed a finger to her temple and closed her eyes.

"What are you doing?" Valre said.

Deep in thought, Efi whispered, "Asking for a favour."

As the helocraft sped north, Jezeer had a smug grin on his face. Romy Gunn was on his way to the penal station. General Hayden Fyr, who he held responsible for his sister's death, was dead, and Field General Jezeer was now one of the most powerful military people in the land. With a smug grin on his face, he retrieved a smack from his pocket and flipped it towards his lips. However, it was an inopportune time for a spot of turbulence, and the pill bounced off his chin into his lap. As he glanced down, his fingers searched for it until it was found under his thigh. As he straightened, he popped the pill into his mouth, but his eyes sprang wide open. The pill caught in his throat until a spasmic cough sent it flying into the windscreen. A great cylinder of water, with green tendrils of electric light shooting through it, had risen from the bay and was directly in his path.

Before the field general could react, the wall of water formed into a giant hand and slammed into the helocraft. He only had time for an, "oh fuck," before his face slammed into the dashboard after which the hand dragged the helocraft into the bay. There was a mighty splash followed by a gurgling whirlpool, but two minutes later, the surface of the bay was once again calm—as if nothing had happened. Field General Brett Jezeer was gone. That was that.

Once the five raiders, supporting Romy, had returned to their ship, the access hatches were closed and the shuttle was disengaged. The entire attack and abduction had taken less than five minutes. The Devil Raider had recloaked, turned and was now heading back into deep space.

Romy regained his senses as the five men pulled him into an elevator. The raiders had removed their head gear. Romy rubbed his eyes as his senses came back to him. He looked from one raider to the other. He realized he had just been rescued, but he had no idea by who, or for what purpose. "What's going on?" he finally managed.

The leader, a man with dark, bushy eyebrows and dirty blonde hair, replied, "You'll find out soon enough."

By now, Romy had fully recovered. His eyes narrowed. "You're the same man who was gardening in the courtyard at the prison." His eyes suddenly widened as he came to a realization. His voice shook and his vibrating finger pointed at the leader. "I know where I've seen you before! You're Barrett Fexman!"

"What if I am?"

"Eighteen years ago, at the Murcia Uprising, my friend Jax was shot in the leg. You were the only person who stopped to help us. You saved his life!" Confusion filled Romy's eyes. "How can this be?"

Barrett smiled warmly. "Someone has always been close to you. We have been watching. I have, so was a friend of mine. His name was Rico."

"Rico…"

Romy's words were cut short as the elevator door opened. Four of the raiders turned left, while Barrett grasped Romy's arm and pulled him in the opposite direction. "This way," he said.

Near the end of the hallway, Barrett stopped in front of a pneumatic door. "This is as far as I go." He pushed a palm button beside the door, and it opened with a *woosh*. "In you go," Barrett urged before he walked away, following in the direction of his fellow raiders.

Romy shuffled into the room that appeared to be a large office. There was seating on his left, but the highlight of the room was a large metal desk. On the other side of it, facing a port hole, was an older man in a claret-red uniform. He rocked back and forth with his fingers intertwined behind his back.

Romy said, "My thanks for saving me, but are you the one who will tell me what's going on?"

The man turned to face Romy. He had shoulder-length, grey hair and a like coloured beard and moustache.

Romy staggered, catching himself with his hands on the desk. Romy still had the longer hair, beard and moustache. As he gazed at the man in front of him, he thought he might as well have been looking in a mirror, albeit one that didn't consider age. The man had the same lips he did, the same eyes and the same strong chin.

Romy's eyes became moist. The older man's eyes were also moist, with a tear falling down his cheek. Ryder Gunn's voice cracked as he said, "Hello, son."

Epilogue

"Why did you stop?"

The man, who yesterday had arranged my abduction, placed the tablet on the coffee table, then turned his gaze to me. He said, "Yevgeni, I've been reading the story of the Korian people to you for six hours."

I had been so enthralled with the tale, I had lost all track of time and, even to a degree, my location. However, the wind had picked up. Shallow rolling waves rocked the 20-metre-long yacht, reminding me it was anchored on Lake Zurich.

"The story is so fascinating," I exclaimed. "You can't stop there and not tell me what happened after Ryder and Romy's reunion. Just try to make it quick."

The man sitting across from me on the rear, open-air deck of the vessel chuckled. "There is more, but there is nothing quick about it. There are many unexpected events in their lives yet to play out."

"I really can't wait," I replied, insisting the story be continued.

Leaning forward, the man lowered his voice. "If women on Earth are anything like Korian women, it's best you don't spend a second, unexpected night away from home."

Laughing, I said, "Good point. However, I have an idea." Pulling my phone from my pocket, I pressed the code for my home. On the second ring, my wife answered.

I explained to her,

"Yes, I'll tell you more about the emergency when I get home..."

My wife rattled off a series of questions I did my best to answer. I watched the man sitting across from me who seemed baffled as the discussion with my wife continued.

"Yes, I'll be home about 5:00 this afternoon...

Dinner? I really don't feel much like going out. How about we order in from the grill around the corner. We haven't had their ribs for a while...

I

Sure, I'll pick up some wine on the way home…

Oh, Darling, we'll be having a dinner guest—a colleague from work. He'll be spending the night, so we can continue with a project from home, tomorrow…

No, don't worry. I'll prepare the guest room when I get in."

As the conversation went on, first, my new-found friend vehemently shook his head. When I ignored him, other than waving away his hesitation, he sighed and rolled his eyes.

"Who is he?"

With a wink to the man, I answered my wife, "His name is Romy Gunn."

Dear Reader:

Reviews are important to every author. We are thankful that many readers take a few moments to return to the purchasing website, in this case, Amazon, and leave a rating and a review.

If you could do so for this story, it would be much appreciated. Keep in mind, a Hollywood style review is not needed. Even a few simple words would be great.

Thanks again, and I hope you enjoyed the story.

Peter Sandor

www.ingramcontent.com/pod-product-compliance
Lightning Source LLC
Chambersburg PA
CBHW031407250626
47155CB00004B/1444